THE
BODY
SNATCHERS

THE SACK-'EM-UP MAN

From a black-and-white drawing, "The Body-snatcher," by H. Meredith Williams
(Reproduced by kind permission of the Scottish Modern Arts Association)

THE
BODY
SNATCHERS

JAMES MOORES BALL, M.D., LL.D.

DORSET PRESS
New York

ISBN 0-88029-397-7

Printed in the United States of America
M 9 8 7 6 5 4 3 2 1

THIS BOOK IS DEDICATED TO THE
COUNCIL AND TO THE FELLOWS OF
THE ROYAL COLLEGE OF SURGEONS
OF EDINBURGH

PREFACE

ALTHOUGH "the Anatomy of Man is an ancient and royal subject of study," as has been stated by the late Alexander Macalister, Professor of Anatomy in the University of Cambridge, it was pursued until quite recently amid surroundings of a most unregal character.

Difficulties attending the study of Anatomy are of two kinds : physical and mental. The latter did not escape observation by Philip Gilbert Hamerton, the gifted author of *The Intellectual Life*, who says : "Studies which from their nature cannot be commonly used are always retained with great difficulty. The study of anatomy is perhaps the best instance of this ; every one who has attempted it knows with what difficulty it is kept by the memory. This is because anatomy lies so much outside of what is needed for ordinary life that very few people are ever called upon to use it except during the hours when they are actually studying it. The few who need it every day remember it as easily as a man remembers the language of the country which he inhabits. The workmen in the establishment at Saint Aubin d'Écroville, where Dr Auzoux manufactures his wonderful anatomical models, are as familiar with anatomy as a painter is with the colours on his palette." They never forget it, because they use it day after day.

For most of us, anatomical details are not easily retained. And no less a man than Sir Astley Cooper, the leading surgeon in London a century ago, daily

visited his private dissecting-room and continued the
study of practical anatomy until near the end of his
career (Mott).[1]

The present volume, however, is concerned chiefly
with the physical and legal difficulties which, prior to
the year 1832, attended the study of anatomy within
the domain of the United Kingdom, and brief mention
is made, *en passant*, of the rise and status of anatomical
science in North America.

It is nothing to the credit of the statesmen of the
United Kingdom, or to the legislators of the United
States, that, less than a century ago, although the
law demanded that surgeons should possess a high
degree of skill, statutory provisions were such that the
knowledge and skill required could be obtained only by
illegal means. No provision for the practical study of
anatomy existed in the United Kingdom prior to the
year 1832—except the scanty and uncertain material
which was supplied by the gallows.

That remarkable advances in anatomy, in physiology,
and in surgery were made in the United Kingdom, in
Canada, and in the United States, during the eighteenth
and in the early years of the nineteenth centuries, at a
time when anatomical material could be obtained only
by stealth, is now a matter of wonderment. It was a
period, however, when individualism was in full bloom.
It was a period when genius was not crushed by enactments like those, which, if he were living in America
to-day, would bar John Hunter from the study of
medicine. It was a period when ambition, initiative,
and prolonged labour in the dissecting-room brought
honour to the workers and surcease of sorrow to the
afflicted. It was a time of freedom of thought and of
action.

[1] Mott, *Travels in Europe and the East* (1834-1841), N.Y., 1842.

It was a time when thinkers could broadcast their views without social ostracism at the hands of the herd —the rabble—described by Dryden :

> " But far more numerous was the *herd* of such
> Who think too little and who talk too much."

It was a time when Adam Smith, later the author of *The Wealth of Nations,* could safely send to Dr Cullen, the famous Edinburgh physician, a letter (dated 20th September 1774) on the subject, " Free Competition in Medicine." However, the celebrated political economist seems to have had some doubts concerning its reception ; for he closes his letter with these words : " Adieu ! my dear doctor ; I am afraid that I shall get *my lug*[1] *in my lufe*[2] as we say, for what I have written." Happy should be the nation which has but few laws, and enforces them.

It was not in richly-endowed institutions, in rooms with tile-covered floors and marble wainscot nor in the presence of full-time instructors, that immortal discoveries were made by such heroes as Andreas Vesalius, Fabricius ab Aquapendente, Julius Casserius, Michael Servetus, William Harvey, Thomas Willis, William and John Hunter, Sir Charles Bell, Thomas Young, Edward Jenner, and the three or four Americans who gave Anæsthesia to a waiting world. And yet these men, who represent the highest type of medical chivalry and intellectual culture, were forced to gain their practical knowledge of anatomy by the dissection of bodies which had been stolen.

This monograph deals with a strange and unique period. It describes the activities of individuals of opposite types. On the one hand were the human hyenas, the most degraded of creatures, the scum

---

[1] Ear.   [2] Palm of hand.

of the earth; on the other hand, however, it mentions the names and records the deeds of not a few men who, in spite of obstacles of the most formidable character, have given immortal service to the world. And yet, strange to say, these extremes were compelled to meet.

If the reading of this account of the "Sack-'em-up Men" should lead a few physicians and surgeons to delve into the fascinating subject of the History of Medicine; or if, perchance, its perusal causes the medical students of to-day to appreciate their opportunities for anatomical study, the author will be pleased, and he will feel that the time, the labour, and the money spent on this book have not been wasted.

My grateful acknowledgments are due to the gentlemen who most kindly have furnished material for, and have assisted in the preparation of, this volume. I trust that the reader will appreciate the difficulties under which an Author, who resides several thousands of miles from the scene of the activities of the "Resurrectionists," and who is trying to describe the events which occurred a century ago, is labouring. This book never could have seen the light of day, but for the help which so cheerfully has been extended by many of the prominent citizens of Edinburgh.

To my friend, D. M. Greig, Esq., F.R.C.S.E., Conservator of the Museum of the Royal College of Surgeons of Edinburgh, I am indebted for many photographs and also for much valuable information and advice.

Dr John D. Comrie, who is an acknowledged authority on medical history in general, and of Edinburgh medical history in particular, has kindly permitted the use of text and blocks from several of his works.

The authorities of Edinburgh University have been most kind in permitting many of their treasures to be photographed.

To Arthur M. Shipley, M.D., of the University Hospital, Baltimore, Maryland, I am indebted for an account of the "Baltimore Burking Case"—a crime which appears to be unique in the annals of American Medicine.

For the portrait of Werner Rolfinck I am indebted to Lt.-Colonel Fielding H. Garrison, of Washington, D.C.

Mr Alan MacEwan, of St Louis, has photographed a number of portraits which are in the Author's collection, in order that they might be the better reproduced by the half-tone process.

It is almost unnecessary to add that Messrs Oliver and Boyd have done their work to the entire satisfaction of the Author.

James Moore Ball.

1st October 1928.

CONTENTS

CHAPTER I

CHAPTER II

CHAPTER III

CHAPTER IV

CHAPTER V

CHAPTER VI

CHAPTER VII

CONTENTS

LIST OF ILLUSTRATIONS

FULL-PAGE PLATES

TEXT FIGURES

INTRODUCTION

TAXES, death, and undisturbed rest for those whose bodies have been interred, are regarded by most people as facts beyond dispute, but not so : taxes must be paid, death is inevitable, but undisturbed rest for one's body is subject to revision.

When and where the vocation of grave-robber arose, and the circumstances under which the members of the Guild first operated, is not known. Violation of mausoleums, graves, and subterranean rooms for the dead, doubtless occurred in ancient times, when gold and silver ornaments, and precious gems, were placed near the body of the deceased. Egypt may have been the birthplace of the practice. The Egyptians, as Herodotus states, neither buried nor burned their dead. They did not bury them, for fear that they would be eaten by worms ; and they did not burn them, because they considered fire like a wild beast that devours everything it can seize upon. Filial piety and respect caused them to embalm the bodies, after which they were deposited in coffins placed in spacious rooms with rich ornaments and utensils (Gannal[1]). That such sepultures often were robbed is now well known. The robbers, however, were not interested in securing anatomical material.

Persons who disturb the dead are called " Resurrectionists." In the broad sense, all of them should be

[1] Gannal, *History of Embalming, and of Preparations in Anatomy, Pathology, and Natural History*, Paris, 1838. Translated by R. Harlan, M.D., Philadelphia, 1840, p. 9.

regarded as outlaws. For, by what right does an alleged scientist of the present day disturb the tomb of the Egyptian ruler who lived three thousand years before Christ? or burglarise the sarcophagus of a later date? Wherein is he less sacrilegious than were the wretches who, less than a century ago, sold hundreds of stolen—and a few dozens of murdered— bodies to the teachers of anatomy? Is there no balm in Gilead? Is there no rest for the dead?

Both types belong to the ever-increasing class of vandals. Both have carried on their work in hope of a reward. The one will find it in the applause of the public, in a royalty from his publisher, or from the satisfaction which comes from seeing his name placed in the latest book treating of ancient history. The other, in bygone days, found it in a cash payment. Both, speciously, may claim to be *aides-de-science* and the promoters of knowledge.

To the relic hunter of churchly or of vulgar note, and to his cousin who is disguised as an anthropologist, nothing ever has been sacred.

The desire for *post-mortem* repose reaches back to the early mists of the morning of the world. The primitive Christians put epitaphs on the tombs of deceased relatives, asking the vengeance of heaven on any and all persons whose hands should disturb the ashes of the dead (MacGregor).[1] Likewise, the same early followers of Christ regarded the crowning of the deceased with chaplets of flowers as little less than idolatry (Kennett).[2] Several of the Popes hurled anathemas against the disturbers of the dead.

[1] MacGregor, *The History of Burke and Hare*, Glasgow, 1884, p. 17.

[2] Kennett, *Romæ Antiquæ Notitia;* or, *The Antiquities of Rome*, second American edition, Baltimore, n.d., p. 325. (Basil Kennett, D.D., 1674-1714, entered Corpus Christi College, Oxford, in 1690. The work mentioned appeared at London, in 1696, and has been frequently reprinted.)

That the omniscient Shakespeare had given thought
to grave-robbing vandals is evidenced by the inscription
on his tomb :

" Good friend, for Jesus' sake, forbear
To dig the dust inclosed here :
Blest be the man that spares these stones,
And curst be he that moves my bones."

Avon's bard, however, has been more fortunate than
were many other historic characters whose osseous
tissues, to say nothing of their internal organs, have
been widely distributed.   No doubt, millimetre-measuring
scientists, as well as reporters for the brass-coloured
press, would give a respectable sum for a look at the
cranium of William of Stratford ; or, for an account like
Sir Henry Halford gave of the head of Charles I.[1]   It
is pleasing to know that, as yet, Shakespeare's body has
not been disturbed.

Many crimes have been perpetrated, and many
foolish projects have been initiated, in the sacred name
of Religion.   Among the long list of extraordinary
popular delusions from which Europe has suffered, a
prominent place must be given to the Crusades.   These
wave-like movements form "the most extraordinary
instance upon record of the extent to which popular
enthusiasm can be carried" (Mackay).[2]

During the period of the Crusades the pious and the
impious alike flocked to Jerusalem.   Eager search was
made for relics, which included such diverse substances
as water from the Jordan, earth from Calvary, pieces of
wood of the True Cross, hems of the garments of the
Virgin Mary, and the toe-nails and hairs of the Apostles.

[1] *British Medical Journal*, 27th January 1906.   Reprinted from Sir
Henry Halford's *Essays and Orations*, 1831.
[2] Mackay, *Memoirs of Extraordinary Popular Delusions*, second
edition, vol. ii., p. 2.   London, 1852.

These were brought back to Europe and were sold by knaves for large sums. "When the relics of saints were first introduced," says D'Israeli, "the reliquemania was universal; they bought and they sold, and like other collectors, made no scruple to *steal* them."

Monks endowed with thaumaturgic power were able to locate the graves of saints and bishops, and to translate their bodies from a subterranean to an appropriate terrestrial location. The term, *translation*, which is found in the writings of the Middle Ages, is a softened expression for grave-robbery.

An account of the miracles which were said to have been performed by saintly relics would fill many volumes. Such was the religious opinion, from the ninth to the twelfth century, which was universally accepted. The pious Canute, the Dane who ruled England in the early years of the eleventh century, encouraged resurrection on earth by commissioning his agent, at Rome, to purchase *St Augustine's arm* for a sum much greater than the finest statue of antiquity then would have brought. A great fall in the price of relics came during the reign of Henry VIII., at the dissolution of the monasteries.[1]

Mummies, which the Egyptians sometimes gave as pledges for the return of borrowed money, have been put to curious uses. In the Middle Ages they were employed as potent remedies in falls, bruises, and other external injuries. Francis I. always carried with him a little packet of powdered mummy and rhubarb, for falls and other accidents. "Mummy," says Sir Francis Bacon, "hath great force in staunching of blood, which may be ascribed to the mixture of balms that are glutinous." When the demand for powdered mummy had become so great that the real article could not be

[1] D'Israeli, *Curiosities of Literature*, London, 1791-1817.

supplied, a substitute was sold "at enormous profits by avaricious Jews in Alexandria " (Keen).[1]

Many individuals who wielded power, changed history, and decided the fate of nations, while they were among the quick, have been accorded scandalous treatment after joining the ranks of the dead.

Powerful as Cromwell had been during life, less than scant courtesy was his lot after death. One of the most disgraceful scenes in English history was staged on 30th January 1661. Evelyn records : " This day (O the stupendous and inscrutable judgments of God !) were the carcases of those arch-rebels, Cromwell, Bradshaw (the judge who condemned his Majesty), and Ireton (son-in-law to the usurper), dragged out of their superb tombs in Westminster among the kings, to Tyburn, and hanged on the gallows there from nine in the morning till six at night, and then buried under that fatal and ignominious monument in a deep pit."

The body of Blake "was removed from its honoured resting-place and reinterred in St Margaret's churchyard." Thus it was that the remains of the "greatest soldier and the greatest sailor that England had produced" were dishonoured (Knight).

Cromwell's bones are supposed to have been scattered. Probably that is true. But there is a legend which runs as follows :—

" Mary, daughter of Oliver Cromwell, in 1657 married Thomas Belasyse, first Earl Fauconberg, Ambassador at Venice and Paris, Councillor of State. The Great Protector occasionally was a visitor to the home of his daughter, and is said to have had a special room there. Legend has it that his remains lie buried in a secret· part of the house, the Countess Fauconberg

[1] Keen, *A Sketch of the Early History of Practical Anatomy*, Philadelphia, 1874, p. 37.

having bribed the guard to secure her father's body when it was disinterred at Westminster Abbey. It was brought to Newburgh secretly, though without the head, which was exposed at Tyburn."

Cromwell's head was stuck on a spike on Westminster Hall. Some twenty-five years afterwards, on a stormy night, it was blown down and was carried home by a sentry on guard. Flaxman, the sculptor, who compared the head with a death-cast of Cromwell's head, declared its features to be precisely similar. On the hard parchment-like skin over the right eyebrow, close to the nose, was a distinct mark—the situation of Oliver's famous wart. This mummied head is still in existence, and a few years ago was in the possession of Mr Horace Wilkinson, of Sevenoaks.[1]

One hundred and fifty-two years (namely, in 1813) after England had disgraced herself by the scenes mentioned above, the rest of Charles I. was disturbed. On 1st April 1813, the vault containing the remains of the unfortunate Charles I. was opened and the head was removed for examination. While the body of Cromwell was dishonoured and his remains were cursed, the examination of the mortal remains of King Charles I. was conducted with the utmost respect and decorum. What a contrast!

The fourth cervical vertebra was found to be cut through transversely. After the head had been returned, and the vault was closed, it was discovered that the portion of the vertebra which had been cut through had separated from the neck, and, escaping notice, had not been restored to the coffin. The Prince Regent, who was present, gave the relic to Sir Henry Halford, who placed it in a case of *lignum vitæ* lined with gold, with an appropriate Latin inscription inside the lid. Possession

[1] *The Practitioner*, London, September 1896, p. 289.

of this relic, however, appears to have been the cause of uneasiness to Sir Henry's heirs ; and it was placed in the hands of the Prince of Wales, by whom, it is understood, it was returned to the vault and was deposited, enclosed in its case, on the coffin of Charles the First.[1]

The head of Richelieu had a somewhat similar, but a more variegated, career than that of Cromwell. In 1793 the body of the great Cardinal was removed by the revolutionists ; the head was cut off and was secured by a citizen who, later, sold it to M. Armez. In 1866, the relic was handed to the Sorbonne, where, with suitable religious rites, it was deposited. M. Armez's claim was disputed by another person, who insisted that he possessed the authentic head of Richelieu. Strange to say, M. Armez had the face, whilst his rival possessed the rest of the head. A noteworthy feature was the height of the forehead, which, though slightly retreating, was very broad at its upper part. The left frontal region was more prominent than the right.

Height of forehead and asymmetry were not the only remarkable features possessed by Richelieu's anatomy. The surgeon who examined the body states that, "in this brain there were twice as many ventricles as usual, each of them having a fellow, which was situated above it, and formed a double stage in front as well as behind, and particularly in the middle, in which are formed the purest spirits of the discursive faculty, subserving the operations of the understanding, the forward ventricles serving for imagination, and those of the backward ventricles serving for movement, emotion, and memory." [2]

Many other historic characters are entitled to the

---

[1] *The Practitioner*, London, September 1896, p. 291.
[2] *Ibid.*

F.S.D.M. degree (Fellow of the Society of Disjected Members). The fifth lumbar vertebra of Galileo rests in the *Gabinetto fiscio* in Padua. It was stolen by the Florentine physician Cocchi, who, in 1757, was entrusted with the removal of the remains of the astronomer to the Church of Santa Croce in Florence.[1] "This bone," says Gould, "which is about the size of a boy's fist, appeared to me to resemble very much the lumbar bones found in the skeletons of other men."[2]

Another "fragment of historic humanity" is the withered finger of Galileo, placed in a glass or crystal vase in the *Museo di storia naturale* at Florence. It was secured by the celebrated antiquary, Gori, upon the opening of the tomb of Galileo in Santa Croce.[3]

Pathetic, indeed, is the history of the heart of Louis de Buade, Count de Frontenac (1620-1698), French Governor of Canada. In his youth Frontenac married a lovely and vivacious girl; but their ecstasy of love soon passed into hatred. Both frequented the French Court, where their unhappiness was apparent to all. Frontenac's first appointment as Governor of Canada was arranged to prevent complications. The proud old ruler of New France, however, always retained a part of his affection for the lady, for, when he was about to die, he requested that his heart be removed from his body and be proffered to his wife as a last tribute. This was done, and the heart that had throbbed with so many emotions was enclosed in a leaden box and was taken across the sea to her. She spurned the gift, and declared she did not want a dead heart which, when beating, did not belong to her. The pitiful relic was returned to Canada and was deposited in

[1] *Handbook for Travellers in Northern Italy*, London, 1843, p. 322.
[2] Gould, *Zephyrs from Italy and Sicily*, New York, 1852, p. 251.
[3] *Handbook for Travellers in Northern Italy*, London, 1843, p. 526.

Frontenac's coffin in the historic chapel of Recollets, in Quebec (Blowden Davies, *Montreal Star*, 6th September 1924).

There is good reason to believe that not all of the organs of Napoleon are housed in his magnificent Parisian tomb. The checkered career of Laurence Sterne, the illustrious author of *Tristram Shandy* and of the *Sentimental Journey*, was ended in London, where he died in poverty, 18th March 1768. He was buried near Tyburn and the corpse, says Sir James Prior in his *Life of Edmund Malone*, was removed by some of the "resurrection men" and was dissected by the professor of anatomy at Cambridge.

Gambetta's *post-mortem* examination, which was made on 2nd January 1883, by Professor Cornil, in the presence of a coterie of distinguished *savants*, afforded to his enthusiastic friends the opportunity to carry off some very select parts of his anatomy. Professor Cornil retained the viscera, M. Lannelongue secured the right arm, the wound of which was the primary cause of death. M. Duval, President of the Société d'Anthropologie, appropriated the brain ; and M. Bertin carried off the heart.[1] Not a few vulgarities have been committed in the name of Science.

The object of this monograph, however, is not to detail the fate of the remains of distinguished men ; but to record the activities of a few of the "resurrectionists" whose lives were spent in securing material for anatomical teaching, to explain the conditions which made body-snatching a necessity, and to preface the whole story with a short account of the history of anatomy.

Medical science seeks the causes of numerous diseases and searches for their remedies. Its far-flung

[1] *The Practitioner*, London, September 1896, p. 288.

battle-line reaches from Winnipeg to Peking, from
Amritsar to Astoria. Colour, caste, condition of
servitude, age, sex, race, nationality, religion, and
geographic location are negligible quantities. The
Modern Crusade for the betterment of the physical
man is not less honourable in conception, and is much
more productive of results, than were the ill-starred and
numerous spiritual movements of European mobs for the
recovery of the Holy Land from the hands of the infidel.
The mediæval crusades ended in disgrace : the modern
crusade, for the prevention of disease, lifts its head
in glory.

Long after the chief nations of continental Europe,
particularly France and Holland, had made legal
provision for an ample supply of material for anatomical
study ; in Great Britain and in Ireland, in the United
States and in Canada, there was practically but one way
of obtaining bodies for dissection—namely, by stealing
them.

In the whole history of Anglo-Saxon jurisprudence,
probably it would be impossible to find a condition more
incongruous than was that which was held by members
of the medical profession during the early years of the
nineteenth century. On the one hand the law demanded
that the surgeon should possess "proper skill" in his
vocation, and subjected him to pecuniary loss, in the
civil courts, at the whim of a dissatisfied patient. On
the other hand, although the only mode of acquiring
that skill was by the dissection of human bodies which
had been "resurrected," this method of obtaining
anatomical material was punishable by fine and
imprisonment. There are times when "The law is
an ass."

Placed thus between Scylla and Charybdis—one the
law, the other the welfare of the patient—all honour

should be given to those valiant souls who, purely for the benefit of science, dared to disturb the repose of the dead in order to prolong the years of the living.

How illogical is man! How childlike and superficial are statesmen! How negligent and ungrateful are nations!

Monuments of imposing grandeur are scattered in reckless profusion in honour of those who have destroyed millions of the earth's inhabitants. The saviours of men are soon forgotten!

THE
BODY
SNATCHERS

PLATE I

GALEN

A most excellent Physitian, born at Pergamus in Asia. He was a great improver of the Hypocratical System of Physick, and the beginner of that Method of Practice w.ch has been used from his time all lately & from him called Galenical &c. as said to have liv.d to a ... under of 100 Summers, & were burned ye temple of pace that contained by Galen among his most noble ... of Work &c. ...

CHAPTER I

DISSECTION of the human body was banned in ancient days. Although the Egyptians and the early Greeks possessed a certain amount of anatomical knowledge, which was gained in the one instance by the practice of embalming, and in the other by an examination of the bones, no real progress in the study of anatomy could be made because of the laws, customs, and prejudices of those ancient peoples. Thus, we find the Egyptians stoning the operator who was employed to open the abdomen, in order that the body might be embalmed ; and the Greeks inflicted the death penalty on those of their generals who, after a battle, neglected to bury or to burn the remains of the slain.

The veneration of the Greeks for those men who had fallen in defence of their country, the honours which it was the custom to pay to their dead, and the manner of conducting the public funeral for those who had died for the glory of Athens—all these matters fortunately have been preserved for us by Thucydides, the historian of the Peloponnesian War. In the winter which marked the end of the first year of that conflict, the Athenians, in conformity to an established custom of their country, solemnised a public funeral for those who had been first killed in that war, in the manner as follows :—

The bones of the slain were brought to a tabernacle erected for the purpose three days before, and all persons were at liberty to deck out the remains of their friends at their own discretion.   Then the grand procession was formed ; cypress coffins were drawn on carriages, one for every tribe ; and one sumptuous bier was carried along empty, for those who had been lost and whose bodies could not be found among the slain.   The remains were deposited in the public sepulchre, which stood in the finest suburb of Athens—for it had been the constant custom to bury there all who fell in war, except the heroes of Marathon, whose extraordinary valour was acknowledged by giving them burial on the field of battle. At the proper moment Pericles, the son of Xantippus, who had been selected by the public voice, as a person in high esteem and worthy of the honour, arose, passed to the lofty pulpit which had been erected for the purpose, and delivered that matchless oration which has come down to us through the centuries without loss of charm.

Imagine such a people, thus honouring the remains of their dead, permitting dissection !   Impossible !

In the time of Hippocrates, whose life extended approximately over the period between 460-377 B.C., Greek medicine began to emerge from the domination of the Asclepiadæ, or priests of Æsculapius, who long had followed it as an hereditary and a secret art. Before this time, in the numerous Asclepia, or Temples of Æsculapius, many votive offerings had been accepted, some of which were of anatomical interest.

It is impossible to determine whether or not the Greek physicians of the Hippocratic period dissected the human body.   " It has long been a matter of debate," says John Bell,[1] "whether the ancients were, or were not, acquainted with anatomy, and the subject, with its various bearings, has been much and keenly

[1] Bell, *Observations on Italy*, Edinburgh, 1825, p. 257.

PLATE II

HIPPOCRATES
From an Ancient Bust

agitated by the learned. If anatomy had been much known to the ancients, their knowledge would not have remained a subject of speculation. We should have had evidence of it in their works, but, on the contrary, we find Hippocrates spending his time in idle prognostics, and dissecting apes to discover the seat of the bile."

Galen states that the ancient physicians did not write works on anatomy ; that such treatises at that time were unnecessary, because the Asclepiadæ—to which family Hippocrates belonged—secretly instructed their young men in this subject, and that opportunities were given for such study in the temples of Æsculapius.

The first systematic dissections seem to have been made by the Pythagorean philosopher Alcmæon, who lived in the sixth century B.C., but it is uncertain whether he dissected brutes or men. The cochlea of the ear and the amnion of the fœtus were named by Empedocles of Agrigentum, in the fifth century B.C. The nerves were first differentiated from the tendons by Aristotle (384-322 B.C.), the most celebrated zoötomist of antiquity, and the man who has been called the father of comparative anatomy. For twenty centuries his views of natural phenomena were held in high esteem.

What the Greek had banned in his own land, he permitted and fostered in a conquered realm. Under the rule of the Ptolemies, who were of Greek descent, human anatomy was first studied systematically and legally. This took place in the famous Alexandrian Museum or University.

Here were assembled the intellectual giants of the earth : Archimedes, the geometer ; Euclid, the mathematician ; Hero, mathematician and machinist ; Apelles, the painter ; Manetho, the historian ; Hipparchus and Ptolemy (Claudius), the astronomers ; Eratosthenes and Strabo, the geographers; Aristophanes, the dramatist; Callimichus and Theocritus, the poets; and Erasistratus and Herophilus, the anatomists—all of whom laboured in quiet near the peaceful banks of the Nile. The posthumous division of Alexander's vast empire placed Egypt under the rule of Ptolemy Soter, founder of the celebrated Library. He it was who brought Greek culture to the valley of the Nile.

In the cosmopolitan city of Alexandria, Erasistratus and Herophilus taught the science of human organisation from actual dissections. The generosity of the Ptolemies furnished them not only with an abundance of dead material, but with condemned malefactors to be used for human vivisection. Celsus[1] states that the Alexandrian anatomists obtained criminals "for dissection alive, and contemplated, even while they breathed, those parts which nature had before concealed."

Herophilus made many anatomical discoveries. He traced the delicate arachnoid membrane into the ventricles of the brain, which he held to be the seat of the soul. He first described that junction of the six cerebral sinuses, opposite the occipital protuberance, which to this day is called the *torcular Herophili*, or the press of Herophilus. He saw the lacteals, but knew not their use. He regarded the nerves as organs of sensation arising from the brain; he described the different tunics of the eye, giving them names which are still retained; and he first named the duodenum and discovered the epididymis. He attributed the pulsation of arteries to the action of the heart; the paralysis of muscles to an affection of the nerves; and he first named the furrow in the fourth cerebral ventricle, calling it *calamus scriptorius.*

[1] Celsus, *De Medicina.*

PLATE III

ARISTOTLE

From *Illustrium Imagines*, Quæ exstant Romæ, major pars apud Fulvium Ursinum
Antverpiæ, ex officina Plantiniana, M.DC.VI.

Erasistratus gave names to the atria of the heart; he declared that the veins were blood-vessels, and that the arteries, from being found empty after death, were air-vessels. He believed that the purpose of respiration was to fill the arteries with air : the air distended the arteries, it made them beat, and in this manner the pulse was produced. When once the air gained entrance to the left ventricle, it became the vital spirits. The function of the veins was to carry blood to the extremities. He is said to have had a vague idea of the division of nerves into sensory and motor. He assigned to the former an origin in the membranes of the brain, while ascribing to the latter a source from the cerebral substance. He recognised the trachea as the tube which conveys air to the lungs ; and he gravely tells us, as a result of his anatomical studies, that the soul is located in the membranes of the brain.

The practice of human dissection did not long exist in the city of its origin, and after the second century was unknown. Then followed the Roman domination. Whatever had survived the sword of the Roman was destroyed by the scimitar of the Mohammedan.

The ancient period closes with Galen (131-201 A.D.), the most celebrated medical practitioner in Rome, and the chief exponent of Greek medicine after Hippocrates. Born in the important Greek city of Pergamus in Asia Minor, Galen acquired a reputation second only to that of the Father of Medicine. He produced numerous treatises which for centuries were the accepted medical authorities.

Galen's voluminous writings form a precious monument of ancient medicine. The writings of the Alexandrian anatomists having been destroyed, we know of their discoveries chiefly from what Galen has said. His treatises show a remarkable familiarity with practical anatomy, although his dissections were made upon the lower animals. Galen advised his pupils to visit Alexandria, where he had studied, in order that they might examine the human skeleton.

Pagan as he was, nevertheless Galen did not fail to recognise the power, the wisdom, and the goodness of an Almighty Architect. In his *De Usu Partium* is this fine and oft-quoted passage :—" In writing these books, I compose a true and real hymn to that awful Being who made us all ; and, in my opinion, true religion consists not so much in costly sacrifices and fragrant perfumes offered upon his altars, as in a thorough conviction impressed upon our minds, and an endeavour to produce a similar impression upon the minds of others, of his unerring wisdom, his resistless power, and his all-diffusive goodness."

Galen's anatomical studies are said to have resulted in his conversion to Christianity—an event which is the subject of an engraving made by J. Caldwall, late in the eighteenth century.

Following the death of Galen came a long period known as the Dark Ages. The few Greek and Arab medical writers who came after Galen did nothing for anatomy. After the end of the fifth century even the works of Galen were forgotten. At this period, when medicine was chiefly in the hands of the Jews, the Arabs, and the clergy, almost nothing was done for science or for art. The whole influence of Christianity was exerted against the schools of philosophy. Illustrious apostles of the Church pronounced anathemas against the reading of the ancient classics [1]; and eminent ecclesiastics regarded disease as a divine penalty, or as an invaluable aid to saintly advancement. Art and

[1] Fort, *Medical Economy during the Middle Ages*, New York, 1883, pp. 102, 103.

PLATE IV

THE CONVERSION OF GALEN

This undated copperplate, engraved by J. Caldwall, is found in vol. iv., third edition, of an anonymous work entitled *Medical Extracts, or the Nature of Health*, London, 1798.   It is credited to Dr Robert John Thornton

anatomy were practically forgotten. Their renaissance occurred almost simultaneously.

During the period from the seventh to the fourteenth centuries the School of Salernum was for medicine what Bologna became for law, and Paris for philosophy. The origin of this institution is unknown. The potent impress made by the medical profession on the little town of Salernum, situated near Naples, is shown by the term *Civitas Hippocratica*, which was applied to it ; and thus its seals were stamped. Here it was that medical diplomas were first issued to waiting students who took a sacred oath to serve the poor without pay. Here, with a book in his hand, a ring on his finger, and a laurel wreath on his head, the candidate was kissed by each professor and was told to start upon his way. Here women were professors and vied with men in spreading the doctrines of our art.

For a period of several hundred years anatomy was taught at Salernum from dissections made upon pigs. Copho, one of the Salernian professors of the early part of the twelfth century, wrote a treatise, *Anatomia Porci*, in which he gives elaborate instructions for the anatomising of the hog.

Legalised dissection of the human body, which had been abandoned for the long period since the days of the Ptolemies, was revived in the early years of the thirteenth century, and then by imperial authority. This was done by a ruler whose acts and deeds, whose broad and liberal views, made him a thorn in the side of the Church ; by a man to whom Italy, the sciences, and literature are deeply indebted—by Frederick II. (1194-1250), Emperor of Germany, King of the two Sicilies, the last one of the Christian Kings of Jerusalem, the author of a treatise which contains a complete account of the anatomy of the falcon ; by a man who was the boon companion of Arab philosophers and scientists.

In the year 1231, Frederick II. decreed that a human body should be anatomised at Salernum, at least once in five years. Physicians and surgeons of the kingdom were required to be present at the dissection. So far as is known, no record has been kept of these demonstrations.

Founded as it was in the darkest, the most bigoted, and the most superstitious period of the Middle Ages, Salernum, says Handerson,[1] *"preserved, amidst the gloom that had settled upon Europe*, a few rays of that intellectual light which had shone so brightly in the golden ages of Grecian and Roman history." In later days Salernum became the mother and model of our modern university system. Yet, strange to say, as Valentine Mott[2] relates, "not a single vestige or relic whatever remains, by which to identify or recall the former glories of this small village and of its celebrated university."

The decline of Salernum began when the city was sacked by Henry VI., in 1194 (Garrison). Perhaps the most serious blow at her supremacy, says Handerson, "was the foundation by Frederick II., in 1224, of the University of Naples, an institution upon which that Prince bestowed unusual privileges." Finally, in 1811, the famous University itself was abolished by Napoleon.

It is difficult to speak in measured terms of Frederick II. Not only did he advance the study of anatomy; not only did he regulate the education of apothecaries and physicians in his kingdom, and protect his subjects from impostors; but he went far

---

[1] Handerson, *The School of Salernum*, New York, 1883, p. 51.
[2] Mott, *Travels in Europe and the East*, New York, 1842, p. 145.

PLATE V

FREDERICK II

From a Medallion in the Church della Porto Santo in Andria. (Allshorn, *Stupor Mundi*, London, 1912)

beyond these bounds and left a definite impress upon the literature and the life of his people.

It was in his splendidly luxurious and semi-Oriental Court, amid an intellectual atmosphere—where Mohammedans, Christians, Jews, and Infidels, all learned men, mingled on terms of equality ; in a place where wine, women, and song were ever present—that the euphonious Sicilian dialect was used for the purpose of poetic expression. Frederick and his secretary, Peter de Vinea, vied with each other in the writing of sonnets. The Sicilian tongue became the vulgar speech of Italy ; and thus Italy owes the beginning of her national literature to one who was a foreigner and an enemy. It was Danté who bestowed upon Frederick the title of "the Father of Italian Poetry." Freeman, the historian, has called Frederick "the most gifted of the sons of men ; by nature the more than peer of Alexander, of Constantine, and of Charles : in mere genius, in mere accomplishments, the greatest prince who ever wore a crown." And yet this great Emperor left but slight impress upon the history of the world (Allshorn).[1] Frederick's vices and cruelties were not different from those belonging to the Kings and Popes of his time.

Following the death of Frederick, in 1250, the study of practical anatomy was abandoned. Although dissection was legalised in Spain in 1283, in Venice in 1308, in Germany in 1347, and in Naples in 1365, practically nothing was accomplished. The revival of anatomical teaching occurred early in the fourteenth century, and must be credited to Mondino of Bologna.

---

[1] Allshorn, *Stupor Mundi: The Life and Times of Frederick II.*, London, 1912, p. 293.

CHAPTER II

MONDINO, known also as Mundinus, Mundini, Raimondino, or Mondino dei Luzzi, was descended from a prominent Italian family. Little is known of his life.[1] The year of his birth is disputed; probably 1276 was near the time. He graduated in medicine in 1290, and in 1306 became a professor in the University of Bologna, holding his Chair with credit until his death in 1326. Like that of the illustrious Homer, Mondino's nativity has been claimed by several rival cities. Guy de Chauliac, writing in 1363, states that Mondino was a Bolognese; *Mundinus Bononiensis* is Chauliac's expression.

In the year 1315, in the old Italian city of Bologna, a wondering crowd of medical students witnessed the dissection of a human cadaver — one of the few procedures of the kind that had occurred since the fall of the Alexandrian University. Acting under royal authority, Mondino, a man who was far in advance of the age, placed the body of a woman upon a table where for two centuries before only the cadavera of apes, of swine, and of dogs had been studied.

The ancients believed that contact with, or even the simple inspection of, a dead body was sufficient to cause an amount of defilement that would require numerous ablutions and other expiatory practices for its effacement.

---

[1] Valuable papers on the life and influence of Mondino dei Luzzi have been written by Fisher, *Annals of Anatomy and Surgery*, Brooklyn, N.Y., 1882; and Pilcher, *Medical Library and Historical Journal*, Brooklyn, N.Y., 1906.

Law and religion were of one opinion on this subject. In holy writ we read : " He that toucheth the dead body of any man shall be unclean seven days " (Numbers xix. 11).

The early Christians denounced the cutting of the dead body in fierce terms ; the Koran forbade the touching of the dead ; and everywhere men were content to learn human anatomy from comparative dissections.

Guy de Chauliac (1300-1370), writing in 1363, gives valuable information concerning the methods of the early anatomist :—" Mundinus of Bologna, who wrote on anatomy, and my master, Bertruccius, demonstrated it many times in this manner :—The body having been placed on a table, he would make from it four readings : in the first the digestive organs were treated, because more prone to rapid decomposition ; in the second, the organs of respiration ; in the third, the organs of circulation ; and in the fourth the extremities were treated." The innovation so auspiciously begun was not continued, and after the death of Mondino the practice of human dissection was forgotten. Although a dissection was made at Prague in 1348, and another was done at Montpellier in 1376, and a few others are on record, yet the practical study of human anatomy did not gain recognition until the sixteenth century.

At the time Mondino began his dissections, Europe was emerging from ten centuries of intellectual darkness. Chaucer was writing poesy ; Friar Bacon, giving a new impetus to correct thought and advancing scientific knowledge in many directions, was regarded as an evil spirit ; Petrarch and Boccaccio were children ; Danté was composing *The Comedy*[1] ; John of Gaddesden,

---

[1] Danté did not write *The Divine Comedy* ; he wrote *The Comedy* (*La Commedia*). More than a century after his death the *Divine* was added to the title.

physician to the King of England, was writing the *Rosa Anglica*; and Arnold of Villanova was delving into the medical lore of the Greeks and Arabs.

Mondino did not himself make the dissections which usually are credited to him. The actual cutting was done by a barber, who wielded a huge knife resembling a cleaver, while the Professor of Anatomy sat upon an elevated seat and discoursed concerning the parts. A demonstrator, who also did not condescend to soil his fingers, stood by the side of the barber and pointed out the different organs and tissues with a staff. Originally Mondino's book contained no figures, but after the art of wood-cutting was introduced in the fifteenth century, a few woodcuts were supplied. These represent Mondino and his method of teaching. One of these early illustrations is found in the *Fasciculus Medicinæ* of Joannes de Ketham, which was printed at Venice in 1493, in Italian, with nine curious woodcuts. An edition of Mondino's *Anathomia*, which was printed at Leipzig, in 1493, has for its title-page a dissection scene. The professor, who is seated in a huge chair, holds an open book in his left hand while his right index finger points to the viscera of the dead man.

In 1316 Mondino issued his treatise on anatomy, a work which remained in manuscript form for more than one hundred and fifty years. The book was first printed at Pavia, in 1478. Small and imperfect though it was, it marks an era in the history of science. By command of the authorities this book was read in all the Italian Universities. Mondino's book passed through numerous editions. The only manuscript extant is in the National Library at Paris. The author's copy, printed at Strassburg (*Argentina*), in 1513, is an exemplar of the eleventh edition, and is a small octavo volume of forty leaves, in old Gothic black-letter type, with ornamental initial letters and no paging. This copy has catch-words, and contains two woodcuts—one

Anathomia Mū dini Emēdata p̄ doctoꝛé melerstat

TITLE-PAGE OF MONDINO'S "ANATOMY" BY MELERSTAT.
(Leipzig, 1493.)

showing a crude diagram of the heart, while the other presents the signs of the Zodiac. The latter has been printed in two places: on the title-page, and also as the colophon. It represents an astrological figure—a cadaver with the thorax and the abdomen opened, surrounded by the signs mentioned. Such was the volume which for more than two hundred years was supposed to contain all that was to be said of human anatomy!

Mondino was much more considerate than are many modern writers, who foist their literary wares upon an unsuspecting public. Mondino is willing to give us the

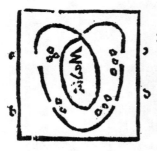

MONDINO'S DIAGRAM OF THE HEART, 1513.

reasons for writing his volume. Here (Pilcher's translation)[1] we have them :—

"A work upon any science or art—as saith Galen—is issued for three reasons : *First*, that one may satisfy his friends ; *second*, that he may exercise his best mental powers ; *third*, that he may be saved from the oblivion incident to old age. Therefore, moved by these three causes, I have proposed to my pupils to compose a certain work on medicine. And because a knowledge of the parts to be subjected to medicine (which is the human body, and the names of its various divisions) is a part of medical science, as saith Averrhoes in his first chapter, in the section on the definition of medicine,

[1] Pilcher, *op. cit.*

for this reason among others I have set out to lay

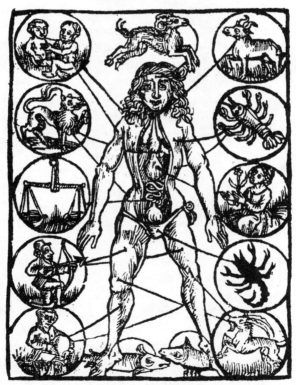

COLOPHON OF THE "ANATOMY" OF MONDINO, 1513.

before you the knowledge of the human body which is
derived from anatomy, not attempting to use a lofty

style, but the rather that which is suitable to a manual procedure."

At the period when Mondino began his dissections, the epoch of Saracen learning had ended; but the influence of Arab medicine, which was exerted by the writings of Albucasis, Avicenna, and Rhazes, had not yet declined. The Arabian physicians, however, had accomplished little for anatomy. In this line the influence of Galen was still potent; and indeed it rarely was questioned until after the publication of the *De Humani Corporis Fabrica* of Andreas Vesalius, in 1543.

Mondino's book contained no new facts. It was compiled largely from the writings of Galen and of Avicenna. The descriptions, to use the words of Turner, "are corrupted by the barbarous leaven of the Arabian schools, and his Latin is defaced by the exotic nomenclature of Ibn-Sina and Al-Rasi." Mondino divided the body into three cavities, of which the upper contains the animal members, the lower the natural members, and the middle the spiritual members. Many of his names are borrowed from the Arab writers. Thus, he calls the peritoneum *siphac*, the omentum *zyrbi*, and the mesentery *eucharus*. His description of the heart is much nearer accuracy than would be expected. Mondino resorted to vivisection, and he tells us that when the recurrent nerves of the larynx are cut the animal's voice is lost.

In Mondino's book we find the rudiments of phrenology. He states that the brain is divided into compartments, each of which holds one of the faculties of the intellect. He describes two membranes of the brain—dura and pia; and three cerebral ventricles—anterior, posterior, and middle: and in these he locates the various intellectual qualities, thus anticipating Gall, Spurzheim, Combe, and other phrenologists. He describes the cerebral nerves—olfactory, optic, motor, oculi, facial, vagus, trigeminal, auditory, and hypoglossal. He calls the innominate bone *os femoris*; the femur, *canna coxæ*; the humerus, *os adjutori*; while the bones of both leg and arm are named *focilia*, majus and minus. For two centuries after Mondino's death, little was done for anatomy.

CHAPTER III

WHO shall define the years which cover the period called "The Middle Ages"? Each thoughtful student should be permitted to make his own chronology. For our purpose this period should begin about the middle of the fifteenth century, and it will continue so far as we wish to continue it. The important events which form milestones in the history of a science cannot be bent to fit a series of dates. It is better that elasticity should be permitted, and in this chapter much elasticity will be in evidence.

The Fifteenth Century.

The fifteenth century was one of the most remarkable epochs of all time. Most of the great events which have influenced European commercial life, and intellectual development, can be traced to that period. For example :—

The invention of printing, the discovery of America, the fall of the Roman Empire in the East, the schism in the Roman Catholic Church ending in the Reformation, the rise of art in Italy, and the beginning of scientific anatomy under the leadership of Leonardo da Vinci and Marc Antonio della Torré—these, and many other innovations belong to the fifteenth century.

At this time almost every city in Italy was a new Athens. The Italian poets, historians, artists, and anatomists vied with the most eminent men of the ancient world in carrying forward the torch of learning.

Florence, Bologna, Milan, Rome, Venice, and Ferrara fought with each other, not for the gains of the battle-field, but for the victories of science and of art. Not so much for the profits of commerce, as for the wealth of genius and of learning. The intellectual development which occurred in Northern Italy under the rule of the House of Medici, and particularly under the auspices of Lorenzo the Magnificent, forms one of the most interesting periods in European history.

The chief anatomical discoveries which were made during the mediæval period must be credited to men who were not of the medical profession—to the artist-anatomists—always, of course, excepting what was done by Andreas Vesalius.

It is quite impossible, in this brief sketch, to trace the steps by which the exquisite taste of the ancients in works of art was revived in mediæval and modern times. Nevertheless, a few words may be devoted to this subject.

While much must be credited to those Greek artists who had left their native country and had settled in the Italian peninsula, yet, it must be conceded that many of the works of art of the native Italians were not the less meritorious. The same circumstances which favoured the revival of letters, operated to further the cause of art; and the same individuals, who were interested in the preservation of the manuscripts of the older authors, also busied themselves with the collection of ancient statues, paintings, gems, and tapestry. The freedom of the Italian republics permitted the minds of men to expand to full fruition; and the encouragement which was given by its rulers to artists, sculptors, and artisans, made the city of Florence, in the fifteenth century, a not less renowned centre of culture than Athens had been in more ancient times.

The close association of Florentine artists with physicians began in the year 1421, when Masaccio was admitted to the Guild of Physicians. Early in this century Art had turned, as in ancient days, to the contemplation of Nature; and then the want was felt of a secure basis for the study of the nude form. Artists then began to look to physicians for instruction in anatomy.

Early in the fifteenth century two Flemish artists, Hubert van Eyck (1365-1426) and his brother John (1385-1441), in their polyptich of *The Adoration of the Lamb*, committed the unheard-of deed of painting nude figures. This example of a new departure in art is found in a polyptich which the van Eycks painted for the Ghent Cathedral. On the outermost panels of the upper zone, Adam and Eve are represented by two nude figures painted with brutal exactitude, direct from living models. Of this polyptich the Ghent Cathedral retains only the central panels. Adam and Eve have found a resting-place in the Royal Gallery of Brussels.

The success of these bold nature studies was so great that the whole pictorial group, in the words of the populace, was named after Adam and Eve. The other beautiful panels, representing God the Father, the Blessed Virgin, St John the Baptist, the Choir of Angels, the Holy Pilgrims, the Holy Hermits, the Knights of Christ, the Just Judges, and the large central group showing the Adoration of the Lamb— all these were forgotten in the charm that was possessed by the rude naked figures of the First Man and Woman.

They stand in stiff posture, without much facial expression. Their muscles, skin, wrinkles, and hair are

PLATE VI

ADAM AND EVE, BY JOHN VAN EYCK.
From *Les Premiers Maîtres des Flandres*, by Fierens-Gevaert.   Bruxelles, 1905

painted in minute detail. The artist seems to have had great difficulty in securing a female model. Eve does not do justice to her sex. She is poorly nourished, her chest is sunken, her prominent abdomen points to an early stage of pregnancy, and, all in all, she seems to be unsuited to the task of perpetuating the human race.

Italy, however, was the birthplace of Art-Anatomy. While the Flemings and others of the North painted everything that they saw, the Italians were the first men of the Renaissance who painted the nude figure before draping it. Leon Battista Alberti (1404-1472), in his treatises on painting, insists that the skeleton must first be drawn and then clothed with its muscles, fat, and skin. This was an important step in advance, since it shows that the Florentine artists were progressing towards realism, and were turning from the symbolism of the early Christian painters and mosaic-workers.

A worthy champion of the new movement in art was Antonio Pollaiuolo (1432-1498), who justly may be named the founder of the scientific study of the nude. Under the patronage of Lorenzo the Magnificent, and the guiding mind of Pollaiuolo, there occurred a revival of pseudo-paganism in art. The old Church subjects were forgotten ; mythological subjects again became the fashion ; draperies were either modified or were laid aside ; and the scientific study of anatomy became the necessary part of the training of the student. Of all the masters of this period, the palm for excellence in drawing the naked figure must be awarded to Luca Signorelli (1442-1524), from whose work Michael Angelo is known to have profited. One of his noblest pictures represents a man carrying a dead youth on his shoulders. Both figures are nude. This work has an allusion to a *touching incident* of Luca's life.   One day his favourite son was brought home dead, having been slain in a duel.   Luca carried the body into his studio, washed away the blood, arranged the light, and, with dry eyes and firm lips, painted the picture of his son (Fletcher).

The statutes of the University of Florence, under the date 1387, set forth the rules under which anatomical demonstrations were conducted.   The authorities were requested to "see to the delivery of not two but three bodies of alien criminals each year; whatever their felonies be, let them be hanged (not burned as the wont is with witches, nor beheaded) and delivered the same day, for corruption comes on apace."[1]   Since artists rarely were admitted to these demonstrations, and public dissections occurred only at long intervals, it is reasonably certain that often artists were compelled to make up "little *post-mortem* parties of their own" (Streeter).   Influential members of the guild were more fortunate—their dissections were made in the dead-houses of the hospitals.   It is believed that the majority of Leonardo's dissections were done in the hospitals of Florence, Milan, and Rome.   No one before him, says Hopstock,[2] "so far as is known, made so many dissections on human bodies nor did any understand so well as he how to interpret the findings."   And no one had so carefully delineated the parts.   Leonardo's anatomical notes and sketches, covering a period of thirty years, show that the painter of *Mona Lisa* and of *The Last Supper* possessed an almost uncanny accuracy, deep physiological insight, untiring zeal, and

[1] Streeter, "The Rôle of Certain Florentines in the History of Anatomy Artistic and Practical," *The Johns Hopkins Hospital Bulletin*, April 1916.

[2] Hopstock, "Leonardo as Anatomist," *Studies in the History and Method of Science*, edited by Charles Singer.   Oxford, at the Clarendon Press, vol. ii., 1921, p. 189.

an unfailing sense of the beautiful.[1] If Leonardo's sketches had been published in his lifetime, or soon thereafter, as Robert Knox[2] remarks, "they would have formed an era, not merely in art, but also in science." The myriad-minded Leonardo was the forerunner of modern science.[3]

Michael Angelo, who carried on his dissections partly in Florence and partly in Rome, for a period of twelve years,[4] hired a house for his purpose and had bodies shipped to him by Realdus Columbus, the celebrated anatomist who first demonstrated the pulmonary circulation. Michael Angelo, unfortunately, often carried his anatomy to an extreme, as witness his picture of soldiers bathing in the Arno when attacked by the enemy. The muscles appear as if devoid of skin.

Quarrels among members of the same guild, fraternity, or profession are of daily note, but who would expect to find rivalries between the anatomising artists and the practical anatomists. Yet, such disputes occurred. Condivi, the pupil and biographer of Michael Angelo, says that his master was so versed in anatomy, "that those who have spent all their lives in that science, and who make a profession of it, hardly know so much of it as he. I speak of such knowledge as is necessary to the arts of painting and sculpture, not of other minutiæ that anatomists observe."

The other side of the shield has been painted by Andreas Vesalius. It is noteworthy that the author of *De Humani Corporis Fabrica*, the most important treatise ever written on human anatomy, which appeared

---

[1] A scholarly evaluation of Leonardo da Vinci as an anatomist is to be found in an Editorial in the *Journal of the American Medical Association*, Chicago, 30th August 1919.

[2] Knox, *Great Artists and Great Anatomists*, London, 1852, p. 164.

[3] Don Gelasio Caetani, *The Scientific Monthly*, November 1924.

[4] Choulant, *Geschichte der anatomischen Abbildung*, Leipzig, 1852.

at Basle in 1543, does not therein state who drew the illustrations, or who cut them in wood. It is only in the *Tabulæ Anatomicæ*, which Vesalius issued in 1538, that the name of Jan Stephan van Calcar is mentioned. Vesalius complains bitterly of the peevishness of the engravers and artists, and says that at times these men so tormented him that he—Vesalius—considered himself to be more unfortunate than the criminal whose body had been dissected (*"neque sculptoribus & pictoribus me ita exercitandum dabo, ut sæpius ob eorum hominum morositatem me illis infeliciorum esse putarem, qui ad sectionem mihi obtigissent"*).[1]

Co-operation of Artists and Anatomists.

Often it has occurred that anatomists and artists have worked together toward a common end, and the close friendships resulting from such co-operative labours are not only interesting, but reflect the highest credit upon the participants.

Affiliations of this kind, for example, existed between Leonardo da Vinci and Marc Antonio della Torré, between Michael Angelo and Realdus Columbus, Benvenuto Cellini and Berengario da Carpi, Jan Stephan van Calcar and Andreas Vesalius, Gaspar Becerra and Juan Valverde di Hamusco, G. Vandergucht and William Cheselden, Sir Robert Strange and William Hunter, Giovanni Battista Piazzetta and Domenico Santorini, Jan Ladmiral and Bernhard Siegfried Albinus, Christian Köck and Samuel Thomas von Soemmering, and between Antonio Serantoni and Paolo Mascagni.

---

[1] Radicis Chinae usus, Andrea Vesalio autore. Lugd., 1547, p. 278. In the 1725 edition of Vesalius's works, edited by Boerhaave and Albinus, this quotation is on p. 680.

We almost unconsciously associate the name of
Rembrandt with that of Tulpius, President of the
Surgeons' Guild of Amsterdam, Johan van Neck with
Frederick Ruysch, Michael Mierevelt with Willem
van der Meer, and Thomas de Keyser with Sebastiaan
Egbertsz.

Relationships of this kind, which long have existed
between the masters of painting and the professors of
anatomy, prove the mutual dependence of art and
anatomy. The practical outcome of such joint labours
justifies the assertion, that the debt which art owes to
anatomy possibly is surpassed only by the obligation
which anatomy owes to art. In every epoch the most
valuable treatises on art-anatomy have been those in
which artists and anatomists of practically equal merit
have been engaged, or they have been produced by
those rare individuals who combined, in their own
persons, the artist and the anatomist. Many of the
most famous painters of the fifteenth and sixteenth
centuries were skilful dissectors, and not a few
anatomists have been able draughtsmen.

Difficulties attending Anatomical Study.

In some instances anatomical knowledge has been
gained by artists at the expense of health, and even of
loss of life. It is related of Bartholomaus Torré, of
Arezzo, whom Vasari calls the greatest Roman artist
of his day, that he constantly kept a cadaver, or parts
thereof in his room, in order that he might make
anatomical sketches. It is not surprising to learn that
no one would live in the same house with him. His
assiduous devotion to the study of anatomy shortened
his days, and he died in 1554, in his twenty-fifth year.
Ludwig Carli, or Civoli,[1] an artist who made wax

[1] Moehsen, *Verzeichnis einer Samlung von Bildnissen*, Berlin, 1771.

models of his own dissections, spent so much time in the dead-house that he contracted epilepsy and lost his memory.   After a period of three years he regained his health and became a famous painter.   When Michael Angelo began to dissect he was so disgusted with the offensiveness of the task that he lost his appetite, and his health became impaired.   For a time he abandoned the dissecting-room, yet he was soon dissatisfied with himself for not being able to do what had been done by others.

Accordingly, he resumed the study, carrying it to the fullest extent necessary to his profession, dissecting not only human bodies but also those of many quadrupeds.   It is related of Arnold Myntens, of the Netherlands School, that he accepted presents from the gallows, dissected these cadavera, and made drawings of the parts.

The Sixteenth Century.

The early part of the sixteenth, like the early years of the twentieth century, was filled with events of the utmost importance to Europe.   The roving mariners of Portugal discovered St Helena and Greenland in 1501, Ceylon in 1507, Sumatra in 1510, Malacca and Java in 1511, and Siam in 1520.   In the same period Scotland was torn by the feuds of the nobility, and late in the year 1513 the power of Scotland was crushed at Flodden, where the loss of 10,000 Scots soldiers made England mistress of the North.   Henry VIII. was England's King, and Wolsey was in the saddle.

In 1513 France, attacked on all sides, was practically driven out of Italy.   In the same year Leo X., second son of the illustrious Lorenzo de' Medici, became Pope, and proved himself a munificent patron of the arts and sciences; and in the same year Charles V. was made

King of Spain and of the Netherlands. In 1514 Hungary declared a crusade against the Turks. Five years later Prussia was at war with Poland. In 1510 Russia was laid waste by the Tartars of Kasan and the Crimea; and four years later the Russians defeated the Poles. In 1514 the Persians were defeated in a decisive battle, and Mesopotamia and Kurdistan were added to the Ottoman Empire.

In the Western Hemisphere important events were taking place. In 1500 the Portuguese, Cabral, while on a voyage to India, by accident discovered Brazil; and in the same year Columbus was sent home in chains. In 1510 the first settlement of the New World was made at Darien. In 1511 Cuba was conquered, and in 1512 Florida was discovered. A few years later Mexico was invaded by Cortez.

In 1571, Don John of Austria, the brilliant illegitimate son of Charles the Fifth, crushed the Ottoman fleet in the Gulf of Lepanto, thus lifting a great fear from the Christian nations of Europe. The bastard's triumph, which threw Europe into a frenzy of delight, has been celebrated in song and story: thus, Chesterton in *Lepanto* :—

" King Philip's in his closet with the Fleece about his neck,
 (Don John of Austria is armed upon the deck.)
 Christian captives sick and sunless, all a labouring race repines
 Like a race in sunken cities, like a nation in the mines.
 (*But Don John of Austria has burst the battle line.*")

The whole world was like a volcano—quiet at times, but pouring out fire and brimstone when least expected.

These were some of the military and political movements of the time; but there were other movements. The early years of the sixteenth century were marked by the beginning of the Reformation, by the birth of the Order of the Jesuits (in 1535), by the extension of the power of the Inquisition, and by the founding of numerous Universities. Surely the period was one of great activity.

Great things were done for medicine in the sixteenth century. Under the scalpel and pen of Vesalius, anatomy was revolutionised. Surgery was guided into new paths by Ambroise Paré; and obstetrics, thanks to the labours of Eucharius Rhodion and Jacques Guillemeau, began to assume its legitimate place among the medical sciences. Servetus, visionary and argumentative, correctly described the pulmonary circulation in a theological work which was burned with its author. Eustachius, Columbus, and Fallopius widened the path which had been blazed by Vesalius. Arantius, Cæsalpinus, Fabricius and Casserius added materially to anatomical science. The labours of these great masters helped to prepare the way for the greatest event occurring in the seventeenth century, namely, William Harvey's discovery of the circulatory movement of the blood.

Andreas Vesalius, the Reformer of Anatomy.

At long intervals a bright particular star appears in the intellectual horizon, endowed with genius of such a superlative order as seemingly to comprise within itself the whole domain of an entire science. These men do not belong to any particular epoch in the development of the human mind. They are not monopolised by race, nor are they tethered by latitude or longitude. They are the eternal symbols of progress. Their history is the history of the science which they profess. Such men were Bacon, Galileo, Descartes, Newton, Young, Lavoisier, and Bichat; and such a man also was Andreas Vesalius, the anatomist.

Young, enthusiastic, courageous, and diligent, Vesalius overthrew the authority of Galen; corrected the anatomical mistakes of thirteen centuries; started anatomical, physiological, and surgical investigation in the right channels; first correctly illustrated his dissections; made many new discoveries; and before his thirtieth year had published the most accurate, complete, and best illustrated treatise on human anatomy that the world had ever seen. This man, Andreas Vesalius of Brussels (1514-1564), deserves the name which Morley has given him—"the Luther of Anatomy."

And this man, whose discoveries have been of untold value to the world, was compelled to steal bones and bodies in order to pursue his studies. His industry, the success which crowned his efforts, the fierce attacks which were made upon him by his contemporaries, the honours which were conferred upon him by Charles the Fifth and Philip the Second, his pilgrimage to the Holy Land, and his tragic death—these, and many other events which deserve to be chronicled, may be studied elsewhere.[1]

The year 1543 marks the date of a revolution which was won, not by force of arms but by the scalpel of an anatomist and the hand of an artist. The whole of

[1] Most of the Vesalian literature which has been written by English and American authors has been in the form of brief articles for the medical press. These oftentimes have been incorrect and unillustrated. Perhaps the best example of this class is Mr Henry Morley's essay, "Anatomy in Long Clothes," which appeared originally in *Fraser's Magazine*, in 1853, and later was published in his *Clement Marot and Other Studies*, in 1871. In modern times the monumental work of Roth, *Andreas Vesalius Bruxellensis*, Berlin, 1892, has surpassed any preceding account of the life and labours of Vesalius.

Other contributions to Vesalian literature are :— Ball, *Andreas Vesalius, the Reformer of Anatomy*, St Louis, 1910. Spencer, "The 'Epitome' of Vesalius on Vellum in the British Museum Library," reprinted from *Essays on the History of Medicine*, presented to Professor Karl Sudhoff. Spielmann, *The Iconography of Andreas Vesalius*, London, 1925.

human anatomy, as concerns correct descriptions and accurate delineations thereof, was founded by Andreas Vesalius and Jan Stephan van Calcar. Light poured into a prism remains unnoticed until it emerges in iridescent hues : so with anatomy, after having passed through the brain of Vesalius it bore rich fruit which has been gathered by many hands. To turn from the writings of Galen, Mondino, Hundt, Peyligk, Phryesen, Berengario da Carpi, and Charles Estienne to the clear text and the beautiful illustrations of Vesalius's *De Humani Corporis Fabrica* is to pass from darkness into sunlight. To both anatomists and artists this book was a revelation. For more than two centuries the osteological and myological figures of the *Fabrica* formed the basis of all treatises on art-anatomy.

The preparatory education of Vesalius was obtained at Louvain ; and it was so thorough that he could read the works of Latin, of Greek, and of Arab authors in the original. In 1533 Vesalius went to Paris, which city then was the medical centre of the world. Here the most famous teachers of the healing art were Jacobus Sylvius (1478-1555), or Jacques Dubois, whose Latinised name is attached to the *aqueduct*, the *fissure*, and the *artery of Sylvius* ; Joannes Guinterius (1487-1574), known also as Winter of Andernach, from the name of the town in which he was born ; and Jean Fernel (1485-1558), of Amiens, who dipped deeply into physiology, philosophy, geometry, and mathematics, and was the author of many books. Fernel was physician-in-ordinary to Henry the Second. Like thousands of other Protestants, Fernel lost his life on St Bartholomew's Night.

Sylvius was noted for his industry, for his eloquence, and above all for his avarice. He was a demonstrative teacher. He was the first professor in France who taught anatomy from the human cadaver. In his lectures on botany he used a collection of plants to elucidate the subject. His chief fault was a blind reverence for ancient authors. He regarded Galen's writings as gospel; if the cadaver presented structures which were unlike Galen's description, the fault was not in the book but with the dead body! Or, perchance, human structure had changed since Galen's time! In one of his early books, Sylvius declared that Galen's anatomy was infallible; that Galen's treatise, *De Usu Partium*, was divine; and that further progress was impossible.

JACOBUS SYLVIUS.

Sylvius was brilliant in learning and contemptible in character. Rough, coarse, and brutal, in controversies he was violent and vindictive—a past-master in the use of bitter language. Jealous of the fame of other anatomists, he was particularly enraged when, in later years, he was opposed by Vesalius. Sylvius spoke of him not as *Vesalius*, but as *Vesanus*, a madman, who poisoned Europe by his impiety and clouded knowledge by his blunders.

Sylvius's avarice led him to endure the cold winters of Paris without the benefit of a fire; in severe weather he would play at football, or engage in other violent exercise in his room, to save the cost of fuel. Once, and once only, did his friends find him hilarious: they wondered, and asked the cause. Sylvius said he was happy because he had dismissed his "three beasts—his

mule, his cat, and his maid." His reputation for miser-
liness followed him beyond the grave, as witness his
epitaph :—

> " *Sylvius hic situs est, gratis qui nil dedit unquàm,*
>   *Mortuus et gratis quod legis ista dolet.*"

("Sylvius lies here, who never gave anything for nothing :
  Being dead, he even grieves that you read these lines for
    nothing.")

Such was the man who, in the mid-part of the
sixteenth century, filled the position of highest honour
in the Medical Faculty of the Collège de France.[1] Such
was the man from whom Andreas Vesalius received his
first instruction in anatomy.

The manner in which Sylvius conducted his anatomical
course is known to us by his own writings, by the
testimony of Moreau,[2] and by that of Vesalius.[3] Thus
the course for the year 1535 began with the reading,
by Sylvius, of Galen's treatise *De Usu Partium*. When
the middle of the first book was reached, Sylvius
remarked that the subject was too difficult for his
students to understand and that he would not plague
his class with it. He then jumped to the fourth book,
read all to the tenth book, discussing a part of the tenth,
and omitting the eleventh, twelfth, and thirteenth, he
took up the fourteenth and the remaining three books.

---

[1] The Collège Royal de France was founded by Francis the First.
This enlightened patron of the sciences and arts recognised the merits of
scientific men and rewarded them with his money and his friendship. He
established the Collège de France with twelve richly-endowed professor-
ships, one of which was devoted to medicine. The lectures were free to
all who desired to attend. The first incumbent of the Chair of Medicine
was Vidus Vidius, Guido Guidi, of Florence, who filled this position from
1542 to 1548. Such success followed his labours that, on his return to
Italy, his experience in Paris was the subject of this witticism : *Vidus
venit, Vidius vidit, Vidus vicit.*

[2] Moreau, *Vita Sylvii, in Sylvii Opera Medica*, Geneva, 1635.

[3] Vesalius, *De radice Chinæ epistola*, 1546, pp. 151, 152.

PLATE VII

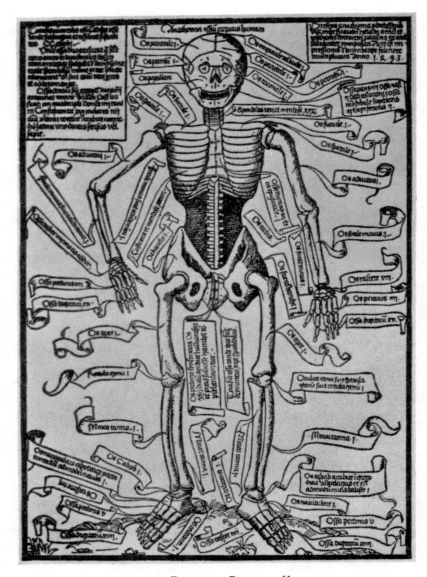

ANATOMICAL FIGURE BY RICARDUS HELA, 1493

Not infrequently the professor was unable to demonstrate in dissection the parts on which he had lectured.

Sylvius, says Northcote,[1] *rendered valuable service in naming the muscles*, which prior to his time were designated by numbers. These, says Northcote, "were differently applied by almost every author; so that it was the description, and not the name, that must lead one to know what part was meant by such authors; and this required a previous thorough knowledge of anatomy." Sylvius is the first writer who mentions coloured injections of the blood-vessels, but he rejects the injection method because the liquid escapes when the vessels are cut and the preparation thereby is spoilt. He gave the first satisfactory descriptions of the pterygoid and clinoid processes of the sphenoid bone, and of the os unguis. He gave a good account of the sphenoidal sinus in the adult but denied its existence in the child, as had been asserted by Fallopius.[2] He wrote intelligently of the vertebræ but incorrectly described the sternum. He observed the valves in the veins; the honour of priority in this discovery, however, belongs to other anatomists—Estienne and Cannanus.

Another famous member of the Paris Faculty of this period, and a man whose life-story reads like a romance, was Joannes Guinterius, the beggar of Deventer, who rose to the rank of a nobleman of Strassburg. Like Sylvius, Guinterius was a teacher of men who became greater than himself—Vesalius, Servetus, and Rondelet sat upon his benches. Like Sylvius, he placed his faith in Galen, and failed to grasp the great truth that anatomical science is based, not on the writings of the fathers but on dissection of the dead body.

---

[1] Northcote, *History of Anatomy*, London, 1772, p. 56.
[2] Portal, *Histoire de l'Anatomie et de la Chirurgie*, Paris, 1770, vol. i., p. 365.

The anatomical teaching in Paris in the early part of the sixteenth century was far from satisfactory.

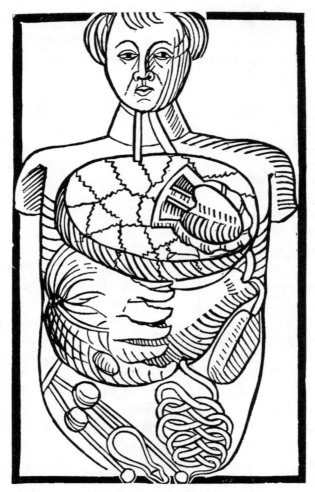

ANATOMICAL FIGURE FROM MAGNUS HUNDT, 1501.

There was too much of lecturing from Galen's texts and too little of actual dissection. Rarely was a human body brought into the amphitheatre, and then the

PLATE VIII

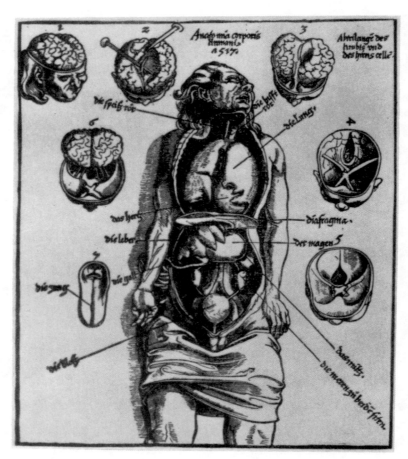

ANATOMICAL FIGURE FROM LAURENTIUS PHRYESEN, 1518

dissection lasted less than three days. The bones, veins, arteries, and nerves were almost wholly ignored. Such teaching did not satisfy the young Belgian who, on more than one occasion, brushed the ignorant prosectors aside, took the knife into his own hands, and carried out the dissection in a systematic manner. His zeal and learning won the admiration of Guinterius who spoke of Vesalius and Servetus in loving terms : "first Andreas Vesalius, a young man, by Hercules! of singular zeal in the study of anatomy ; and second, Michael Villanovanus (Servetus), deeply imbued with learning of every kind, and behind none in his knowledge of the Galenic doctrine. With the aid of these two I have examined the muscles, veins, arteries, and nerves of the whole body, and demonstrated them to the students."[1]

Realising that the great lights of the Paris profession were totally unfit to give him what was his heart's desire, Vesalius resolved to devote his energy, his talents, and his life to the mastering and the teaching of anatomical science. He dreamed of the time when he might rival the great masters who had taught anatomy in the Alexandrian University, and he knew that he must secure an abundance of material for dissection, and secure it personally and at his own peril. "Never," he says, "would I have been able to accomplish my purpose in Paris if I had not taken the work into my own hands." The Book of Nature which Sylvius lauded, but kept his pupils from studying, was now opened by Vesalius. In his search for a skeleton he haunted the Cemetery of the Innocents. On one occasion, when he went to Montfauçon, the place where the bodies of executed criminals were deposited and bones were plentiful, Vesalius and his

[1] Guinterius, *Anatomicarum Institutionum*, 1539.

fellow-student were attacked by fierce dogs. They came near leaving their own bones to the hungry scavengers. But he gained his objective and became so versed in osteology that he could play "blind-man's buff" with a dead man's bones, articulating a skeleton solely by the sense of touch. During the short period of his stay in Louvain—late in the year 1536 or early in 1537—Vesalius conducted the first public anatomy that had there been held in eighteen years. Here, accompanied by his friend, Regnier Gemma, he made secret nocturnal visits to the gallows outside the walls of the city of Louvain, in order to secure the bones of a robber who had been chained to the top of a high stake and roasted alive. Vesalius climbed the gallows and secured the prize.

Vesalius left Louvain and journeyed into Italy, in which country his greatest scientific triumphs were to be attained. It was in the year 1537 that he entered the prosperous and enlightened city of Venice, where the study of anatomy was encouraged, particularly by the Theatin monks, who devoted themselves to the care of the sick. At the head of this Order stood two remarkable men—J. Peter Caraffa, who later ascended the Papal throne as Paul IV., and Ignatius Loyola, the founder of the Jesuits. It is a strange circumstance that two strong characters so dissimilar as were Vesalius and Loyola should meet as co-workers in the same field. The one was dreaming of the day when his *opus magnum* should revolutionise anatomy; the other was enthused with visions of the world-wide acceptance of Catholicism. They met again, in 1543—the year which marks three important events, namely, the publication of the *Fabrica;* the full recognition of the Jesuits by the Pope; and the appearance of the *De Revolutionibus Orbium Cœlestium*, by which, to use the words of

PLATE IX

JOANNES GUINTERIUS, WINTER OF ANDERNACH

Dr Harvey Cushing, "Copernicus, at a stroke, dethroned the Aristotelian theory of a fixed and immovable world."

In order to gain all the rights and privileges of a full-fledged physician, Vesalius settled in Padua. On the 6th day of December 1537, shortly after having

INITIAL LETTER BY VESALIUS.
From the *Fabrica*, 1543.

received his degree as Doctor of Medicine, Andreas Vesalius of Brussels was appointed Professor of Surgery with the right to teach anatomy, in the famous University of Padua. This was the first purely anatomical Chair ever instituted.

The years which Vesalius spent in Padua were years of intensive activity: anatomy was taught by day, and anatomical dissections, drawings, and writings occupied many hours of the night. Here, as he had done previously at Louvain, Vesalius dismissed the ignorant barbers and himself acted as lecturer, demonstrator, and dissector.   All possible means were employed to secure anatomical material, much of which was obtained by stealth.

The aula in which Vesalius conducted his course was built of wood and was capable of holding 500

INITIAL LETTER BY VESALIUS.
From the *Fabrica*, 1543.

persons.   Here, before an audience of distinguished laymen and students, a strenuous anatomical course was given, occupying practically the entire day for a period of three weeks, and comprising not only human but also much of comparative anatomy.   Vivisection of dogs, pigs, and rarely of cats, was a regular part of the course.   Drawings were used in the teaching, and many of these pictorial aids were made by the master himself. Few instruments were employed in his dissections.

PLATE X

TITLE-PAGE OF THE "FABRICA," 1543

An astonishing output came from the pen of Vesalius during his Paduan years. His first work was a set of anatomical plates, *Tabulæ Anatomicæ*, issued as loose sheets, or *Fliegende Blätter*, for the use of his students, comprising six engravings which are now among the rarest of medical works. These, printed at Venice in 1538, show three views of the skeleton ; the portal system and the organs of generation ; the venæ cavæ and chief veins ; and the great artery—*arteria magna*—and the heart. All were of large size, measuring over sixteen inches in length, and were cut in wood. The skeletons were drawn by van Calcar ; the other illustrations probably were by Vesalius. The beauty of these plates, their fidelity to nature, and the skill with which they were cut in wood, were features which showed the world that a real master of anatomy had been born. In the same year, for the further benefit of his class, he edited an edition of Guinterius's *Institutionum Anatomicarum*, which was issued in April 1538. For a while the press slumbered, but not for long.

Suddenly, in the month of June 1543, the scientists of Europe were astounded to have presented to them, almost simultaneously, two treatises on anatomy, both written by the young professor in the University of Padua. The one, a thin book called for short the *Epitome*,[1] may be likened to the herald who goes in advance to announce the impending arrival of the king. The other, a huge folio volume with magnificent illustrations cut in wood, and carefully printed by Joannes Oporinus (1507-1568) of Basel, is known as the *Fabrica*,[2] and is by far the greatest work of its

---

[1] The title is, *Andreæ Vesalii Bruxellensis, Scholæ medicorum Patavinæ professoris, suorum de Humani corporis fabrica librorum Epitome. Basil, ex officina Joannis Oporini, Anno 1543, mense Junio.*

[2] The title is, *Andreæ Vesalii Bruxellensis, Scholæ medicorum Patavinæ professoris, de Humani corporis fabrica Libri Septem. Basileæ, MDXLIII.*

kind that ever came from the brain and the pen of any one man. This is the treatise on which modern anatomy has been founded.

This is not the place in which to list the anatomical

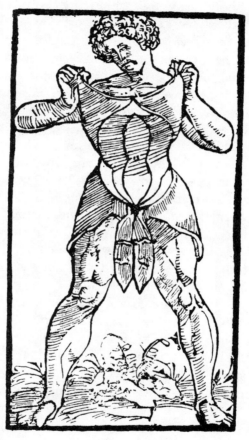

MUSCLES BY BERENGARIO, 1521.

discoveries of Andreas Vesalius. It is not the place in which to recount the many interesting and exciting episodes of his life. But this much we can do: just as the eye can grasp a picture quicker than the mind can

PLATE XI

JOANNES OPORINUS

interpret a printed text, so we may let the reader draw his own conclusions from some of the anatomical illustrations of the pre-Vesalian period, comparing them with some of the pictures in the *Fabrica*.

MUSCLES BY BERENGARIO, 1521.

Berengario da Carpi (1470-1550), who was a member of the Bologna Faculty from 1502 to 1527, must be given the credit of furnishing some of the first anatomical illustrations that were published, and that were made

SECOND VESALIAN PLATE OF THE MUSCLES.
From the *Fabrica*, 1543. (Reduced one-half.)

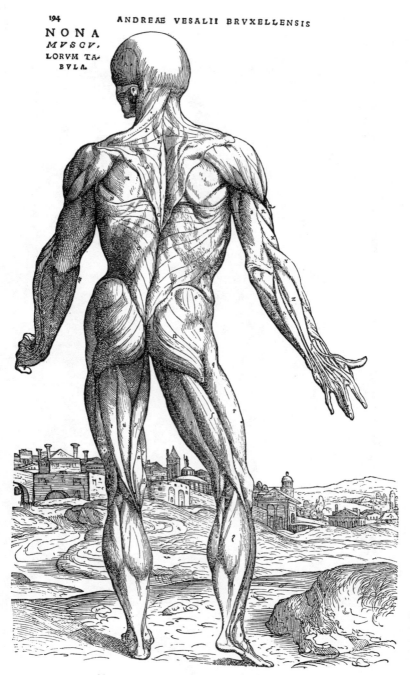

NINTH VESALIAN PLATE OF THE MUSCLES.
From the *Fabrica*, 1543. (Reduced one-half.)

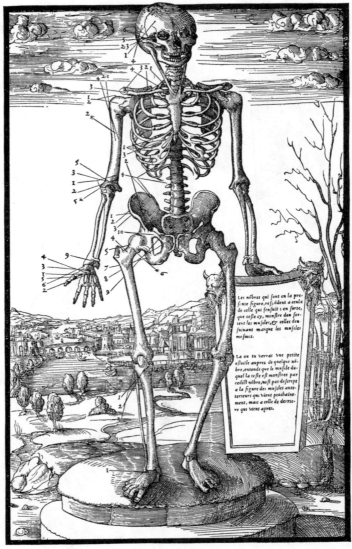

SKELETON BY ESTIENNE, 1545.
(Reduced one-half.)

from actual human dissections. (See figs. on pp. 40 and 41.)

Let us compare Berengario's representation of the muscles with what is shown in the second and ninth Vesalian plates of myology. The difference in years is twenty-two : otherwise, what ?

One of the most meritorious of the pre-Vesalian works on anatomy was written by Charles Estienne (Carolus Stephanus), who belonged to that noted Huguenot family of scholars and printers who have made the Estienne name famous. His anatomical treatise, *De Dissectione Partium Corporis Humani*, which appeared at Paris in 1545—two years after the publication of the *Fabrica*—is really a pre-Vesalian book. The work was printed as far as the middle of the third book as early as the year 1539 : some of the sixty-two full-page plates, well cut in wood, are dated as early as the year 1530. They combine anatomical clearness, beauty of form, and artistic representation. The gifted author suffered for his faith, was thrown into a dungeon, and died therein in the year 1564.

CHAPTER IV

RESURRECTION DAYS

THE term "Resurrection Days" is applied to the period when the Irish, the Scottish, and the English teachers of anatomy were compelled to deal with grave-robbers. In the early part of the nineteenth century, and long prior thereto, an adequate supply of material for dissection could not be obtained legally. In this respect the United Kingdom and Ireland were far behind the nations of continental Europe.

It was not until after the passage of the Warburton Anatomy Act in 1832 that the vocation of body-snatching, which long had been regarded as a despised but a necessary evil, was gradually abandoned. Prior to the date mentioned above, the only legalised source of material for dissection was that small and variable supply resulting from the execution of criminals. It was not until the reign of George II. in 1726 that the bodies of *all* executed criminals were given for dissection in England. "In all Great Britain, from 1805 to 1820, there were executed eleven hundred and fifty criminals, or about seventy-seven annually; and at the same time there were over one thousand medical students in London and nearly as many in Edinburgh"[1] (Keen).[2] The natural result was the

[1] The number of students of medicine, entered in the matriculation list of the University of Edinburgh, has been compiled for decennial periods from 1770 to 1820. The yearly average in the decennium from 1770 to 1780 was 301 ; from 1810 to 1820 it was 849. (Struthers, *Historical Sketch of the Edinburgh Anatomical School*, Edinburgh, 1867, p. 30.)

[2] Keen, *A Sketch of the Early History of Practical Anatomy*, Philadelphia, 1874, p. 17.

rifling of graves. As the demand for anatomical material was a permanent one, there arose a class of desperadoes who were called "Sack-'em-up Men," "Resurrectionists," or "Resurrection-Men"; and the several decades during which they were most active have been given the incongruous appellation of "Resurrection Days."

To understand the rise of the "Resurrectionists," it is necessary to give an account of the early history of anatomy in Ireland, Scotland, and England.

Early History of Anatomy in Ireland.

To the city of Dublin belongs the honour of having been the birthplace of the first incorporation of medical practitioners in the United Kingdom.

On 18th October 1446 King Henry VI. established by Royal Charter a Fraternity, or Guild of Barbers. The next one was that of the London Barber-Chirurgeons in 1461.[1]

The charter of King Henry cannot be found. It may have been surrendered when it was succeeded by one granted to barber-chirurgeons by Queen Elizabeth in 1572. This new document, which gave to women the freedom of the guild, stated that the incorporation "from henceforth for ever" should be known "by the name of Master Wardens and Fraternity of Barbers and Chirurgeons of the Guild of St Mary Magdalene within our City of Dublin." This was followed by a charter, granted 10th February 1687, in the third year of the reign of James II.

In this document, "Barbers Chirurgeons Apothecayres and Perriwigmakers of the citty of Dublin" are scattered about in tiresome profusion. Its redeeming

---

[1] Cameron, *History of the Royal College of Surgeons in Ireland*, Dublin, 1886, p. 60.

feature is this—the names of eight men are set down as "physicians and readers of Anotomy." [1]

The union between the barbers and the surgeons, says Cameron,[2] was dissolved *de facto*, though perhaps not *de jure*, in 1784, by the creation of a Royal College of Surgeons in Ireland.

ARMS OF THE DUBLIN BARBER-SURGEONS' COMPANY.

Although the robbery of graves for dissection purposes, in and near Dublin, was common in the mid-part of the eighteenth century, it was not until nearly a century later that the Irish could boast of anatomists, physicians, and surgeons who commanded the respect of the world.

Exportation of bodies from the north of Ireland to Glasgow and Edinburgh was carried on for many years prior to its detection in 1827. Many bodies also were shipped to London. The demands of Edinburgh and London were imperative. In 1827, says Cameron, the

---

[1] Cameron, *History of the Royal College of Surgeons in Ireland*, Dublin, 1886, p. 72.　　　　　[2] *Ibid.*, p. 183.

PLATE XII

JAMES BORTHWICK (1615-1675), the first special Demonstrator of Anatomy in Edinburgh

From a Portrait in the Royal College of Surgeons, Edinburgh

number of medical students was about 900 in each of these cities.

In Dublin and in its vicinity the stealing of bodies was easily accomplished. Several of the ancient burial-grounds were either insufficiently enclosed, or they had walls which were easily scaled. The graveyard which probably supplied the largest number of subjects was one known, in popular parlance, as " Bully's Acre," owing to the large number of rowdies or bullies who have been buried in it. It was a free burial-ground where the lowest and poorest persons brought their dead. Since the graves were unguarded at night the "sack-'em-up men" could work here with impunity. For many years prior to the passage of the Warburton Anatomy Act, bodies from this "Acre" were regularly shipped from the north of Ireland to the schools in Glasgow and Edinburgh. They were landed from boats on lonely parts of the coast, particularly that of Ayrshire.

Early History of Anatomy in Scotland.

To the credit of Scotland it must be said that provision for dissection was made at a comparatively early period. The evidence of this is contained in the first charter to the Surgeons of Edinburgh, which was granted by the Town Council, 1st July 1505, and was ratified by James IV. in the following year.

This was one hundred and twenty-three years prior to the appearance of Harvey's book in which he announced the discovery of the circulation of the blood—a circulation which he did not live to see in its entirety.[1] It was nine years before the birth of Vesalius. Charles V., who many years later called a consultation of divines at

[1] Harvey died 3rd June 1657; Malpighi discovered the capillaries in 1661.

Salamanca,[1] to know whether in good conscience a human body might be dissected, for the sake of comprehending its structure, was little more than five years of age.

Long before the granting of the charter of 1505, in Edinburgh, as in other towns, there were guilds of barber-surgeons as of other trades; and in fifteenth-century Edinburgh, the Brethren of the Guild of Surgeons and Barbers maintained an altar where daily service was held in the Collegiate Kirk of St Giles, under the patronage of St Mungo.[2]

The charter stipulated that the candidate, before he became a freeman and master of the craft, should pass an examination in a number of subjects, particularly "thatt he knaw anotomea, nature and complexioun of every member In manis bodie," etc. A noteworthy concession by the Town Council, as indicating the beginning of public teaching, is the grant to the guild "that we have anis in the yeir ane condampnit man efter he be deid to mak antomea of quhairthrow we may haif experience Ilk ane to instruct utheris."

Thus the early study of practical anatomy in Scotland hinged upon, or rather completed, the work of the law: the surgeons were given for dissection "ane condampnit man"—one condemned man—each year.

The words, "efter he be deid," indicate that, prior to the reign of James IV., cases had occurred in which incomplete strangulation by hanging was followed by revival. History has recorded several such instances, of which one of the most interesting was that of Patrick Redmond in Cork, in 1766, who was resuscitated by Glover, a play-actor.

In the evening following his incompleted execution

---

[1] Hutchinson, *Biographia Medica*, London, 1799, vol. ii., p. 472.

[2] Comrie, "Early Anatomical Instruction at Edinburgh," *Edinburgh Medical Journal*, December, 1922.

PLATE **XIII**

THE "TENEMENT" IN DICKSON'S CLOSE

The stair and walls are still standing, though the overhanging timber in front
has been removed

Redmond, effervescing with gratitude and fortified by whisky, went to the playhouse, and on Glover's appearance, jumped upon the stage, where he returned his profuse thanks to his preserver, to the no small terror and astonishment of the audience.[1]

The fact that the bodies of hanged criminals were to be "left for dissection" increased the natural horror of the populace against the practice; and for three centuries it retarded the study of practical anatomy in Scotland and in England (Lonsdale).[2]

It is presumed that the annual anatomical demonstration was conducted after the plan which Mondino, two centuries earlier, had employed at Bologna. Since there was much travel in the sixteenth century between Scotland and the Continent, probably, as Comrie[3] suggests, either Mondino's small text-book or that of his contemporary, Henri de Mondeville, of Paris and Montpellier, was used.

The yearly demonstrations made by the master surgeons in rotation were succeeded, in 1645, by those given by a definite teacher of anatomy, named James Borthwick, who had served abroad "as a surgeon along with Alexander Penicuik," who had been surgeon to General Bannier (Commander of the Swedish Forces in the Thirty Years' War), and later Chirurgeon-General to the Auxiliary Scots Army in England (during the Civil War).[4]

[1] Lonsdale, in his *Life of Robert Knox, the Anatomist*, London, 1870, p. 50, relates this incident and cites as authority T. Crofton Croker, *Researches in the South of Ireland*, p. 191.

[2] Lonsdale in 1870 cites an instance: "Upwards of forty years ago a man was hanged in Carlisle; and the friends of the culprit determined to revenge themselves on the doctors who engaged in the post-mortem examination. All the medical men sustained personal injuries, and of a severe kind." One was shot in the face; another was thrown over the parapet of a bridge and was killed.

[3] Comrie, *op. cit.*   [4] *Ibid.*

Up to that time it had been the custom to hold the meetings of the craft in the house of the deacon. However, in 1647, David Kennedy and James Borthwick reported that they had taken as a place of meeting, "three rowmes of ane tenement of land in Diksone Close, for payment of fourtie poundis zeillie" (Comrie).

Early recognition of the importance of dissection by the Town Council of Edinburgh bore but little fruit. For a period of nearly two centuries after the granting of the charter of 1505, nothing of value for anatomy was done in Scotland.

For many years Scotland was so much engrossed with her political status ; was so much concerned with theological disputes ; was so much occupied with the destruction of witches (nine of whom were burned together, at Leith, in 1664), that but slight if any energy could be expended on the medical sciences. The revival of anatomical study in Edinburgh can be traced to the University of Leyden, and to the activities of Dr Archibald Pitcairne, a Scot, who, for a brief period, was Professor of Practice of Physic in the famous Leyden school. It was his hope that in Edinburgh there might be built up a school of medicine which should rival that of Leyden. It now is time to consider the circumstances under which the University of Leyden was born.

How did it occur that Edinburgh became a famous centre for anatomical instruction? The answer follows :—

The torch of medical science does not remain permanently in any one city or country ; it is as elusive as a will-o'-the-wisp, and it has been known to appear when and where it was least expected. Nor is there any one university or other institution of learning that is sacrosanct, albeit some of them childishly think that

PLATE **XIV**

Archibald Pitcairne (1652-1713)
From a Portrait in the Royal College of Physicians, Edinburgh

PLATE XV

VIEW OF LEYDEN UNIVERSITY, as it appeared in 1614
From Lacroix's *Science and Literature in the Middle Ages*

they are such ; and that all learning, refinement, and culture will expire coetaneously with their demise.

Just as the financial centre of the world has moved from Venice to Amsterdam, from Amsterdam to London, and then, as some persons claim, from London to New York City, so has been the migration of anatomical science—which means medical science in general.

Early in the sixteenth century, Paris was the medical centre of the world.   Then, thanks to the brilliant anatomical discoveries made by Vesalius, Padua and other Universities in Northern Italy, in which he taught, came to the front.   Next, strange to say, the palm for excellence in medical teaching passed suddenly from old Padua to new Leyden.   Why ?

In the long and terrible religious war which Charles V. and his son and successor, Philip II., conducted against the heretical Netherlanders : a war in which the people of the *Pays bas*, or Low Countries, finally defeated the Spanish monarchy, which till then was the greatest power in Christendom ; a war which ended in giving to Spain a staggering and almost mortal blow, a slowly evidenced wound—from which she will not recover in our day and generation—of all the Hollandish cities there was not another which had put up so heroic a defence as did the city of Leyden.   And when peace had been declared, the citizens of Leyden—the few who survived—were offered an alternative reward : they might have an absolute remission of taxes for a long period of years, or they might have a University established in their city.

To their lasting credit be it said, that the citizens of Leyden chose the University.   The University of Leyden was established in 1575, by William I. (1533-1584) of Nassau, Prince of Orange, who was murdered at the instigation of Philip II. of Spain.   In a brief period the medical department of this University became the most famous institution of its kind.

It was here, in the year 1589, that Pieter Paaw, Professor of Anatomy and Botany, built the first anatomy theatre in the Netherlands. Andreas Stog's engraving of this structure is shown in the following plate.

For nearly two centuries Leyden remained the medical centre of the world. Here, as elsewhere in their domain, Dutchmen made discoveries of supreme importance in many different lines. It may suffice to mention only a few names: Erasmus (1467-1536), whose literary activities were widespread and whose collected works (Basel, 1540) had the honour to be condemned to the flames by Pope Paul IV.; Grotius (1583-1645), whose writings founded the international law of the seventeenth and eighteenth centuries; Boerhaave (1668-1738), who, for many years, was the most celebrated physician in Europe; Huyghens (1629-1695), geometer, astronomer, and author of the undulatory theory of light; and Van Leeuwenhoek (1632-1723), the father of microscopy. Late in the eighteenth century, the palm for excellence in anatomical teaching passed from Leyden to Edinburgh.

Although anatomy was taught in Edinburgh by several individuals during the twenty-six years following Pitcairne's return from Leyden, the foundation of Edinburgh's fame as a centre for anatomical study dates from the 29th day of January 1720, when Alexander Monro *primus* was elected by the Town Council "Professor of Anatomy in this City and College," with a yearly salary of £15. Thus it was that, one hundred and seventy-seven years after Andreas Vesalius had given his monumental *Fabrica* to the world, the systematic teaching of anatomy was begun in Scotland!

PLATE XVI

ANDREAS STOG'S ENGRAVING OF PIETER PAAW'S THEATRE OF ANATOMY, 1589

Since that time (1720) Scotland has produced many famous exponents of this subject.[1]

To Alexander Monteath, who was the close friend of Archibald Pitcairne, belongs the merit of having made the first effort to open a school of anatomy in Edinburgh ; and to him is due the credit of having secured, on 24th October 1694, a grant from the Town Council of Edinburgh, of "those bodies that dye in the correction-house," and of "the bodies of fundlings that dye upon the breast."[2] This special grant to Monteath (who was encouraged by Pitcairne) aroused other members of the College of Surgeons, and caused them to request that they be given other subjects than those which already were assigned.

The petition was granted, with what ultimately proved to be an important condition : that the petitioners shall, "befor the terme of Michaelmas 1697 years, build, repair, and have in readiness, ane anatomicall theatre, where they shall once a year (a subject offering) have ane anatomicall dissection, as much as can be showen upon one body, and if the failzie thir presents to be void and null."

The petition of the surgeons is dated 2nd November 1694. On 17th December 1697, the Surgeons' Anatomical Theatre being reported to the Town Council as completed, the Council ratified its grant of 1694, and the same day the surgeons chose a "committee to appoint the methods of public dissections and the operators." I am indebted to Mr D. M. Greig for a photograph of this building taken from a picture in the Royal College of Surgeons of Edinburgh.

---

[1] After centuries of strife, England accomplished the military conquest of Scotland. The intellectual conquest of England by the Scots is still in progress.

[2] Struthers, *Historical Sketch of the Edinburgh Anatomical School*, Edinburgh, 1867, p. 9.

The first Anatomical "Course" (November 1702) was conducted by James Hamilton, Deacon of Surgeons' Incorporation. It lasted for eight days. Each day a different part of the body was demonstrated by a different lecturer appointed for the purpose.[1]

Monteath's grant was for thirteen years, but after three years he began to teach chemistry. If he taught anatomy during the intervening three years there is no evidence of it (Struthers). Certain it is, however, that the merit of being the first who endeavoured to give anatomical instruction in Edinburgh belongs to him; and to Monteath, along with Pitcairne, belongs the credit of starting the movement which led ultimately to the formation of a medical school in Edinburgh. Both of these men could see far into the future; and both realised that a medical school, which their dreams displayed as a rival to that in Leyden, could be established in Edinburgh only on the firm foundation of excellence in the teaching of anatomy.

In the fifty years following the chartering of the "Surregeanis" and "Barbouris" of Edinburgh, in 1505, no great character had appeared in Scottish physic (Lonsdale).

It is said that the ignorance of the Scottish physicians and surgeons of that time was the reason for the long journey which, in 1552, brought Jerome Cardan from Pavia to Edinburgh, as consultant in the case of John Hamilton, Archbishop of St Andrews.[2] And it is a matter of record that, in 1671, the presentation of a human skeleton to the University of Edinburgh excited fear and wonder.[3]

[1] Cresswell, "The Royal College of Surgeons: Anatomy in the Early Days," *Edinburgh Medical Journal*, 1914, p. 144.

[2] Waters, *Jerome Cardan*, London, 1898, p. 111; Dana, *Annals of Medical History*, Brooklyn, N.Y., 1921.

[3] Lonsdale, *Life of Robert Knox, the Anatomist*, London, 1870, p. 51.

PLATE XVII

THE SURGEONS' HALL OF 1697. From a Sketch in the Royal College of Surgeons, Edinburgh

The wall was built hurriedly after the disastrous Battle of Flodden, 3rd September 1513. The English army did not march on Edinburgh, as had been expected

(Photograph by D. M. Greig, Esq., F.R.C.S.E.)

PLATE XVIII

JAMES HAMILTON
From a Painting in the Royal College of Surgeons, Edinburgh

PLATE XIX

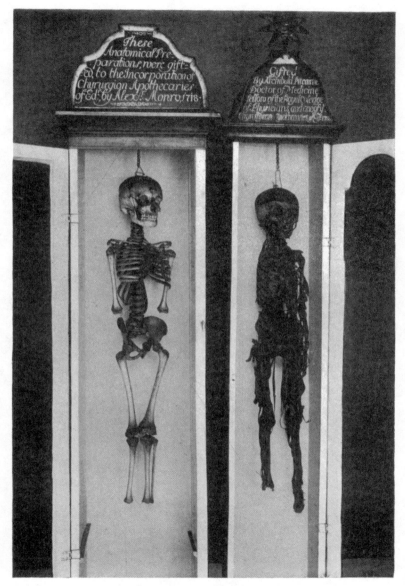

SKELETON AND DISSECTION
Presented to the Museum of the Royal College of Surgeons of Edinburgh, by
Monro *primus*, in 1718, and by Archibald Pitcairne, in 1702
(Photographs by D. M. Greig, Esq., F.R.C.S.E.)

PLATE XX

ALEXANDER MONRO *primus* (1697-1767). Professor of Anatomy, 1720-1754
From an engraving by J. Basire

PLATE **XXI**

ALEXANDER MONRO *secundus* (1733-1817). Professor of Anatomy, 1758-1798
Engraved by J. Heath from a picture by Raeburn

PLATE **XXII**

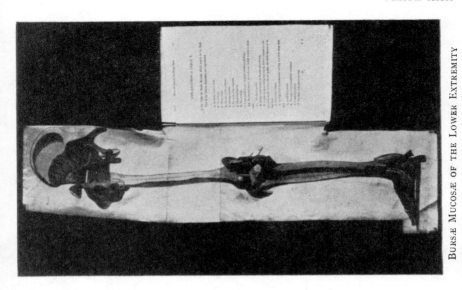

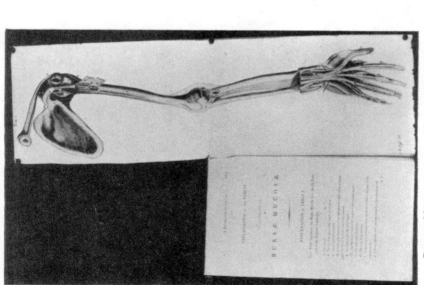

Bursæ Mucosæ of the Lower Extremity

Photographs by D. M. Greig, Esq, F.R.C.S.E.

Monro *primus* was succeeded by his son, Alexander *secundus*, who taught anatomy from 1758 to 1798. Toward the end of the year 1798, Monro *secundus* petitioned the Town Council of Edinburgh to appoint his eldest son, Alexander *tertius*, who then was in his twenty-fifth year, to the Chair of Anatomy. He was elected, but the less said of him as a teacher the better—although it will be necessary to mention him later in this narrative.

All of the Monros lived to old age, Alexander *primus* dying at seventy, Alexander *secundus* at eighty-four, and Alexander *tertius* at eighty-six years. All were professors early in life: at twenty-three, twenty-one, and twenty-five years respectively. All of them taught for long periods: thirty-eight, fifty-four, and forty-eight years respectively. Father, son, and grandson, they held the Anatomical Chair in Edinburgh University from 1720 till 1846, a period of one hundred and twenty-six years.

Not a little credit, as Miles[1] points out, was due to the foresight of John Monro, the father of Monro *primus* and a President of the Royal College of Surgeons of Edinburgh, for the local preparation of opinion which ensured for his son, whom he had guided and trained for that purpose, the appointment as lecturer on and later Professor of Anatomy at Edinburgh. "To John Monro belongs by right the honourable title of 'Father of the Edinburgh Medical School' usually assigned to his son."

Both Monro *primus* and *secundus* were brilliant teachers of anatomy. Both made valuable contributions to the literature of comparative and human anatomy. It is a striking fact, says Comrie, that the original anatomical contributions made by Monro *secundus* did not

[1] Miles, "The Dynasty of the Monros," *University of Edinburgh Journal*, 1926, p. 54.

appear until after he was fifty years of age.   One of the best of his original works, *Description of the Bursæ Mucosæ of the Human Body*, was published in 1788, when Monro was in his fifty-fifth year.

Alexander Monro *primus* immediately initiated a course of instruction which lasted from October to May, and embraced the history of anatomy, descriptive and surgical anatomy, much comparative anatomy, operations on the cadaver, the use of bandages and other surgical appliances, and ended with several lectures on physiology.

He lectured in the Hall of the Surgeons from 1719 (a few months before he was elected professor) till 1725, when, following upon a public riot directed against body-snatching, he removed his preparations for greater security within the walls of the University, as the town's college had come by that time to be called.

During the regime of the first two Monros, the number of students attending the anatomy class showed a gradual and substantial increase.   Monro *primus* had lectured to 57 students in 1720, to 130 in 1740, and to 158 in 1750.   Under Monro *secundus*, during the decennium 1780-1790, the average was 342 students per annum, and after the year 1800, the yearly average was over 400.

Anatomy in England prior to the Year 1832.

From time immemorial small and aristocratic guilds of surgeons, and large fellowships of barbers—many of whose members practised surgery—have existed in London and in the larger of the provincial towns of England.   Sir D'Arcy Power, F.S.A., says that the smaller guild seems to have been recruited from the military surgeons; that it was most active in the intervals of truce during the long French wars of Henry V. (1388-1422) and Henry VI. (1422-1471),

PLATE XXIII

WILLIAM CHESELDEN (1688-1752)
Painted by Richardson and engraved by Ridley

whilst in times of peace there are scarcely any traces of its existence; that the larger and more wealthy guild of barbers was entirely civic, and consisted of citizens who sometimes attained high municipal office.[1] After the oligarchy of London was replaced by democratic government during the Wars of the Roses, many of the old guilds received a new lease of life as Livery Companies. The Barbers' Guild was enfranchised as the Barbers' Company in 1462 by Edward IV. The barbers and surgeons had been united in practice for many years, but it was not until 1540, in the thirty-second year of the reign of Henry VIII., that an Act of Parliament formally united the Barbers' Company with the Fellowship of Surgeons. The Bill was passed on 12th July and received the Royal assent on Sunday, 24th July (South).[2]

The incorporation thus formed was known as "The United Company of Barbers and Surgeons." It was the official representative of surgery in London until 1745. The rights and privileges of the old were confirmed to the new Company, and several new rights were added. The United Company was permitted to take the "Bodyes of ffoure condemned persons yerely for anatomies."[3]

The exclusive right to conduct anatomical demonstrations was given to the Company. The teaching of anatomy was jealously guarded by that corporate body for a period of one hundred and seventy-five years.[4]

---

[1] Power, "The Centenary of the Royal College of Surgeons of England," *Practitioner*, London, 1900.

[2] South, *Memorials of the Craft of Surgery in England*, London, 1886, p. 90.   [3] *Ibid.*, p. 91.

[4] In 1564 Elizabeth gave similar anatomical privileges to the College of Physicians which, in 1581, created the lectureship on anatomy. Here, in 1615, William Harvey was elected reader in anatomy, and here, about one year later, he gave his first public demonstrations of the circulation of the blood (Macmichael, *The Gold-Headed Cane*, Reprint, New York, 1919, p. 91).

The "ffoure deade bodies" could not always be obtained without difficulty. Often riots were started when the beadles of the Company went to Tyburn for the bodies of murderers, and in 1713 the clerk was ordered to go to the Secretary at War for a guard of soldiers to protect the beadles. Often bodies were carried away by unknown persons before the beadles reached the place of execution. Evidently anatomical material was in great demand.

Private anatomies were forbidden by the Company, yet private demonstrations were carried on. In 1573 John Deane was fined "for havinge an Anathomye in his howse." In 1714 this restriction was enforced against no less a man than William Cheselden (1688-1752), the celebrated English anatomist, author, surgeon, and oculist.

Although the union of barbers and surgeons was a *mésalliance*, of which few details are known, the event was the motive for one of the best known pictures which Hans Holbein (1498-1554) produced, whilst enjoying the patronage of Henry VIII. The monster who "cut off the heads of the fair damsels whose true knight he had been," who destroyed "ancient monuments, and Gothic piles, and painted glass, by the suppression of monasteries," and who was the author of a so-called reformation which "antiquaries almost devoutly lament," was a lover of art (Walpole).[1]

The manner of conducting anatomical demonstrations in the early part of the seventeenth century is shown in the engraved title-page of the *Mikrokosmographia* of Helkiah Crooke, which first appeared in London in 1616. Crooke was a member of the "Worshipfull Company of the Barber-Chirurgeons of London." He had studied anatomy in Holland under

---

[1] Walpole, *Anecdotes of Painting in England*, London, 1862, vol. i., p. 59.

PLATE **XXIV**

TITLE-PAGE OF HELKIAH CROOKE'S "MIKROKOSMOGRAPHIA." London, 1631

This title-page is a copperplate engraving, measuring $7 \times 11\frac{1}{2}$ inches. In the centre, occupying a comparatively small space, is the title of the book, supported by a skeleton on one side and by Father Time on the other. At the lower part of this profusely ornamented title-page is a picture which shows an anatomical demonstration, doubtless such as Crooke, when "Professor in Anatomy and Chirurgery, was accustomed to hold in the presence of the "VVorshipfull Company of the Barber-Chyrurgeons," in London

PLATE XXV

THOMAS LINACRE (1460-1524)
From Pettigrew's *Medical Portrait Gallery*, vol. i., London, n.d.

Pieter Paaw, of whom he speaks as "that excellent and oculate anatomist Petrus Pavius of Leyden, my master and moderator in anatomy."

The scene is laid in a room containing a long table, at which Crooke and two assistants are seated. The professor is demonstrating the brain which rests in a head placed upright upon the table. As in the Holland *Lessons in Anatomy*, so here many of the auditors have their gaze directed toward the observer and away from the dissection. The first edition of Crooke's book was printed by W. Jaggard, printer of the first edition of Shakespeare's plays.[1]

That the Barber-Surgeons' Company believed in heralding its activities to the public is evidenced by the following extract from the *Daily Advertiser* of 15th January 1742 :—"Notice is hereby given that there being a publick Body at Barbers and Surgeons Hall, the Demonstrations of Anatomy and the Operations of Surgery will be at the Hall this evening and to-morrow at six o'clock precisely in the Amphitheatre."

In 1752 it was ordered that the bodies of murderers who were executed in London and in Middlesex should be conveyed to the Hall of the Surgeons' Company to be anatomised, and any attempt to rescue such bodies was made a felony.[2]

Prior to the reign of Elizabeth medical science in England was far behind that of the continental countries, and the dearth of English medical literature in the sixteenth century was in keeping with the state of literature in general. "The Renascence had done little for English letters" (Green). The two men who may be regarded as the Fathers of English medicine were

---

[1] The question, "How came Shakespeare to refer to the *pia mater* in the play of *Twelfth Night?*" has been answered by Benjamin Ward Richardson in *The Asclepiad*, London, 1888, p. 386.

[2] Bailey, *The Diary of a Resurrectionist*, London, 1896, p. 21.

Thomas Linacre and John Kaye (Caius).[1] Both were native-born Englishmen who travelled into Italy, and there sought to master the mysteries of the new learning. Both received the M.D. degree from the famous University of Padua. Both carried back to their native land an abundant store of the learning and the culture of the Renaissance. Both were the founders of medical and of other institutions which have had a powerful influence in the advancement of letters in England. The one is best known as the introducer of the Greek language, the other as the founder of anatomy in England.

Thomas Linacre[2] (1460-1524), a Fellow of All Souls' College, Oxford, "was amongst the earliest of his countrymen to whom learning owed its revival and propagation in the fifteenth century" (John Noble Johnson).[3]

Caius entered Gonville Hall, Cambridge, in 1529. Ten years later he went abroad, and received a thorough medical training in the Universities of Padua and Bologna. For some months he lived in the same house with Andreas Vesalius. In 1542 Caius delivered lectures from the text of Aristotle, at Padua. Returning to England, Caius was summoned by Henry VIII. to deliver anatomical lectures to the surgeons of London. It was Caius whose influence secured to the United Company the privilege of dissecting four felons annually. "Caius, on his return from Italy, imbued with the spirit of inquiry and enlightened by the lamp of science lately kindled in that country, taught anatomy to the

---

[1] The name of Caius was spelt in many ways—Gauius, Gavius, Kaius. Anglicè—Kaye, Keye, Cay (*The Gold-Headed Cane*).

[2] His name has been frequently written Lynacer, Lynaker, Lynakre (Pettigrew, *Medical Portrait Gallery*, vol. i., London, n.d. The last volume (iv.) is dated 1840).

[3] Johnson, *The Life of Thomas Linacre*, London, 1835.

PLATE XXVI

JOHN KAYE (CAIUS) (1510-1573)
From Pettigrew's *Medical Portrait Gallery*, vol i , London, n.d.

surgeons in their own hall.   Here, beyond the precincts of the College of Physicians, reflecting great honour upon that body, adding to his own reputation and conferring no small advantage on the surgeons, he laid that solid foundation for the study of anatomy, to which may easily be traced the glory and after-discoveries of Harvey." [1]

In time, with the increase in surgical knowledge, association of educated and skilful surgeons with illiterate barbers created an intolerable situation.   In 1745, by wish of the surgeons, the United Company was separated by Act of Parliament.

The surgeons were incorporated under the title of "The Masters, Governors, and Commonality of the Art and Science of Surgery."   To the surgeons were given the bodies of malefactors for dissection.   The building of the Surgeons' Company—as the corporation usually was called—was in the Old Bailey.

By the Act of separation the surgeons had retained their dignity and their self-respect, but their financial position was most unfortunate.   Their assets consisted of two small bequests dating from the seventeenth century, known as the Arris (1645) and the Gale (1698) foundations for public dissections and lectures.   The foundations are still in existence, and give their name to the Arris and Gale Professor who delivers an annual course of lectures at the Royal College of Surgeons of England.

The Surgeons' Company seems to have been fore-ordained to disaster.   Emptiness of its treasury, lack of business ability of its rulers, and its failure to keep abreast of the surgical progress of the time, were most serious handicaps.   Finally, after an inglorious career

[1] Macmichael, *The Gold-Headed Cane*, second edition, London, 1828 (Reprint, New York, 1919), p. 87.

of fifty years, its existence was ended 7th July 1796, by reason of the fact that the death of one governor, and the inability of another to attend a meeting for the election of officers, caused the corporation to lose its charter. Loss of the charter was followed by a fight of such bitterness as only members of a learned profession are competent to conduct.

Parliament steadfastly refused to sanction a new charter which would exclude members of the College from a share in its government. What Parliament had refused was soon secured by courtly intrigue through the Duke of Portland. And thus, finally, on 22nd March 1800, the Royal College of Surgeons in London obtained its charter from George III. This charter sanctioned most of the monopolistic and objectionable provisions contained in the Bill rejected by the House of Lords. The courtiers and the medical politicians had scored, but the victory of 22nd March 1800 was destined to be destroyed thirty years later.

Under this charter the Company was reinstated in its former position on condition that it resigned its municipal privileges, and the titles of master, governors, and court of assistants, which the Surgeons' Company had inherited from the United Company of Barbers and Surgeons, were retained. The present style of " The Royal College of Surgeons of England" dates from 14th September 1843, when a charter from Queen Victoria was granted.

Attempt to Legalise Anatomy in England.

After the end of the Napoleonic wars, numerous social and political reforms engaged the attention of the people of England, and Medicine naturally was not overlooked. The Navy and Army Medical Departments, the Royal Colleges of the United Kingdom, and not

PLATE XXVII

HENRY VIII. PRESENTING A CHARTER TO THE BARBER-SURGEONS OF LONDON. (From the Painting by Holbein) From *Memorials of the Craft of Surgery in England*, by John Flint South, edited by D'Arcy Power, F.R.C.S. Eng. (Cassell & Company, Ltd., 1886)

less the general public, were active in advocating such extensions in the medical curriculum as would place anatomy, surgery, pathology, and therapeutics upon a better foundation. And it was hoped that anatomy would obtain such legalised footing in Britain as would enable the English medical schools to compete with those of the Continent—but in vain. The wishy-washy Government played fast and loose with the profession. The authorities demanded a higher standard of anatomical and surgical knowledge, and then did nothing to facilitate the acquirement of such skill. The law against the practice of exhumation, says Lonsdale,[1] "was kept in full force all the while ; there were not less than fourteen convictions in one year in England." While the politicians had their minds fixed upon party and personal interests, "Medicine, the most valued of all sciences, was left out in the cold, or resolutely thwarted in its progress by the rule of Tory fogyism" (Lonsdale).

Rise of the Private Medical Schools in London.

England and Scotland were united 1st May 1707. In 1714, the crown passed to George I. During his reign, which ended with his death in 1727, several private schools of anatomy and surgery were opened in London ; but the most influential of such institutions were founded during the time of George II. (1714-1760).

So long as the United Company of Barbers and Surgeons was able to enforce its monopoly of teaching anatomy and surgery, there could be no need for the "resurrection - men." Monopolies often carry within themselves the seeds for their own destruction.

For many years before its final dissolution, the authority of the United Company had been on the

---

[1] Lonsdale, *Life of Robert Knox, the Anatomist*, London, 1870, p. 58.

wane.[1]   The rise of independent medical schools was a thorn in the flesh; and, in 1695, formal complaints were made "against breeding soe many Illiterate and unskillful pretenders to Chyrurgery att St Thomas's hospitall or wherever else y⁰ like ill Practises are used."[2] No doubt the Company suffered a monetary loss by reason of the establishment of medical schools in connection with St Bartholomew's and St Thomas's Hospitals.   The hospital medical schools, however, were able to offer what the United Company had failed to furnish.   It was an easy matter for the Company to deal harshly with John Deane and William Cheselden, for conducting a private "Anathomye"; it was a different story when the staffs of two important hospitals decided to give instruction in anatomy and in surgery.

The founding of the private schools of anatomy in London was a natural and inevitable response to the inefficient and monopolistic teaching of that day. Hospital appointments and lectureships only too often had been secured by nepotism or by financial gifts. Many a man of superior talents was ignored.   The position which he desired and which he could have filled with credit to himself, with honour to the profession, and with benefit to sick and injured persons, often was given to an individual of inferior merit.   The great hospitals of London were managed in that day, just as now some few in America are conducted, not for the benefit of suffering humanity, or for the advancement of medical science, but to further the selfish ends of a few individuals.

This anomalous, corrupt, and illogical system of hospital management had existed in London for many

---

[1] South, *Memorials of the Craft of Surgery in England*, London, 1886, p. 246.

[2] *Ibid.*, p. 246.

years. It was strongly entrenched. It grew pompous with its own importance. Its beneficiaries laughed at, and jeered, and ridiculed, the good and true men who asked for reform. But a day of reckoning at last was born. A Knight of the True Cross put on his armour; he went into the battle; and he finally destroyed the infamous system.

That man was Thomas Wakley, best remembered to-day as the founder of *The Lancet*. In the first number of this journal, issued 5th October 1823, the vicious system was attacked. Week after week Wakley fired his editorial broadsides. He continued until the victory had been won. The courageous editor did not hesitate to expose the weak spots in the armour of such idols as Abernethy and Sir Astley Cooper.

Neither the burning of his home by incendiaries, the attempt to assassinate him, the occurrence of personal encounters, the bringing against him of numerous suits at law, nor the efforts at ostracism, could cause this valiant knight to stop his fight for medical reform. Wakley's career was a stormy one. His opposition was most powerful and influential. His life reads like a romance. It has been well written by Sprigge.[1]

Although William Cheselden was compelled to abandon his course of private anatomical lectures in 1714, three years after their inauguration, his example bore good fruit. About 1730 Mr Edward Nourse, of St Bartholomew's Hospital, delivered anatomical lectures at London House, in Aldergate Street, where he then lived; and he employed Percivall Pott, his apprentice, to act as his prosector. Mr Nourse was one of the first persons to deliver public lectures at his own house. This arrangement probably became inconvenient, as we find Mr Nourse's advertisement, in 1739, worded as follows:—

[1] Sprigge, *Life and Times of Thomas Wakley*, London, 1897.

"ANATOMY.

"Designing to have no more lectures at my own house, I think it proper to advertise that I shall begin a Course of Anatomy, Chirurgical Operations, and Bandages, on Monday the 11th of Nov., at St Bartholomew's Hospital.

"EDW. NOURSE, Assistant Surgeon
and Lithotomist to the said Hospital."[1]

Dr Frank Nicholls, in 1737, and Percivall Pott, about 1747, advertised similar courses. The advertisement of Cæsar Hawkins, Surgeon to St George's Hospital, appeared early in the year 1739. Samuel Sharpe, Edward and Richard Grainger, William and John Hunter, Joshua Brookes, Benjamin Brodie, and Sir Charles Bell, won their spurs while teaching anatomy and surgery in the private schools.

It was under the leadership of William Hunter (1718-1763), a young Scot who was poor in purse but rich in intellect, that the profession soon broke away from the shackles of the Surgeons' Company. Samuel Sharpe, who had been giving lectures to a "Society of Navy Surgeons," gave up his teaching duties. He was succeeded by William Hunter, whose announcement, from the *London Evening Post*, 12th January 1748, states[2]:—

"On Monday, the 1st of February, at Five in the Afternoon

WILL BEGIN

A COURSE of ANATOMICAL LECTURES. To which will be added, the Operations of SURGERY, with the Application of BANDAGES.

By WILLIAM HUNTER, SURGEON.

"Gentlemen may have an Opportunity of learning the Art of Dissecting, during the whole Winter Season, in the same Manner as at Paris."[3]

[1] Bailey, *The Diary of a Resurrectionist*, London, 1896, p. 41.
[2] Richardson, *The Asclepiad*, London, 1888, p. 349.
[3] The same paper contains announcement of the publication of Smollett's *Roderick Random*, and of Hogarth's *Two Apprentices*.

From this humble beginning there arose the Great
Windmill Street School, which ended its glorious career
in 1833. On a lot in Great Windmill Street, London,
opposite the Haymarket, William Hunter built a
dwelling-house, an anatomical theatre, dissecting-rooms,
and a museum. Here great things were done. Here
William Hunter collected his museum, now in Glasgow,
at the cost of £100,000; here his brother John assembled
his own collection, now the chief ornament of the
Museum of the Royal College of Surgeons of England,
at a cost of £70,000. Here Hewson, Baillie, Cruikshank,
Wilson, Brodie, Charles Bell, and others, instructed
thousands of young men in anatomy and surgery. Who
can estimate the value of such an institution? The
Great Windmill Street School was a foster-mother;
new schools of anatomy and surgery sprang up in the
hospitals; and, in addition thereto, in the winter of
1825-6, London could boast of no less than seven
private schools of anatomy (Keen).[1]

Thus, in the one hundred years preceding the
Anatomy Act of 1832, the two factors of greatest
value in the advancement of medical science in the
United Kingdom were: (1) the rise of the private
schools of anatomy and surgery; and (2) the founding
of *The Lancet*, in 1823, by Thomas Wakley. True it
is that many important discoveries in anatomy and
surgery were made during this period; but they were
made outside the walls of the Royal College of Surgeons.

It is to be regretted that a complete history of the
private schools never will be written, "for no succinct
record of them has been handed down by anyone with
personal knowledge of them" (Sprigge).[2] However,

---

[1] Keen, *A Sketch of the Early History of Practical Anatomy*, Philadelphia,
1874, p. 4.   A list of these schools is printed in *The Lancet*, 1825, pp. 26 *et seq.*
[2] Sprigge, *Life and Times of Thomas Wakley*, London, 1897, p. 17.

a most interesting account of these institutions has been given to us by D'Arcy Power.[1]

The rise and multiplication of the private schools was spectacular. No licence was required for opening an anatomical school in Great Britain, their number was not limited, there was no regular and dependable legal supply of subjects for dissection—hence the advent of the Resurrectionists.

The keen competition existing among the teachers of anatomy in London, in Edinburgh, and in Dublin,[2] the development of medical teaching in such centres as Glasgow, Manchester, and Leeds, and the activities of individual members of the profession, who wished to add to their knowledge of the human structure, caused such a demand for *matériel* as could be supplied only by the robbery of graves.

[1] Power, "The Rise and Fall of the Private Medical Schools in London," *British Medical Journal*, 1895, vol. ii., p. 141. This has been reprinted, with other articles, in a pamphlet entitled *The Medical Institutions of London*.

[2] Cameron, *History of the Royal College of Surgeons in Ireland*, Dublin, 1886, p. 513. A private school of anatomy was advertised in the *Dublin Weekly Journal* for the 19th of October 1728. The first private school of anatomy opened in Dublin in the nineteenth century was established (1804-1813) by Mr (later Sir) Philip Crampton.

CHAPTER V

General Considerations.

THE resurrection-men were not all of the same litter. They were of two classes, whose respective members had but one thing in common: the securing of anatomical material. The distinction between the two groups is founded upon the motive for their illegal acts. The one class was animated by a desire to advance the cause of science; the other was actuated purely by greed for money.

In the one class were those individuals—medical students, physicians, surgeons, and anatomists—whose zeal for the advancement of science was the sole reason for the robbing of graves. Most of their activities were for the purpose of securing anatomical material for dissection, in order that the professor of anatomy might clarify his didactic instruction by demonstrations made on the cadaver. In a few instances the insatiable desire to possess the body of a congenital or of an acquired monstrosity, or to secure organs presenting unusual pathological changes, has led a John Hunter,[1] or a Robert Liston,[2] to commit lawless acts. The names of many other distinguished surgeons and anatomists, whose labours have been of supreme value to suffering humanity, could be added to those mentioned.

To the other class belonged those depraved

[1] John Hunter's successful quest for the body of the Irish giant, O'Brien, or Byrne, is mentioned on p. 128.

[2] For one of Liston's adventures, see p. 131.

individuals who systematically engaged in the stealing of bodies solely for the sake of gain.   These traffickers in human flesh were called "resurrectionists," or "sack-'em-up men." Neither the place of their origin nor the date of their initial activities can be stated. Their period of greatest importance and prosperity was the first third of the nineteenth century.

So long as the resurrectionists confined their activities to the filching of dead bodies, their illegal acts, although exciting disgust and horror, did not approach the magnitude of crime.   But some of the guild, tempted by the thirty or forty pounds for which a body could be sold, reduced murder to a fine art and made of it a lucrative business.   Such persons were Burke, Hare, and their paramours, in Edinburgh, and Bishop, Williams, and May, of London.   Exposure of their crimes aroused public sentiment to such an extent that the Parliament, which long had ignored the prayers and petitions of anatomists and surgeons for the legalisation of anatomical study, was compelled to action.   The breed of "sack-'em-up men" became extinct shortly after the year 1832, when the Anatomy Act was adopted.

Bodies were taken sometimes for other than dissection purposes.   Bailey[1] cites an item printed in the *Universal Spectator and Weekly Journal*, 20th May 1732, which states : "John Loftas, the Grave Digger, committed to prison for robbing of dead corpse, has confess'd to the plunder of above fifty, not only of their coffins and burial cloaths, but of their fat, which he retail'd at a high price to certain people, who, it is believed, will be call'd upon on account thereof.   Since this discovery several persons have had their friends dug up, who were found quite naked, and some mangled in

[1] Bailey, *The Diary of a Resurrectionist*, London, 1896, p. 88.

so horrible a manner as could scarcely be suppos'd to be done by a human creature."

Southey, in his ballad, *The Surgeon's Warning*, refers to this, where he makes the surgeon say :

"I have made candles of infants' fat."

Organotherapy is of ancient origin. Savage tribes have eaten the hearts of lions and tigers to acquire the courage of those beasts, and a similar instinct, says Wootton,[1] would suggest that the heart and other organs be used for medicinal purposes. Our forbears came to the logical conclusion that, the higher the rank of the animal the more potent and curative should be its tissues.

Motley, when describing the repulse of the Spaniards at Ostend and Antwerp in 1585, and the terrible slaughter consequent thereon, has this to say : "The Dutch surgeons sallied forth in strength after each encounter and brought in great bags filled with *human fat*, which was then esteemed the sovereignest remedy in the world for wounds and diseases."

Instances of hatred extending further than death itself are on record. Mention has been made of the indignities to which "the carcases," as Evelyn calls them, of Cromwell and others were subjected after the Restoration. Cromwell's body was given a brief period of repose in Westminster Abbey. But no such honour was accorded to the remains of Sir William Wallace, the national hero of the Scottish people. After having been beheaded, portions of his mangled body were exposed at various places—his head in London and the quarters in Newcastle, Berwick, Stirling, and Perth. Six hundred years later, at Westminster Hall in London, where he had appeared before judges whom

[1] Wootton, *Chronicles of Pharmacy*, London, 1910, vol. ii., p. 1.

Edward I. had appointed not to try but to condemn him, a skilfully wrought and embellished brass tablet is now set to record the greatness of Sir William Wallace! This dramatic reconciliation of history recalls the belated honours which have been accorded to the Maid of Orleans, and to Giordano Bruno, whose statues recently have been erected on the very spots where they were burned to death.

A curious story of *post-mortem* hatred, inspired by a love affair, is related by MacGregor,[1] in which the hand of a Miss Wilson was sought by two young men from the north, named Ferguson and Duncan. Ferguson was preferred, and was hated by his rival. The successful suitor died, and his body was interred in Buccleuch burying-ground. Duncan "employed a well-known snatcher, who rejoiced in the cognomen of 'Screw,' on account of his cleverness at raising bodies, and they went together to the cemetery for the purpose of conveying the corpse of Ferguson to the rooms occupied by Dr Monro. When they arrived there they found Miss Wilson beside the grave, overwhelmed with grief at the loss of her lover. At last she went away, and soon the body was within the precincts of the college."

Rise of the "Sack-'em-up Men."

Activities of the resurrection-men were confined almost entirely to the British Isles. In the continental countries material for dissection was furnished by the legally constituted authorities. In Paris, for example, the anatomical schools were licensed institutions. A law passed during the Revolution has consolidated several Boards of Management into one body, *Administration des Hôpitaux*, which carried into effect the law

---

[1] MacGregor, *History of Burke and Hare*, Glasgow, 1884, p. 43.

passed by the Legislative Assembly, whereby the bodies unclaimed at hospitals were distributed among the various schools. This distribution of anatomical material was carried out in a fair and systematic manner. In Italy, Austria, Germany, and in the Low Countries, there was an ample supply of bodies for dissection, and there the resurrection-men were unknown.

In Great Britain and in Ireland, however, the situation was different. At this period no licence was required; and any man or set of men could open a school of anatomy, but material for dissection could be obtained only by illegal means. And thus it was that the activities of the resurrectionists were carried on chiefly in the vicinity of London, Dublin, Glasgow, and Edinburgh.

The multiplication and the growing importance of the private schools of anatomy, the increase in the number of their students, and the keen rivalry which existed amongst these institutions, were all factors ever increasing the demand for bodies for dissection.

The absolute necessity of having an ample supply of material for the use of students, so as to keep them from migrating to rival schools, caused the teachers of anatomy to offer unheard-of prices for subjects. At first the traffic was carried on by a few men, who seem to have had a sense of decency, and whose work was done without public scandal. It was stated by the police that, in 1828, the number of persons in London who lived regularly on the profits derived from grave-robbing did not exceed ten; but, in addition to these there were about two hundred men who were occasionally employed in this kind of work.

The larger number of these human ghouls were thieves of the lowest grade, belonging to the most abandoned and desperate class of the community.

They were devoid of the proverbial "honour" which thieves are supposed to possess. The fights and brawls of these men often occurred in churchyards, and caused more scandal than the actual robbing of graves.

Increased demand, and the larger prices paid for subjects, caused a greater number of vicious characters to engage in the traffic. The competition existing among rival gangs of resurrectionists often led to desperate fights and unusual reprisals. If a body were secured from an outside source, the regular resurrectionists would sometimes break into the dissecting-room and so mutilate the corpse that it would be unfit for dissection. If this attempt should fail, the police were told that a stolen body could be found in the rooms of the offending teacher of anatomy. The lot of the anatomist who dared to break with the resurrection-men was anything but a bed of roses.

Business Methods of the Resurrectionists.

The resurrection-men were past-masters in the gentle arts of extortion and blackmail. They held the whip-hand over the teachers of anatomy, for two reasons : the need of material for dissection, and the illegality of its source.

The extortion began prior to the opening of the session, in the demand for an advance payment, or *douceur*; it was continued during the session ; and it ceased, temporarily at least, with the payment of "finishing-money" at the end of the session.

These, however, were not the only demands of the resurrection-men. If one of them were imprisoned, the teacher was obliged to contribute to the support of the man's wife and family whilst he served his sentence. A *solatium*, or compensation, was also expected on his release from gaol. Mr R. D. Grainger spent £50 in this way for one man. Sir Astley Cooper's account books show such entries. For example, the following : " 1829, May 6th. Paid Vaughan's wife 6s. Paid Vaughan for twenty-six weeks' confinement at 10s. per week, £13 0s. 0d."

The amount of money that could be made by trafficking in bodies can be judged from the testimony which was given by a body-snatcher before a Select Committee of the House of Commons in 1828. A gang of six or seven men disposed of three hundred and twelve bodies during the regular winter session. The average price of an adult body was £4, 4s. Thus these men reaped an income of 1328 guineas (about six thousand dollars), or nearly one thousand dollars apiece. It is almost needless to add that the pound sterling then would buy much more than to-day.

Vengeful Acts of the Resurrectionists.

The "sack-'em-up men" generally worked in gangs, and competition was most keen. One gang would do anything in its power to nullify the success of its rivals. What these gangsters did to one another is of little consequence in this narrative. We are concerned, however, with what the resurrection-men did to the teachers of anatomy.

It is the old story of trying to maintain a monopoly at any cost, and by any means—fair or foul. It may seem unreasonable to mention the banditti of art in the same sentence with the "sack-'em-up men"; but nevertheless, the methods of suppressing competition, which Ribera and other Neapolitan artists employed in the seventeenth century, differed from those used by the resurrectionists two hundred years later, not in principle but only in manner and in character. The followers of Caravaggio disposed of their rivals either by the skilful

use of the stiletto, or by submersion in the Bay of
Naples ; and thus they maintained their monopoly
of art.

The resurrection-men, who also were artists in their
exclusive sphere, maintained their monopoly in a different
manner.   If any teacher of anatomy dared to refuse the
extortionate demands of the ghouls, that teacher immediately became a marked man.   The experience of Joshua
Brookes (1761-1833), proprietor of the Blenheim Street,
or Great Marlborough Street, School, will serve as an
example.

Joshua Brookes had proved himself to be the best
practical anatomist in England (Sprigge).[1]   His disputes
with the London resurrectionists caused him much
trouble and notoriety, and on several occasions his life
was endangered.

Joshua Brookes often was the victim of vengeful
acts.   At one time, because he had refused five guineas
as a *douceur* at the beginning of the session, the
"third degree" was conferred upon him by disgruntled
resurrectionists.   At each end of the street on which
Brookes's School was located, during the night a badly
decomposed body was placed.   In the early morning,
two young ladies having stumbled over one of the
bodies, such a commotion was raised that only the
protection of the police saved the anatomist from the
fury of a mob.

On another occasion Mr Brookes had an experience
which is described by Bransby Cooper,[2] as follows :
" One night he was knocked up by a man who informed
him that he had a Subject for him.   Mr Brookes
himself arose to receive it, according to his custom

---

[1] Sprigge, *The Life and Times of Thomas Wakley*, London, 1897, p. 17.
[2] Bransby Blake Cooper, *Life of Sir Astley Cooper*, London, 1843,
vol. i., p. 399.

PLATE **XXVIII**

JOSHUA BROOKES, ESQ., F.R.S., F.L.S., F.Z.S., ETC., ETC.
Painted by T. Phillips, R.A., and engraved by H. Cook

upon such occasions, and, without first inspecting the Subject to see if it were perfect, as was usually done, desired the man to bring it in, paid him a portion of the money, for which he was particularly anxious, and desired him to call the next day for the remainder. He then with a kick rolled the parcel down six or seven steps which led to his dissecting-room, and turned away.

"As he was ascending the stairs to his bedroom, Mr Brookes was surprised to hear what seemed to him to be complaints issuing from the package which he had just so unceremoniously dismissed into the passage leading to the dissecting-room. He listened attentively and was soon perfectly satisfied that his suspicion as to the source of the noises he had heard was correct. On the instant, the thought crossed his mind that the sack contained the body of someone who had attempted to be murdered for the sake of his body, and in whom life was not yet quite extinct. He turned to resolve these doubts, and on coming within view, was not a little astonished to see, in place of the parcel, a man standing erect, with the sack lying empty by his side. Mr Brookes was one who knew not fear, and immediately advanced towards him. The man, alarmed, did not wait any question from Mr Brookes, but at once, in a tone of supplication, begged him to let him go, saying he had been put into the sack when he was drunk, and that it was a trick which had been played upon him. Mr Brookes, who did not believe one word of the fellow's story, but felt that it was a preconcerted scheme of the resurrectionist to rob him of as much money as he could get from him, opened the door, and at once kicked the Subject into the street."

The vengeful character of the resurrection-men did not change with clime, country, latitude, or longitude.

It was the same in the United States as it had been in the United Kingdom.

Among the noted American resurrectionists was "Old Cunny," a raw-boned Irishman, with muscles like those of Hercules, whose duty it was to supply anatomical material to the Ohio Medical College, Cincinnati, Ohio. His ghoulish nature was shown when he took a horrible revenge on a few students who had played some sort of trick on him. He dug up the body of a small-pox victim and succeeded in infecting many of the students with this horrible disease.[1]

Dental Activities of the Resurrectionists.

The business acumen of the resurrection-men was shown by their alliance with the dentists, which has been mentioned by Bransby Cooper, as follows :

"The graves were not always disturbed to obtain possession of the entire body, for the teeth alone, at this time, offered sufficient remuneration for the trouble and risk incurred in such undertakings. Every dentist in London would at that time purchase teeth from these men, and the public can have but little idea of the immense sums of money which persons thus occupied could earn." It is a matter of record that one wretch, who had gained access to a vault, was able to carry away enough front teeth to give him the neat sum of sixty pounds.

Stealing of teeth was not confined to dead subjects. Scarcely more than a century ago, the resurrection-men haunted the battlefields in the Peninsula, further adding their tortures to the horrors of war. Several of the well-known body-snatchers of London supplied wealthy clients with teeth which were extracted from soldiers

[1] Juettner, *Daniel Drake and His Followers*, Cincinnati, 1909, p. 395.

PLATE XXIX

WILLIAM BURKE AS HE APPEARED AT THE BAR
Drawn by Lutenor and engraved by T. Clerk.   Edinburgh, 1829

who were wounded in the Peninsular battles. When one of the ghouls was asked by what means he would obtain teeth, he answered Bransby Cooper as follows :

"Oh, sir, only let there be a battle, and there'll be no want of teeth. I'll draw them as fast as the men are knocked down." [1]

That the vile breed who traffic in the appurtenances of dead men is still in existence is evidenced by the following account which appeared in the *Evening Dispatch*, Edinburgh, 28th July 1925 :—

DESPOILING THE DEAD.

Extraordinary Story from Germany.

Occurrences which are regarded even in Germany as being of an extraordinary nature are reported from Dresden. The attendants at the crematorium there, who are municipal officials, have for some years past enriched themselves by stealing from the bodies entrusted to them to be burned articles of value left on them, says the *Morning Post* Berlin correspondent.

Not only did these attendants take rings and other jewellery, but they broke off teeth that had gold fillings or settings. The attendants also removed the clothes and burial sheets from the bodies and sold them with the help of receivers at good prices in distant towns.

Furthermore, the attendants considered that it was wasteful to have the coffins burned, so they put only the bodies into the fire and sold the coffins. To save trouble they sometimes burned two bodies at the same time and simply divided the ashes among the respective relatives.

These facts have been communicated by the President of the Dresden Police, who has informed the population of the Saxon capital that the persons implicated have been removed from their posts, and that proceedings are being taken against them.

[1] Bransby Blake Cooper, *Life of Sir Astley Cooper*, London, 1843, vol. i., p. 399.

CHAPTER VI

THE EDINBURGH MURDERERS : BURKE AND HARE

To read the history of most of the existing nations of the world is like bathing in a tub of blood. The countless examples of treachery, of oppression, of torture, and of lesser crimes, which often were committed in the name of *Religion*, or under subterfuge of *Law*, make one sick at heart and despondent for the future.

History, as Philip Gilbert Hamerton—the gifted author of *The Intellectual Life*—observes, "is hardly ever written disinterestedly. Historians write with one eye on the past and the other on the pre-occupations of the present." Failing to tell the pure truth, and all the truth, "they fall short of the intellectual standard." Probably an ideal history never will be written.

The pages of Irish, English, and Scottish history are befouled with a vast array of crimes. Scotland has had her full share of acts of injustice and intolerance, which often were perpetrated to satisfy personal ends, ambition, or avarice ; or were consummated under the pretence of making for the welfare of the people.

In the long list of criminal events that have occurred in Scotland, there are few that have caused so deep, so enduring, and so widespread an interest as the murders committed by Burke and Hare, dealers in fresh anatomical material.

In Edinburgh the progress of anatomical teaching was hampered by law and by superstition. Always there was a shortage of material ; and bodies often

PLATE XXX

WILLIAM HARE AS HE APPEARED AT THE BAR
Drawn by Lutenor and engraved by Clerk.   Edinburgh, 1829

brought from £10 to £20 each.[1]   While every educated
person knew that, "as the rule and the square were to
the architect and builder, and the compass to the sailor,
so was anatomy to the surgeon," yet only by illegal
acts could the material for acquiring such knowledge be
obtained (Lonsdale).   Whilst Protestant England and
Scotland boasted of their advanced civilisation, and did
nothing to legalise the study of human anatomy, the
great Catholic countries of the world long had been
aiding the advance of medical science.

A full realisation of the extent of the traffic in
human bodies, and the news that persons had been
murdered for the sake of the sale of their bodies for
dissection, came like a flash of lightning from a cloudless
sky, when, in the latter part of the year 1828, the crimes
of Burke and Hare were exposed in Edinburgh.

These men were too cowardly to rob graves.   In
the true sense they were not "resurrectionists."   They
did not hesitate, however, to commit murder by
smothering their victims.   Fifteen times the "deil's
luck" befriended them : the sixteenth turn of the wheel
proved fatal to the murderers.

The career of Burke and Hare, as purveyors of
anatomical material, began on the 29th day of November
1827, when an old pensioner of the name of Donald
died in Tanners' Close, in the West Port, Edinburgh.
He died in debt to the extent of £4, and William Hare,
his creditor, thought to collect it by selling the old
man's body to the anatomists.   Hare found a ready
accomplice in William Burke, another of his lodgers.
The body was removed from the coffin, a bag of tanners'
bark took its place, and the funeral was duly held.   The
same night Hare and Burke stealthily repaired to the

[1] Frank, "Resurrection Days," *Interstate Medical Journal*, St Louis,
No. 3, 1907.

College, and, on meeting a student in the quadrangle, asked for Dr Monro's rooms. The student, who was a loyal member of Dr Knox's anatomical class, on discovering their errand, advised them to try No. 10 Surgeons' Square. There the body of the old pensioner was sold for £7, 10s.

So large a sum, and one obtained so easily, was a temptation. The two Irishmen loved their labour less and their whisky more, from the hour of selling their friend's body. Waiting for such another death was "awfu' tedious." Hare and Burke were too cowardly to attempt the mode of the resurrectionists. Hare, the viler member of the firm, suggested a stroke of business, namely, to entice the old and infirm into his den and "do for them."

Then there followed a career of crime which rarely has been equalled. Imbeciles, street-walkers, widows, and orphans, were murdered by Burke, Hare, and their paramours.

Well might the house, into which the victims had been enticed, have had inscribed over its door Dante's lines :—

> "*Lasciate ogni speranza, voi ch' entrate.*"
> (Leave all hope, ye that enter.)

So expert did Burke and Hare become, so certain was their method, that of them it well might have been said, that they had demonstrated the correctness of De Quincey's notion of "murder being one of the fine arts."

The career of the murderers lasted for one year. Very appropriately it came to an end on Hallowe'en, 1828—a time which Burns describes as "a night when witches, devils, and other mischief-making beings are all abroad on their baneful midnight errands." As

PLATE XXXI

HELEN MCDOUGAL AS SHE APPEARED AT THE BAR
Drawn by Lutenor and engraved by Clerk. Edinburgh, 1829

PLATE XXXII

MARGARET LAIRD OR HARE AS SHE APPEARED IN THE WITNESS-BOX
Taken in Court. Drawn by Lutenor and engraved by Clerk. Edinburgh, 1829

Lonsdale, the biographer of Robert Knox, the anatomist, says: " Burns little fancied that his poetical definition would be realised to the full by devils in human shape, living in the year of grace 1828, under the shadow of Edinburgh Castle."

The last one of the West Port tragedies was the murder of a poor old woman by the name of Docherty. Burke, Hare, Mrs Hare, and Helen M'Dougal were all in at the death. Discovery of the body of the little old woman, lying under a mass of straw, in Burke's house, was made by former lodgers, Mr and Mrs Gray. The Grays were frightfully poor, but they were honest. They refused the offer of hush-money and reported what they had found to the authorities.

The next morning the authorities instituted a search. The first place visited was the dissecting-room of Dr Robert Knox, and here was found the body of the woman Docherty. The police had to cut the ropes binding the tea-chest in which the body was contained. In other words, no one connected with the establishment had seen the body.

Anatomical material was received at No. 10 Surgeons' Square during the hours of the night, sometimes by the door-keeper Paterson, who later turned against his master; but usually it was taken in charge by two of Robert Knox's assistants, Thomas Wharton Jones, who later narrowly escaped giving the ophthalmoscope to the world, and William (later Sir William) Fergusson, who became a distinguished surgeon and practised in London.

When it became known on 2nd November 1828 that a woman had been murdered for the sake of the sale of her body to an Edinburgh anatomist, there was created a consternation which extended far beyond the limits of that city. Publication of the acts of Burke and

Hare sent a thrill of horror throughout the United Kingdom and Ireland. It hastened legislation for the purpose of legitimately securing subjects for dissection. In the city of Dublin, from which place many bodies had been shipped to Glasgow and Edinburgh, it caused such a scarcity of material as seemed for a time to threaten the very existence of anatomical teaching in that metropolis. It placed a new verb, "to burke," in the dictionary. It created a new and an ephemeral literature—in the form of broadsides, chap-books, and narratives—and it gave to the writers of fiction a new theme on which to harp and by which to display their talents. Needless to say it wrecked the life of the anatomist in whose rooms the body of the woman Docherty had been discovered.

Edinburgh, however, was the chief centre of the disturbance. That such a crime should have been committed in the Athens of the North—in "Scotia's darling seat"—in the very city where John Knox, the iconoclastic reformer, had fired his thunderbolts against Papal authority, and by his harsh words often had brought tears to the eyes of "bonnie Queen Mary"— seemed to be worse than a crime.

Dreadful as was the West Port discovery, were not worse things in store for poor Scotland? "In the perfect unanimity that there was something 'rotten in Denmark,' everybody in authority came in for a share of the blame, from the wicked George IV. down to the hateful exciseman. The 'General Assembly of the Kirk,' the religious Parliament of Scotland, was accused of having lost its sterner attributes. The pulpit was not so warm and edifying in its exhortations to the elect, and not sufficiently vehement in denunciations of the sinner. The common folk were crying reform and reading newspaper trash, instead of reforming them-

PLATE XXXIII

SOUTH-WEST CORNER OF SURGEONS' SQUARE IN 1829

Drawn by Thos. H. Shepherd and engraved by T. Barber. At the left is Surgeons' Hall. At the right is the Royal
Medical Society's Hall. In the centre is Knox's (formerly Barclay's) Class Room

selves and studying 'The Book.' Burke and Hare were but the carnal weapons of Satan, their concubines the alluring servitors of Romish priests, keenly alive to the selection of fitting instruments for plotting and effecting mischief" (Lonsdale). Such was the public sentiment of the time.

The rifling of graves had been sad enough, but murder now had added new terrors. It furnished food for wild exaggeration, and gave to gossiping creatures of both sexes an endless topic of conversation. Each family collected its members long before sundown, doors were locked and barricaded with the utmost care; labourers came home at night only in groups, and even "the unfortunates" were seen but rarely on the streets. Many persons were fearful that, suddenly as well as unwillingly, they might be converted into anatomical material.

Fate of the Edinburgh Murderers.

The trial of Burke and M'Dougal began at ten o'clock in the forenoon of Wednesday, 24th December 1828. It was continued, with certain intervals for refreshment, until nearly ten o'clock the next morning.

The slaughter-house of Burke and Hare had been conducted for a whole year in the metropolis of Scotland without a breath of suspicion having been aroused. When the news was out, the public mind was excited to such an unprecedented degree that, had it not been controlled, it might have interfered with the legal administration of justice. Under the circumstances it was necessary for the fair fame of Edinburgh that the prisoners should be ably and powerfully defended. It ever must be a source of satisfaction to Scotsmen to know that the trial of Burke and M'Dougal was conducted along just, legal, and honourable lines. And it is pleasing to know that the head of the Bar of Scotland, in conjunction with some others of its most respected luminaries, offered their services gratuitously on this memorable occasion.

Burke was defended by Sir James W. Moncrieff, Bart., *Dean of the Faculty;* Patrick Robertson, Duncan M'Neill, and David Milne. For M'Dougal appeared Henry Cockburn, Mark Napier, Hugh Bruce, and George Patton.[1] And certainly "never was there a defence in any case conducted with more consummate ability."[2]

It was on Christmas morning 1828 that the jury, after an absence of fifty minutes, returned the following verdict :—

"The jury find the pannel, William Burke, *guilty* of the *third charge in the indictment;* and find the indictment *not proven* against the pannel, Helen M'Dougal."[3]

The Lord Justice-Clerk then addressed William Burke, saying (in part) :

"The only doubt that has come across my mind is, whether, in order to mark the sense that the Court entertains of your offence, and which the violated laws of the country entertain respecting it, your body should not be exhibited in chains, in order to deter others from the like crimes in time coming. But, taking into consideration that the public eye would be offended with so dismal an exhibition, I am disposed to agree that your sentence shall be put in execution in the usual way, but accompanied with the statutory attendant of the punishment of the crime of murder, viz.—that your body should be publicly dissected and anatomized."

[1] Roughead, *Burke and Hare* (Notable British Trials Series), Edinburgh, 1921, p. 95.
[2] *West Port Murders*, Edinburgh, 1829, p. 7.
[3] Roughead, *Burke and Hare* (Notable British Trials Series), Edinburgh, 1921, p. 253.

PLATE XXXIV

EXECUTION OF WILLIAM BURKE
From an Etching by Walter Geikie.   Edinburgh, 1829

His Lordship then pronounced sentence of death in the usual form, a part of which was as follows :

"The Lord Justice-Clerk, and Lords Commissioners of Justiciary, in respect of the verdict before recorded, decern and adjudge the said William Burke, pannel, to be carried from the bar, back to the Tolbooth of Edinburgh, therein to be detained, and to be fed upon bread and water only . . . until Wednesday the 28th day of January next to come, and upon that day to be taken forth of the said Tolbooth to the common place of execution, in the Lawnmarket of Edinburgh, and then and there, between the hours of eight and ten o'clock before noon, of the said day, to be hanged by the neck, by the hands of the common executioner, upon a gibbet, until he be dead, and his body thereafter to be delivered to Dr Alexander Monro, Professor of Anatomy in the University of Edinburgh, to be by him publicly dissected and anatomized."

His Lordship then addressed Helen M'Dougal as follows :

"The jury have found the libel against you *not proven;* they have not pronounced you *not guilty* of the crime of murder charged against you in this indictment. You know whether you have been in the commission of this atrocious crime. I leave it to your own conscience to draw the proper conclusion. I hope and trust that you will betake yourself to a new line of life, diametrically opposite from that which you have led for a number of years."

Execution of William Burke.

On the morning of Tuesday, 27th January 1829, at four o'clock, Burke was taken off the *gad*,[1] and was removed in a coach from the gaol on the Calton Hill to the Lock-up-house, a prison immediately adjacent to the place of execution. The unusual hour was chosen to avoid annoyance from a riotous crowd.

During all of Tuesday, and far into the night, work-

[1] The *gad* is an iron bar fixed in the wall of old Scottish prisons about a foot from the ground to which criminals were chained by the ankle.

men were engaged in building the scaffold. Regardless of the "pelting of the pitiless storm," many spectators watched the erection of the gallows, and not a few persons passed the night in the adjacent closes and stairs, lest they might miss seeing the execution. The din of the workmen, the clanging of hammers, the lurid glare cast by the torches, and the soughing of the storm, made a weird and impressive scene. When all had been finished and the fatal beam was placed in proper position, the crowd expressed its abhorrence of Burke and his associates by giving three tremendous cheers.

Shortly after eight o'clock on the morning of Wednesday, 28th January 1829, Burke was hanged in the presence of an enormous crowd, estimated by various writers at from 20,000 to 37,000 persons. All had assembled to show their delight. The unknown author of *West Port Murders* says : "Every countenance bore an expression of gladness that revenge was so near, and the whole multitude appeared more as if they were waiting to witness some splendid procession or agreeable exhibition."

When Burke arrived on the platform of the scaffold, his composure left him amid the jeers, the curses, and the taunts of the assembled multitude. Defiant cries of "Hang Hare too!" "Where is Hare?" and "Hang Knox!" were mingled with curses against Burke.

Early on Thursday morning, in the presence of a select audience (Robert Liston, surgeon ; Mr George Combe, phrenologist ; Sir William Hamilton, the Scottish philosopher and metaphysician ; and Mr Joseph, an eminent sculptor), Burke's body was examined in one of Dr Monro's rooms.

At one o'clock in the afternoon, in pursuance of the sentence of the Court, Alexander Monro *tertius* publicly

PLATE XXXV

ALEXANDER MONRO *tertius* (1773-1859)

dissected the body of Burke. The anatomical theatre was crowded to its capacity. It was perhaps the most exciting and riotous *anatomical afternoon* recorded in Scotland's history. The audience was mixed and impatient. A huge crowd besieged the class-room door. Although the registered students of anatomy had been given tickets of admission, it was with great difficulty that these could be honoured even with the aid of the police.

The lecture concerned the brain, a portion of the anatomy of the human body on which Monro was supposed to have bestowed especial attention. After the calvarium had been removed, "the quantity of blood that gushed out was enormous, and by the time the lecture was finished, which was not till three o'clock, the area of the class-room had the appearance of a butcher's slaughter-house, from its flowing down and being trodden upon."[1]

It is a matter of record that philosophers, surgeons, phrenologists, medical students, rich men, poor men, vagabonds, policemen, and the better class of the ordinary public touched elbows and struggled for vantage spots from which to view the body of Burke. Professor Monro dismissed his audience and then tried, to the best of his ability, and to the utmost extent that his amphitheatre would permit, to satisfy the curiosity of the crowd. Shortly before the end of the lecture, a large body of young men—some of whom were students—demanded admission *en masse*, which was quite impossible. The police were summoned. This simply added fuel to the flame and a fierce contest ensued, hard blows being exchanged. The Lord Provost tried to quell the riot, but was glad to retire with whole bones. After the riot had lasted for nearly two hours,

[1] *West Port Murders*, Edinburgh, 1829, p. 254.

it was suddenly ended by the good sense of Robert (later Sir Robert) Christison, Professor of Materia Medica in the University of Edinburgh, who addressed the mob, announcing that he had arranged for their admission in units of about fifty at a time, giving his own personal guarantee for their good behaviour. The effect was electric; riot at once was converted into order; and, so long as daylight lasted, a constant stream of persons passed the table on which the body of Burke was exposed. It is recorded that seven females pressed in among the crowd which viewed the corpse. These women were roughly handled by some of the men. On the following day not less than twenty-five thousand persons viewed the remains of the murderer. Burke's body was carefully dissected. His skeleton now hangs in the Anatomical Museum of the University of Edinburgh, where all who wish may see it.

The phrenologists were not slow to seize this opportunity to extol their favourite views for the edification of the public. Elaborate measurements were made of Burke's head, and appropriate deductions were drawn therefrom, with the result that a violent controversy arose between phrenologists and anti-phrenologists —all of which added to the gaiety of nations and improved the financial standing of the printers of pamphlets; but it got Science nowhere

Fate of Hare, Mrs Hare, and Helen M'Dougal.

It is now time to recount briefly the fate of the remaining members of this infamous quartette. Hare and his wife saved their necks by turning King's evidence. The public and the newspapers demanded the execution of Hare. After careful study of the question, the Lord Advocate decided that he was "the prisoner of his word"; he had found it necessary to promise immunity to Hare in order to receive the whole information that Hare could give, and reluctantly his Lordship came to the conclusion that he was legally barred from prosecuting either of the persons concerned.[1]

It was with the greatest difficulty, and under the protection of the authorities, that Hare got out of Scotland into England. His identity was discovered by a body of workmen who promptly threw him into a vat of lime, with the result that his sight was destroyed. For a period of forty years he existed as a blind beggar, moving about on the north side of Oxford Street in London.

Mrs Hare managed to get to Glasgow. There, while waiting for a vessel to sail to Belfast, her presence became known, and only by the strenuous efforts of the police was she saved from a mob which would have torn her to pieces. She was escorted to Greenock, and was placed on the steamer *Fingal* for Belfast. She reached port safely, after which all trace of her was lost. Alexander Leighton, author of *The Court of Cacus*, (London, 1861), thinks that she died in Paris, where she was employed as a nurse.

Helen M'Dougal had the audacity to show her face around her old haunts, and was promptly mobbed. She left Edinburgh and suffered terrible hardships and injuries on her way south. She is supposed to have reached a vessel bound for Australia and to have died there.

"Burke and Burking."

The English language often has been enriched by reason of tragedies. Burke's crimes have added to the contents of the dictionary. "Burking" means (1) "To

---

[1] Roughead, *Burke and Hare* (Notable British Trials Series), Edinburgh, 1921, p. 68.

murder by suffocation, or to murder so as to produce few marks of violence, for the purpose of obtaining a body to be sold for dissection ": and (2) "to dispose of quietly or indirectly; to suppress; to smother; to shelve; as, to *burke* a parliamentary question" (Webster). "Burkism" is defined as "The practice of killing persons for the purpose of selling their bodies for dissection" (Webster).

According to Bailey (*The Diary of a Resurrectionist*, London, 1896, p. vii.), the newspapers of the period applied the term "Burking" to a much broader field. For example, "When any fresh scandal had given prominence to the doings of the resurrection-men, the newspapers saw 'Burking' in every trivial case of assault. If a child were lost, the paragraph announcing the fact was headed, 'Another Supposed Case of Burking.' Reports of the most ridiculous character were duly chronicled as facts by the newspapers of the day."

In some of these accounts over one hundred bodies were supposed to have been found in a single building; it was expected that persons of eminence would be arrested, but no further mention can be found of the case. Such was the yellow press in the early years of the last century.

Poisoning by arsenic inhaled in snuff was mentioned as "Burking by means of snuff." A wild tale was printed to the effect that a man named John Wilson was "supposed to have been two or three years in this abominable practice, and to have realised a considerable sum" from the sale of the bodies of his victims. However, careful inquiry shows that no such case occurred (Bailey).

Long before the time of Burke and Hare, Werner Rolfinck (1599-1673), Professor of Anatomy, Surgery,

PLATE **XXXVI**

WERNER ROLFINCK (1599-1673)
(Courtesy of the Librarian, Surgeon-General's Office, Washington, D.C.)

and Botany in the University of Jena, showed such enterprise in dissection that Jena criminals, just before they were turned over to the hangman, entreated that their remains should not be placed at the disposal of the anatomist,[1] and the peasants in near-by territory had the graves of their friends watched lest the dead should be " Rolfincked."

[1] Puschmann, *History of Medical Education*, London, 1891, p. 400.

CHAPTER VII

ROBERT KNOX, THE ANATOMIST, 1791-1862.[1]

ROBERT KNOX—a great, strong, outstanding, and valiant character ; the most eloquent, the most versatile, and the most thorough teacher of anatomy that Scotland, a country which long has been noted for the excellence of its anatomical instruction, ever has produced : Robert Knox—he who was designated as "*Knox, primus et incomparabilis,*" had his life wrecked, ruined, and embittered by the fortuitous circumstances which caused the murderers, Burke and Hare, to cross his path.

What a pity, that a man who made many original observations in both comparative and human anatomy ; a man endowed with a superior intellect and possessed of unusual industry ; a man who lectured extra-murally to larger classes than those of Monro *tertius* ; a man who wrote *The Races of Men, A Manual of Artistic Anatomy, Great Artists and Great Anatomists*, and several other works ; a man who translated the anatomical writings of several foreign authors—what a pity, that such a man as Robert Knox, the anatomist, should have been dragged into an abyss.

Robert was the eighth child and the fifth son of Robert and Mary Knox. At an early age the boy had smallpox in so virulent a form that it left him with a blinded left eye. In due time he was sent to the famous

[1] Dr Knox's birth-date is given as 4th September 1791, in the family Bible ; and the same date is in the records of the Royal College of Surgeons of Edinburgh. In the obituary notice written by Dr Druitt (*The Medical Times and Gazette*, 27th December 1862) it is given 1793, which date appears in many documents.

PLATE XXXVII

JOHN BARCLAY, M.D., F.R.C.S. Ed.

High School of Edinburgh, where, in obtaining his classical education, competing with the brightest youths of Edinburgh city and the adjacent districts, he rose to the head of every class, and came out as Gold Medallist in 1810. He joined the medical classes in November of the same year. On his first examination for the degree of Doctor of Medicine, Knox was plucked for his anatomy. And no wonder—the Professor of Anatomy in Edinburgh University was Alexander Monro *tertius* —he who, the incompetent descendant of a distinguished father and grandfather of the same name whose anatomical teaching had made the Edinburgh University famous throughout the world, repeated the lectures and experiments of Alexander Monro *primus*, palming them off as his own!

Fortunately, outside the supposed-to-be-sacred precincts of the University, there was a famous private school of anatomy, conducted by Dr John Barclay (1760-1826). If there were need for extra-mural teaching in anatomy during the reign of Monro *secundus*, as John Bell[1] had stated, that need now was increased by the inefficiency of Monro *tertius*.

Barclay, who had been a licensed preacher in the Church of Scotland, and had spent some years as a tutor, was drawn to the study of medicine. After graduation at Edinburgh, where he had served as

[1] John Bell (1763-1820), elder brother of Sir Charles Bell, was noted as an excellent classical scholar, as a lover of art, and as a rapid and skilful operator. He observed that the application of anatomy to surgery was neglected in the lectures of Monro *secundus*, and resolved to remedy the defect. He saw that not merely demonstration but actual dissection was required. In his own words : " In Dr Monro's class, unless there be a fortunate succession of bloody murders, not three subjects are dissected in the year. On the remains of a subject fished up from the bottom of a tub of spirits, are demonstrated those delicate nerves, which are to be avoided or divided in our operations ; and these are demonstrated once at the distance of one hundred feet " (*Letters on the Education of a Surgeon*, 1810).

assistant in anatomy to John Bell, Barclay went to London and there continued his anatomical studies. He returned to Edinburgh, and began to teach anatomy in 1797, in the thirty-seventh year of his age. He began in a small and modest way. He elucidated his lectures by means of a few specimens, some of his own dissections and others obtained by purchase. During the first seven years (1797-8—1803-4) his classes were small, due to two facts: (1) they were not recognised by a licensing board; and (2) Monro *secundus* taught on one side of Barclay's school and the two Bells— John and Charles—on the other. After Charles Bell had departed for London, in the summer of 1804, a clear field remained for Barclay, whose lectures were recognised, on 19th June, by the College of Surgeons. Barclay had an extensive knowledge of comparative anatomy; and an attempt was made by his friends, in 1817, to create for him a Chair of Comparative Anatomy in the University. Although the attempt was unsuccessful, it gave John Kay an opportunity to produce *The Craft in Danger*, which is one of his most admired medical caricatures.[1]

It was to Barclay's school that Knox went to learn anatomy. Knox's second appearance before the examiners caused a sensation greater than his previous rejection. Anatomy, described in the choicest of Latin words, seemed to ooze from his finger-tips. He graduated in 1814. In 1815, Knox, as assistant-

---

[1] Kay: A Series of Original Portraits and Caricature Etchings by the late John Kay, miniature painter, Edinburgh, 1877, vol. ii., p. 448.

Sir George Ballingall, while serving in India, prepared the skeleton of an elephant which subsequently was presented by him to his old master, Dr Barclay. In the plate Dr Barclay is trying to enter the University gate on the skeleton of the elephant, supported by Dr Gregory and welcomed by Mr Robert Johnston (a member of the Town Council). The cavalcade is opposed by Dr Hope, Dr Monro *tertius*, and Professor Jameson, who resented the encroachment on their respective departments.

PLATE XXXVIII

SIR CHARLES BELL (1774-1842)

Painted by Ballantyne and engraved by Thomson.   From Pettigrew's *Medical Portrait Gallery*, vol. iii., London, n.d.

surgeon in the army, was sent to Brussels to aid the wounded of Waterloo. Two years later, accompanying the 72nd Highlanders, he sailed to the Cape of Good Hope, where he remained until the autumn of 1820. Late in September 1821, having obtained permission from military headquarters to be absent from the United Kingdom for one year, Knox went to Paris. Here he found every department of medicine, surgery, and natural science ably represented. Cuvier (1769-1832) was developing the science of palæontology; Geoffroy St Hilaire (1772-1844) was elucidating his *Philosophie Anatomique*; De Blainville (1778-1850) was lecturing on Comparative Osteology, which lectures later were translated and corrected by Knox and were published (beginning on 26th October 1839) in *The Lancet*; and Baron Dominique-Jean Larrey (1766-1842), the greatest French military surgeon of his time, was adding to the literature of his profession. With all these men Knox formed valuable friendships. The knowledge of ethnology and of natural history which Knox had acquired by his researches in South Africa, was greatly increased by his studies in the *Jardin des Plantes* and the museums of Paris.

Robert Knox returned to Edinburgh in December 1822. It was "amid the zoological treasures obtained by Napoleon, and the osteological collections of Cuvier," says Lonsdale,[1] that "Knox became imbued with a grand emulation for biological study." This spirit was his guiding star throughout his whole professional life.

Knox's original contributions to science began in 1815, the year following his graduation. They were continued for many years and are too numerous to be catalogued here. Knox had been at home but a few days when, on 28th December 1822, he read to the

[1] Lonsdale, *A Sketch of the Life and Writings of Robert Knox, the Anatomist*, London, 1870, p. 23.

Wernerian Natural History Society, a "Notice relative to the Habits of the Hyæna of Southern Africa," in which he opposed the view that bones of animals found in caves had been dragged there by hyænas. Other papers which followed in rapid succession were : "Observations on the Anatomy of the Beaver considered as an Aquatic Animal," "Inquiry into the Original and Characteristic Differences of the Native Races inhabiting the extra-tropical part of Southern Africa," etc., etc. An important paper on "The Foramen of Soemmering, as seen in the Eyes of certain Reptiles," was read by Knox, on 15th November 1823.

Of the many original papers which were written by Knox during the years 1822-1825, perhaps the most remarkable one was the valuable essay he read to the Royal Society of Edinburgh, on 17th June 1823, entitled, "Observations on the Comparative Anatomy of the Eye." In this paper, which is drawn from the wide field of comparative anatomy, Knox concluded that the so-named "ciliary ligament" is a muscle ; that "it is the muscle by which the eye adapts itself to the perception of distant objects ; and that, by it in conjunction with the iris, all the changes which take place in the interior of the eyeball are effected." This paper alone should give to Robert Knox a niche in the temple of medical history.[1]

[1] Knox *reasoned* that the so-called ciliary ligament must be a muscle. Actual microscopic demonstration of the muscular nature of this part of the eye dates from 1835, and must be credited to an American, Dr William Clay Wallace (*Amer. Journ. of Sciences and Arts*, 1835, xxvii., pp. 219-222). It is not to the discredit of Knox that he *reasoned* concerning the nature of the ciliary muscle. William Harvey, who described a circulation which he never saw in its entirety, *reasoned* that there must be small vessels connecting the terminal arteries with the beginning veins.

Harvey died 3rd June 1657. Marcello Malpighi (1628-1694), in 1661, published an account of the capillaries which he had observed, during the preceding year, while studying the lung of the frog. A few years later (in 1668), these minute vessels were better described by Antonj van Leeuwenhoek (1632-1723), of Delft.

ANATOMY

AND

Physiology.

DR KNOX, F.R.S.E. *(Successor to* DR BARCLAY, *Fellow of the Royal College of Surgeons and Conservator of its Museum,)* will commence his ANNUAL COURSE of LECTURES on the **ANATOMY** and **PHYSIOLOGY** of the Human Body, on Tuesday, the 4th November, at Eleven A. M. His Evening COURSE of LECTURES, on the same Subject, will commence on the 11th November, at Six P. M.

Each of these Courses will as usual comprise a full Demonstration on fresh Anatomical Subjects, of the Structure of the Human Body, and a History of the Uses of its various Parts ; and the Organs and Structures generally, will be described with a constant reference to Practical Medicine and Surgery.

FEE for the First Course, £ 3, 5s.; Second Course, £ 2, 4s. ; Perpetual, £ 5, 9s.

N. B.—*These Courses of Lectures qualify for Examination before the various Colleges and Boards.*

PRACTICAL ANATOMY

AND

OPERATIVE SURGERY.

DR KNOX'S ROOMS FOR **PRACTICAL ANATOMY** and **OPERATIVE SURGERY,** will open on Monday, the 6th of October, and continue open until the End of July 1829.

Two DEMONSTRATIONS will be delivered daily to the Gentlemen attending the Rooms for PRACTICAL ANATOMY. These Demonstrations will be arranged so as to comprise complete Courses of the DESCRIPTIVE ANATOMY of the Human Body, with its application to PATHOLOGY and OPERATIVE SURGERY. The Dissections and Operations to be under the immediate superintendance of DR KNOX. Arrangements have been made to secure as usual an ample supply of Anatomical Subjects.

FEE for the First Course, £ 3, 5s. ; Second Course, £ 2, 4s.; Perpetual, £ 5, 9s.

N. B.—*An Additional Fee of Three Guineas includes Subjects.*

. *Certificates of Attendance on these Courses qualify for Examination before the Royal Colleges of Surgeons, the Army and Navy Medical Boards, &c.*

EDINBURGH, 10. SURGEONS' SQUARE,
25th September 1828.

HANDBILL ANNOUNCING DR KNOX'S LECTURES, SESSION OF 1828.
From the original in the University of Edinburgh.

In April 1824 Dr Knox submitted to the College of Surgeons a plan for the formation of a Museum of Comparative Anatomy and offered to give his whole time to the project. This generous offer was accepted. Thanks to Knox's industry and ability the Museum of the College of Surgeons soon became worthy of a Royal College which could boast of its Bells, Listons, and Symes.

Among the former anatomists of Edinburgh there are few names that rank with that of Dr Barclay. He had conducted an extra-mural school of anatomy for many years. He had built up a large and valuable museum ; he had assembled an extensive library ; he had framed a new anatomical nomenclature ; many of his pupils had attained eminence in the profession—but the dim shadows began to steal over Barclay. He looked around for a successor who should be worthy to fill his shoes, and he chose Robert Knox.

Dr Knox's first course of lectures on anatomy and physiology was delivered during the winter of 1825-1826, with satisfaction to the students, credit to himself, and honour to Dr Barclay. There was a new Richmond in the field. "From 1826 to 1835 there was but one temple worthy of the name in Edinburgh, in which aspiring youths might worship in the spirit of Galen, and sing the hymns that the anatomico-theosophist delighted in, and that temple was the old 'Surgeons' Hall,' where Robert Knox presided as high priest, oracle, and philosopher" (Lonsdale, p. 162).

For some men, as Thomas Carlyle has said, the clock does not advance to the meridian by hourly sounds, but at once it strikes twelve. It was so with Knox.

Anatomical teaching in Edinburgh has presented different characteristics with the passing years. The somewhat primitive anatomical teaching of the first

PLATE XXXIX

ROBERT KNOX (1791-1862).

This picture, showing Knox in his fiftieth year, has been made from a calotype which forms the frontispiece of Lonsdale's *Sketch of the Life and Writings of Robert Knox, the Anatomist*, London, 1870.

Monro was followed by the more minute descriptions of the second Monro. Surgical anatomy was brought to the fore by John Bell. Charles Bell emphasised the teleological and artistic features of anatomy. The gentle, pious, and classic Barclay set the example of teaching anatomy as a vocation. Others were noted as delvers into the physiological, the histological, or the plodding, demonstrative phases ; and still others laboured diligently in the compilation of text-books, in the translation of foreign literature, or in the production of pictorial representations of the human structures.[1] Knox, however, presented anatomy under a different light and clothed it with fresh draperies. " His forte as an anatomist was, not in detail or the relation to surgery and medicine, but in bringing comparative anatomy to the explanation of human anatomy " (Struthers).[2]

Looking at anatomy as a subject worthy of the attention of a philosopher ; recognising its broad divisions — anatomical science and anatomical art ; building on the comparative anatomy of Barclay, the inductions of Cuvier, and the then despised views of Geoffroy St Hilaire—Robert Knox was able to arouse a new interest in anatomy. Within a short period his lectures were attended by the largest class that Edinburgh had known.

No medical lecturer in the United Kingdom ever enjoyed such popularity, or won his spurs so quickly, as Robert Knox. "From 1826 to 1835, over a period of nine years, his students annually averaged 335, and in the session of 1828-9 he had 504 pupils. No such

[1] The overcrowded condition of the Edinburgh school, and the impossibility of securing an adequate supply of bodies for dissection, accounts for the numerous engravings which were issued by the anatomists of that city. A long list of such works is found in Struthers's *Historical Sketch of the Edinburgh Anatomical School*, Edinburgh, 1867, pp. 90-91.

[2] Struthers, *op. cit.*

anatomical class ever assembled in Britain.   The old
lecture room of Dr Barclay would not admit of more than
200 persons, so Knox was obliged to lecture three times
daily, and on the same subject each time" (Lonsdale).

How, then, under such wearying conditions, could
Dr Knox have done otherwise than to turn over to his
doorkeeper, and to student-assistants, many of the
details of his establishment, such as the reception and
preparation of anatomical material?

The fall of Dr Knox was tragic.

Discovery of the body of the woman Docherty in
Knox's establishment spelt ruin for the anatomist.   It
linked his name with the names of Burke and Hare.
That was enough.   Useless were the searching inquiries
made by the Procurator-Fiscal of Edinburgh and the
Lord-Advocate of Scotland, by whom nothing to the
discredit of Knox could be found—the rabble demanded
its prey ; and the rabble—with shame be it said—was
encouraged by some of the clergy, by a hostile press,
and by rival members of the medical profession.[1]

---

[1] The Edinburgh physicians and surgeons had long been famous for
the ferocity of their quarrels.   The esteemed Dr James Gregory, Professor
of the Practice of Medicine in Edinburgh University, late in the eighteenth
century expressed his opinion of the greatest Edinburgh surgeon of that
period, in these words : "Any man, if himself or his family were sick,
should as soon think of calling in a mad dog as Mr John Bell, or any who
held the principles he professes."

Another malignant attack against John Bell "was stuck up like a
play-bill in a most conspicuous and unusual manner, on every corner of
the city" (Struthers, p. 41).

And at so late a date as the middle of the last century this ferocity was
voiced by John Lizars, in his *Use and Abuse of Tobacco*, wherein, "while on
the subject of cancer of the tongue, [he] indulges in some conjectures
regarding the minute structure of that organ, and enters his caveat against
its removal when affected with malignant disease.   He refers to two cases
in which the tongue was excised by Mr Syme, both of which terminated
fatally, and he evidently introduces the notice in order that he may give
that gentleman a thrust under the rib" (Gross, *The North American
Medico-Chirurgical Review*, vol. iii., 1859, p. 1031).

PLATE **XL**

CARICATURE OF ROBERT KNOX

Was Dr Knox in any way to blame for the West Port murders? This question has given rise to a mass of controversial literature. To epitomise this would require a separate volume, and, now that a century has passed since the crimes were committed, it were a fruitless task. All the players have disappeared: the murderers, the rival anatomists, yea, even their students are no more. Let the dead rest.

It is appropriate, however, to quote the words of a man who lived during those stirring days and who had access to the facts. For example, Lord Cockburn, one of the judges of the Court of Session in Scotland, long accustomed to the sifting of evidence, having had personal knowledge of all the facts, has said[1]: "No case ever struck the public heart or imagination with greater horror. And no wonder. For the regular demand for anatomical subjects, and the high prices given, held out a constant premium to murder, and when it was shown to what danger this exposed the unprotected, everyone felt himself living in the midst of persons to whom murder was a trade. All our anatomists incurred a most unjust, though not an unnatural odium; Dr Knox in particular, against whom not only the anger of the populace, but the condemnation of more intelligent persons, was specially directed. But tried in reference to the invariable, and the necessary practice of the profession, our anatomists were spotlessly correct, and Knox the most correct of them all."

The mob wished to apply to Dr Knox that form of judicial procedure which is known as "Jeddart justice,"

---

[1] Cockburn, *Memorials of His Time*, Edinburgh, 1872, p. 395. Henry Cockburn (1779-1854) has given a charming account of Scottish manners, and of important events which had marked the progress of Scotland, or at least of Edinburgh, between the years 1821 and the close of the year 1830.

which is founded on the principle "to hang first and try afterwards." The name is derived from the town of Jedburgh, where the magistrates as well as the barons had the power of life and death. This arbitrary power was exercised so late as the year 1715, when some suspected rebels were brought before the zealous magistrates. Only one crime could be clearly "proven," which was that the suspects were "real natural-born Irishers," on which conviction they were quickly taken to "the goose pool, and hadden doun, and drownit till they were dead." [1]

The conduct of Alexander Monro *tertius*, who read the lectures and performed the experiments which had been initiated by his grandfather, often palming them off as his own, could not fail to excite the contempt and derision of the free-lance who taught anatomy at No. 10 Surgeons' Square.

Knox possessed a facile pen and a ready tongue, both of which often were directed toward his rivals. There was little of friendship, and much of quarrelling, among the Edinburgh teachers of anatomy during the early years of the nineteenth century. When, however, the West Port murders were out, all could unite in condemnation of Knox. The hostile flame often was fanned by his confrères.

The desire of the rabble to "hang Knox"; the march of the mob—composed largely of boys, rowdies, and street-walkers of the Old Town—from the Calton Hill to Knox's residence, carrying an effigy which bore the words, "Knox, the associate of the infamous Hare"; the stoning of the anatomist's house; the frequent attempts which were made to do him bodily harm, and the many annoyances and insults to which he was subjected — all these are matters which, for their

[1] Gordon, *The Home Life of Sir David Brewster*, Edinburgh, 1870, p. 5.

explanation, require thought. Two points should be considered : (1) the activities of rival anatomists, which we will ignore ; and (2) the condition under which Scotsmen had lived at the end of the eighteenth, and under which they now were living in the early years of the nineteenth, century.

Life in Scotland, in the early years of the nineteenth century, was for the most part hard and undelectable. Strange to say, so late as in the year 1799, there were slaves in Scotland, for such was the condition of the colliers and salters, who "could not be killed nor directly tortured ; but they belonged, like the serfs of an older time, to their respective works, with which they were sold as a part of the gearing." [1]

Free speech did not exist in Scotland, since the Government, mindful of the '45 rebellion, did not approve of it. A meeting against West Indian Slavery was held in Edinburgh in July 1814. "Except for victories and charity," says Lord Cockburn, "*this was the first assembling of the people for a public object that had occurred here for about twenty years*" ; and if it had been purely a political matter, it could not have been held in Edinburgh, even in 1814. Fancy such a repression, when given a free rein, without the possibility of a depressing aftermath. No wonder the mob was brave. Its members had nothing to fear. [2]

Burke made two confessions. The first one, 3rd January 1829, he dictated before the Procurator-Fiscal and other officials ; and on the 22nd of the same month he added a short statement to it. On 21st January, however, the condemned man made another and fuller confession, but this time unofficial. This is known as the "*Courant*" confession, the document having found

[1] Cockburn, *Memorials of his Time*, Edinburgh, 1872, p. 67.
[2] *Ibid.*, p. 242.

its way, by mysterious channels, into the sanctum of the *Edinburgh Courant*.

This document reflects credit on the journalism of that day. The securing of it was a " scoop," whose publication, however, was postponed by order of the High Court. A full account of the matter has been given by MacGregor.[1]

For us the *Courant* confession is of interest, by reason of its concluding paragraph, as follows :

" *Burk deaclars that Docter Knox never incoureged him, nither taught or incoreged him to murder any person, nether any of his asistents, that worthy gentleman Mr Fergeson*[2] *was the only man that ever mentioned anything about the bodies. He inquired where we got that yong woman Paterson.*

"(Sined)   WILLIAM BURK, prisner."

" *Condemned Cell, January* 21, 1829."

It is unnecessary to go into the details of the life of Dr Knox. His biography has been admirably written by Lonsdale.[3]   The effect of the Edinburgh murders has been described by a former member of the editorial staff of *The Lancet*, Mr J. F. Clarke,[4] as follows :—

" The popular fury against Knox was wild and

---

[1] MacGregor, *The History of Burke and Hare*, Glasgow, 1884, p. 185.

[2] When, late in December 1827, Burke and Hare were diverted from Monro to Knox, they turned the body of old Donald, who died a natural death, to several young men at Knox's establishment.   The names of two of them—William Fergusson (1808-1877), and Thomas Wharton Jones (1808-1891)—are worthily recorded in the annals of medical history.

Fergusson (the *Fergeson* of Burke's confession) was the founder of conservative surgery.

Thomas Wharton Jones was a noted physiologist and ophthalmic surgeon, who narrowly escaped the honour, accorded to von Helmholtz of introducing the ophthalmoscope (see *British and Foreign Medico-Chirurgical Review*, October 1854).

[3] Lonsdale, *A Sketch of the Life and Writings of Robert Knox, the Anatomist*, London, 1870.

[4] Clarke, *Autobiographical Recollections of the Medical Profession*, London, 1874, p. 424.

— Burke Declares that doctor Knox Never incowreged him Neither thought [?] or incoureged him to murder any person Sethos any of his contends that worthy gentleman Mr. fergeson was the osely man that ever mintioned any thing about the bodies he inquirded where we got that yong womans nuchnos —

Sined William Burke prisoner

FACSIMILE OF BURKE'S ADDITION TO THE "COURANT" CONFESSION.
(MacGregor, *The History of Burke and Hare*, Glasgow, 1884, opposite page 229.)

savage. He was charged in so many words as a *particeps criminis*, and held up to public odium and indignation. He bore with the accusation for a time in silence, but eventually replied to it in a dignified and somewhat haughty manner. That he was entirely innocent of the dreadful charge made against him, it is scarcely necessary, perhaps, to say ; but so grave was his position, that a committee of persons of the highest position and character thought it desirable, on his behalf, and for the interests of the public, to inquire fully into the matter. This they did, completely exonerating Knox, but considered, under the circumstances, that he should have exercised 'greater vigilance.' Notwithstanding this acquittal,[1] however, Knox was exposed to great personal danger from the populace, and more than once had occasion to display a coolness and a courage never surpassed."

Not only was Knox endangered by mobs, assailed by the press, denounced by every class of the "unco guid," and covertly criticised by rival anatomists—he had also to withstand the assaults of the literary muck-rakers of the day. Chief among these was John Wilson, *alias* "Christopher North."

Two months after Burke's confession, exonerating Knox from all blame, had been given to the world, the pious "Christopher North," Professor of Moral Philosophy, vented his spleen in *Blackwood's Magazine* (March 1829), in its "*Noctes Ambrosianæ.*" The savage attack of the literary ruffian, as Lonsdale calls him, was not confined to his effort to destroy Knox. "Literary ruffianism," says Lonsdale, "is too mild a term to apply

---

[1] "The Committee who, at the request of Dr Knox, undertook to investigate the truth or falsehood of the rumours in circulation regarding him" made its report on "13th March 1829." Like a bee, or an epigram, it leaves a tender but non-lethal spot. This may have been placed purposely —to soothe the rabble.

to the foul words used by Wilson, who, not content with
holding up Knox to public execration, rushed with the

𝕎𝖊𝖘𝖙-𝕻𝖔𝖗𝖙 𝕸𝖚𝖗𝖉𝖊𝖗𝖘.

CHARACTERS

OF

BURK, HARE, AND Dr. KNOX.

[*From the Noctes Ambrosianæ of Blackwood's Magazine
for March 1829.*]

BEING PART OF A CONVERSATION BETWEEN NORTH, TICKLER,
AND THE ETTRICK SHEPHERD.

Shepherd.—Did you ever see sic a preparation o' a skeleton o' a turkey ? We maun send it to the College Museum,
to staun in a glass case aside Burk's.

North.—What did you think, James, of the proceedings
of these two Irish gentlemen ?

Shepherd.—That the were too monotonous too impress the
imagination. First ae drunk auld wife, and then anither
drunk auld wife—and then a third drunk auld wife—and
then a drunk auld or sick man or twa. The confession got
unco monotonous—the Lights and Shadows o' Scottish
Death want relief—though, to be sure, poor Peggy Paterson,
that Unfortunate, broke in a little on the uniformity ; and
sae did Daft Jamie ; for whilk last murder, without ony
impiety. ane may venture to say, the Devil is at this moment
ruggin' that Burk out o' hell fire wi' a three-prong'd fork,
and then in wi' him again, through the ribs—and then stirring up the coals wi' that eternal poker—and then wi' the
great bellows blawin' up the furnace, till, like an Etna, or
Mount Vesuvius, it vomits the murderer out again far ower
into the very middle o' the floor o' the infernal regions.

R. Menzies, Printer, Edinburgh.

FACSIMILE OF "CHRISTOPHER NORTH'S" ATTACK ON DR KNOX.

savagery of the war-whoop and tomahawk upon an
unoffending anatomical class for showing an affectionate

regard for their great teacher." A fine example of Christian charity, which is more often forgotten than remembered!

Throughout his whole professional career, Robert Knox conducted himself like a Knight of Old, ever ready to expose the false and to defend the true.

A distinguished member of the Royal College of Surgeons of Edinburgh recently has written (personal communication) :— " I fancy that what underlay Christison's denunciation of Knox was the University jealousy of Knox's success. Everybody thought Knox was careless, everybody thinks so still; but in those far-off days no anatomist dared ask his suppliers where they got their subjects, far less how they got them. Christison overlooks the fact that Knox's men received the bodies, handled them, and injected them. Knox paid for them. If the bodies had been rotten Knox would have been warned that they were not worth the money and the suppliers told to bring them fresher. Knox's business was to get on with his lectures and demonstrations, not to get handling the bodies until they came into the dissecting-room itself. If the local committee which was formed for the express purpose of bringing home Knox's criminality failed to find reasons then to impeach him, we may be pretty certain that there was not a shred of evidence that could be a cause of complaint. Before the occurrence Knox was not a society man. That he was ruined afterwards no one denies, but far less would ruin a man to-day just as certainly. The anatomical world was the poorer for the popular virulence against Knox."

This was the Edinburgh whose medical profession, denying to him "a place in the sun," drove Mr Charles Bell to London, where his brilliant discoveries in anatomy and physiology caused his name to become a

household word throughout the civilised world. This
was the Edinburgh which, in later years during one of
its spasmodic spells of repentance, begged *Sir* Charles
Bell to return and to accept a Chair in its University.
This was the Edinburgh whose pulpit orators denounced
James Y. Simpson as a co-partner of the devil, because
he had dared to make labour painless by the inhalation
of chloroform. A little less of the outward cant and
form of religion, and a little more of the milk of human
kindness, would have prevented many a heartache. The
Scot, however, seems to be foreordained to take his
religion as he takes his whisky—neat.

John Calvin, in 1553, had caused Michael Servetus
—physician, biblical student, enthusiast, and discoverer
of the lesser, or pulmonary, circulation—to be burned
alive, together with his books, on a hillside near Geneva.
The twentieth century Calvinists, in the Athens of the
North, were running true to form.

Dr Knox died, 20th December 1862, from apoplexy.
An admirable notice of Knox appeared in the *Medical
Times and Gazette*, 27th December 1862, as an editorial.
It was written by Dr Druitt.

It was by the merest accident that Knox was brought
in relation with Burke. If the West Port subjects had
gone to the University rooms, as Hare intended, Monro
tertius, then in his decadence, would have been the
object of popular wrath; and likely Dr Knox would
have succeeded to his professorial Chair.

By virtue of his success as a teacher, Knox from the
start was placed in a dangerous situation. All other
Edinburgh anatomists looked with envious eyes upon
the ever-increasing number of his students. All teachers
of anatomy were accepting from the resurrectionists any
bodies which were offered—no questions being asked.
A century ago, no anatomical teacher in Edinburgh,

in London, or in Dublin, dared to quarrel with the
"sack-'em-up men." To have done so, at once would
have caused the ruin of the anatomist's school—to say
nothing of the loss of time and credits to the students.
Knox was unfortunate in having had directed to him
a body which the murderers, Burke and Hare, intended
to deliver to Monro *tertius*. This was the body of old
Donald, who died a natural death. Thus began an
acquaintance which ended in destruction for all parties
concerned.

Poor old Knox had a sufficient amount of censure
whilst he was amongst the living. It seems cruel to
think that Sir Robert Christison, whose *Life*, published
in 1885—edited by his sons, from manuscript written
"at intervals between 1870 and 1879"—should have
said of Knox that: "One of his last occupations was
that of lecturer, demonstrator, or showman, to a travelling
party of Ojibbeway Indians."[1]

Knox, who had written *The Races of Men*, could
have had only a scientific interest in the original
Americans, whose visit to Europe, in 1839, created a
sensation. Members of the Royal family, as well as
lesser lights, were delighted to see and to talk with
these descendants of what is now a fast-vanishing race.[2]

Of all the so-called *non-civilised* aboriginal races, the
North American Indian was the noblest. His nobility
was destroyed by so-called *civilised* peoples, who gave
to him syphilis, smallpox, and rotten whisky. They
extended the make-believe hand of friendship whilst
planning to steal his lands.

[1] *The Life of Sir Robert Christison*, Edinburgh 1885, vol. i., p. 311.
[2] Catlin, *Adventures of the Ojibbeway and Ioway Indians in England,
France and Belgium*, London 1852, third edition, vol. i.

PLATE **XLI**

CAST OF THE HUMAN BODY BY JOHN GOODSIR (1814-1867), a pupil of Robert Knox, and who succeeded Monro *tertius* as Professor of Anatomy in the University of Edinburgh

(Photograph by D. M. Greig, Esq., F.R.C.S.E.)

CHAPTER VIII

THE crimes of the resurrection-men were so well known that one naturally asks why the Government did not at once pass a Bill which would legalise dissection and simultaneously abolish the robbing of graves? Such legislation was earnestly desired by the teachers of anatomy; to them the existing system was both degrading and ruinous. After a deputation had called his attention to the matter the Home Secretary answered "that there was no difficulty in drawing up an effective Bill; the great obstacle was the prejudice of the people against any Bill."[1]

Such an answer was to be expected of a Government which played fast and loose with the profession. Whilst the Eldons and Castlereaghs had their minds directed toward party and personal interests, and learnedly discussed such subjects as the State Church and the "glorious Constitution," the progress of medical science was resolutely thwarted by the ineptitude of the Tory politicians.[2] Evidently the public must be educated to demand the passage of such an Act as would legalise dissection.

To show the advantages of anatomy Sir Philip Crampton in Dublin lectured with open doors, and explained the mysteries of the human structure to all, rich or poor, educated or ignorant, who would attend his demonstrations. The same plan was also tried in

---

[1] Bailey, *The Diary of a Resurrectionist*, London, 1896, p. 89.
[2] Lonsdale, *Life of Robert Knox*, London, 1870, p. 58.

London.   Unfortunately, however, attempts to educate the public, by quiet and sane methods, often end in intellectual bankruptcy.   It is only from sudden and volcanic eruptions that public sentiment undergoes a quick change of front.

Horrible as were the crimes which had been committed by Burke and Hare, something more was needed to arouse the English.   The first Anatomy Bill, which Mr Henry Warburton introduced into the House of Commons in March 1829, was passed with slight modifications; but when Lord Calthorpe introduced it into the Upper House, it was opposed by a group of peers headed by the Archbishop of Canterbury and was withdrawn.[1]   Lord Calthorpe's intention to present the same Bill in 1830 was abandoned by reason of the impending dissolution of Parliament.

The increasing frequency of grave-robberies, the persistent pleas of the teachers of anatomy, the virile and thunderous editorials that Wakley set forth in *The Lancet*, the exposure of the crimes of "the sack-'em-up men" by the public press—all these were important factors in changing public sentiment.   The change, however, was of slow growth.   A shock was needed. Nothing less than a foul murder, committed at its very doors by the resurrection-men of London, was sufficient to arouse the British Government to the absolute necessity for a change in the law.

The London Murder.

Infamous as were the Edinburgh crimes, another one occurred in London three years later which stirred the English public against the "resurrection-men" and the anatomists, and finally aroused Parliament to a realisation that some determined step must be taken to

[1] Sprigge, *Life and Times of Thomas Wakley*, London, 1897, p. 436.

prevent not only the wholesale spoliation of graves, but also the practice of "burking."

On 5th November 1831 two men, named Bishop and May, asked the porter of the dissecting-room at King's College if he "wanted anything." When interrogated as to what they had for sale, May replied, "A boy of fourteen." For this body they asked twelve guineas, but ultimately agreed to accept nine guineas for it. Later in the day they returned with another man named Williams, *alias* Head, and a porter named Shields, who carried the body in a hamper. The appearance of the subject caused Mr Hill, the porter at King's College, to suspect foul play and to mention his suspicion at once to Mr Partridge, the demonstrator of anatomy. Examination of the body by Mr Partridge confirmed the porter's suspicions. To delay the men, so that the police might be informed, Mr Partridge produced a £50 note, and asked the men to wait until he could secure change for it. Soon after, the police arrived and the men were given into custody. At the coroner's inquest a verdict of "Wilful murder against some person or persons unknown" was brought in, the jury adding that there was strong suspicion against Bishop and Williams.

A vivid account of the *post-mortem* examination has been given by Mr J. F. Clarke,[1] who for many years was a member of the editorial staff of *The Lancet*. The examination was conducted by Mr Wetherfield, a surgeon. The others present were Mr Mayo, then lecturer on anatomy at King's College; Mr Partridge, his demonstrator; Mr Beaman, parish surgeon; his assistant, D. Edwards; and Mr Clarke, who says :— "The boy's teeth had been removed for sale to a

[1] Clarke, *Autobiographical Recollections of the Medical Profession*, London, 1874, p. 101.

dentist, and with this exception there were no external marks of violence on any part of the body. The internal organs were carefully examined : there was no trace of injury or poison. Mr Mayo, who had a peculiar way of standing very upright with his hands in his breeches pockets, said, with a kind of lisp he had—'By Jove! the boy died a nat*h*ral death.' Mr Partridge and Mr Beaman, however, suggested that the spine had not been examined, and after a short consultation it was determined to examine the spinal column. Upon this being done, one or more of the upper cervical vertebræ were found fractured. 'By Jove!' said Mr Mayo, 'this boy was murthered.'"

To Mr Partridge and Mr Beaman are due the discovery that this subject had been murdered. Bishop, Williams, and May had their trial at the Old Bailey, in December 1831. The body was proved to be that of an Italian boy, named Carlo Ferrari, who made his living by showing white mice. The two ruffians— Bishop and Williams—had enticed the lad to their den in Bethnal Green, where he was murdered. Their method, according to Clarke,[1] was as follows :—" It was the custom of the murderers to strike their victim on the upper part of the spine, and when insensible to place him head foremost in a water-butt." A different version is given by Bailey,[2] who states that the guest was first drugged with opium and then was let down a well until suffocated.

In the rooms of Bishop and Williams, whose house might well be likened to the cave of Cacus,[3] was found

[1] Clarke, *Autobiographical Recollections of the Medical Profession*, London, 1874, p. 102.

[2] Bailey, *The Diary of a Resurrectionist*, London, 1896, p. 109.

[3] Cacus was a huge giant who inhabited a cave on Mount Aventine and plundered the surrounding country. He was slain by Hercules (Bulfinch, *The Age of Fable*).

the empty mouse-cage which belonged to the Italian boy. This, says Packard,[1] was made to furnish evidence, as follows : Mr Partridge suggested an ingenious and successful plan by which the little animals which had been his support in life proved silent though eloquent witnesses against his murderers. Some cheese was placed in the rooms to which the boy had been decoyed and in which his empty mouse-cage was found, and the little creatures came forth to eat it."

Bishop, Williams, and May had their trial at the Old Bailey, December 1831. The three prisoners were found guilty and were sentenced to death. May, however, escaped the penalty.

The execution of Bishop and Williams, 5th December 1831, caused a scene of tremendous excitement. Extra fuel was added to the flame when, by mistake, three chains were suspended from the gallows : as soon as the error was noticed, one of them was removed, and the crowd took this as a sign that May had been reprieved. The execution of Bishop and Williams marks the end of the system of "burking." The case of the Italian boy aroused the public, but, as Clarke says, there is much reason to believe that "burking" was carried on to a great extent in London. "Many persons had been missed, and were never afterwards heard of," says Clarke, "and it was naturally supposed they had been murdered, and their bodies sold for dissection."[2]

The fate of Bishop and Williams has been mentioned above. May was respited, and was sentenced to transportation for life. On hearing of his good fortune, May

[1] Packard, "The Resurrectionists of London and Edinburgh," *The Medical News*, New York, 12th July 1902.

[2] Bishop and Williams confessed, also, to the murder of a woman named Fanny Pigburn, and a boy, whose name was supposed to be Cunningham (Bailey).

went into a fit, and for a time was near death. He made a partial recovery, but was much annoyed by the gibes he received from the other convicts on board the hulks. He died on board the *Grampus* in 1832.

Shields, who was porter to the gang, had been watchman and grave-digger at the Roman Catholic Chapel in Moorfields, and was most useful to the other resurrectionists. No evidence was offered against him in connection with the murder of the Italian boy. Soon after the trial, when he attempted to get work as a porter, Shields was recognised by a crowd of working men who raised the cry of "burker," and came near killing him. This incident shows the state of public feeling towards the resurrection-men, and that feeling, says Bailey, "was quite as bitter towards the anatomists."

The bodies of Bishop and Williams were removed from Newgate to Surgeons' Hall on the evening of the execution, the Royal College being by charter entitled to the bodies of all convicts found guilty of murder and sentenced "to be dissected and anatomised." The bodies were not really dissected by the Royal College of Surgeons. The demands of the charter of the College were met by the receipt of the murderer's body and by making in it a simple incision. The body was then handed over to one of the teachers of anatomy. After the passing of the Anatomy Act, in 1832, the College no longer had to share with the hangman the duty of carrying out the sentence on murderers.

CHAPTER IX

SIR ASTLEY PASTON COOPER (1768-1841), of Norfolk, the son of a clergyman, and one of John Hunter's pupils, became the most noted surgeon in London during the first quarter of the nineteenth century. His passion for anatomical study was appeased only by daily dissections, for which purpose a special room was used in his own house. Sir Astley was deeply versed in comparative anatomy, and his dissections were carried out on animals which ranged in size from a mouse to an elephant.

Removal of the elephant from the Menagerie of the Tower to Cooper's house caused great excitement and obstruction in traffic. The articulated skeleton of this quadruped may be seen in the museum at St Thomas's Hospital.

Sir Astley Cooper's career as a teacher began in 1791 and ended in January 1825. During this period his relations with the resurrectionists were constantly maintained. When Mr Cooper commenced lecturing at St Thomas's Hospital, there were comparatively few students in anatomy; only three or four men in London lectured on the subject, and the persons who supplied bodies for dissection "had no distinct denomination, nor indeed was their existence known to the public generally."[1] Within a few years, however, there was a sixfold increase in the number of students; new

---

[1] Bransby Blake Cooper, *The Life of Sir Astley Cooper*, London, 1843, vol. i., p. 344.

teachers of anatomy appeared on the scene ; the demand for bodies became imperative ; the "sack-'em-up men" became more numerous, and the name "resurrectionists" was given to them by an aroused public.

Under the encouragement of Sir Astley Cooper and other teachers, who paid high prices for anatomical material, the violation of graves in and near 'London became a horrible trade. The business passed into the hands of men of the most degraded character : men who, for the sake of gain, if they could not obtain their objects by the ordinary method of disinterment, would adopt any means to effect their purpose.

The shameful and criminal acts of the London and Edinburgh resurrection-men resulted in their undoing. The demands of an outraged public finally secured what the teachers of anatomy long had desired, namely, an Anatomy Act. This justly is called the Warburton Act. Its history is mentioned elsewhere in this monograph.

In December 1831 Mr Warburton for a second time introduced a Bill into the House of Commons, to legalise the study of anatomy. This became a law on 1st August 1832. That date marks the end of the vocation of the resurrection-men. Violent oscillations of the pendulum are followed at last by rest in the vertical meridian.

Sir Astley Cooper's opinion of the resurrectionists was expressed before the Committee on Anatomy of Parliament.[1] He said that they are "the lowest dregs of degradation. I do not know that I can describe them better ; there is no crime they would not commit,

---

[1] *Report from the Select Committee* [*House of Commons*] *on Anatomy*, folio, London, 1828. This is, perhaps, the best source of information respecting the resurrectionists. Many important documents are printed in this volume, in addition to the evidence and the report (Bailey).

and, as to myself, if they should imagine that I would make a good subject, they really would not have the smallest scruple, if they could do the thing undiscovered, to make a subject of me."

Sir Astley Cooper led an active, a laborious, a useful, and an honourable life. He was a pioneer in the surgery of the great vessels, in the surgery of the ear, and in experimental surgery. His ligations of the common carotid and the external iliac arteries for aneurysms, the ligation of the abdominal aorta, his amputation at the hip-joint, and his operation of perforating the tympanic membrane for deafness due to obstruction of the auditory tube—all these procedures, which were done without the aid and solace of anæsthetics—entitle him to the everlasting gratitude of mankind. Nor was this all! His students, who flocked to London from the ends of the earth, profited from the words of wisdom which dropped from his lips and carried back to their respective lands the latest and most approved methods of surgery. One of them was Valentine Mott (1785-1865), by whom, in 1818, the innominate artery was ligated for the first time in the history of surgery. In addition to this, Mott made one hundred and thirty-eight ligations of great vessels for aneurysm, and had many original operations on bones and joints to his credit.

Sir Astley Cooper's usefulness to the world was based on his profound knowledge of anatomy—and this was gained by the careful dissection of bodies which were supplied by the resurrectionists. Thus did the end justify the means.

When Dr Valentine Mott, of New York City, revisited London after an absence of thirty-five years, he found Sir Astley Cooper (who then was in his sixty-eighth year) deeply engrossed in dissections of the thymus gland.[1] Of such men as Sir Astley Cooper is the Kingdom of Medicine made.

The large sums, which were given to the resurrectionists for subjects, not infrequently led persons, while alive, to offer to sell their bodies for dissection. It rarely happened, however, that the proposal was accepted, for such an agreement, even if made in good faith, could not be enforced, the law not recognising any right of property in a dead body. Among Sir Astley Cooper's papers, preserved in the Stone collection at the Royal College of Surgeons of England, is the following epistolary gem :—

"SIR,—I have been informed you are in the habit of purchasing bodys, and allowing the person a sum weekly ; knowing a poor woman that is desirous of doing so, I have taken the liberty of calling to know the truth.

"I remain your humble servant,

————."

Sir Astley's reply was this :—

"The *truth* is that you deserve to be hanged for making such an unfeeling offer.   A. C."

This brave answer was chiefly bluff. Under other circumstances the famous London surgeon opened his purse widely.

Sir Astley's accounts for 1820 show the following entries in regard to obtaining the body of a man on whom he had operated twenty-four years before : " Coach for two there and back, £3, 12s. ; guards and coachmen, 6s. ; expenses for two days, £1, 14s. 6d. ; carriage of subject and porter, 12s. 6d. ; subject, £7, 7s. ; total, £13, 12s."

This body was to be obtained, we read, "cost what it may." It is no wonder, then, that of Sir Astley it

[1] Mott, *Travels in Europe and the East*, New York, 1842, p. 19.

PLATE XLII

SIR ASTLEY COOPER (1768-1841)
Painted by Sir T. Lawrence and engraved by W. H. Mote. From Pettigrew's
Medical Portrait Gallery, vol. i., London, n.d.

might be said, that no man knew so much of the habits, the crimes, and the few good qualities of the "resurrection-men." He could obtain any subjects he pleased, however guarded, and indeed offered to do so. No one could go further than he did before a Committee of the House of Commons, to whom he plainly avowed : " There is no person, let his situation in life be what it may, whom, if I were disposed to dissect, I could not obtain. The law only enhances the price, and does not prevent the exhumation."

Hypothecation of the body during life, in return for a monetary subsidy, is still thought possible among the more illiterate of the general public by whom the kindnesses towards the sick and hurt, to which the medical profession is so prone, are shorn of their disinterestedness and given the vilest interpretation. The persistence of this belief is evidenced by the following letter, received so recently as 29th June 1925 by the Conservator of the Museum of the Royal College of Surgeons of Edinburgh :—

"—— STREET,
DUNFERMLINE, FIFE.

" Dear Sir, just a few lines to ask you if I could get 5 or Ten pounds on my body as I have a 100 pounds worth of silver on me as I was wounded in the War and I am an ExSoldier but I do not want any body to know I want it kept quiet when should I call please let me know yours Truly

JAMES C——."

Even the subtle combination of an appeal to anatomical zeal, pathological curiosity, and personal cupidity failed in this instance to bring off a deal or evoke an answer.

Selling the body during life was referred to by Tom Hood, who lived in body-snatching days (1799-1845), in his poem, "Jack Hall," where he makes the dying resurrectionist confess—

> "'Alas,' he said, 'I'm sore afraid,
> A dozen pangs my heart invade;
> But when I drove a certain trade
>   In flesh and bone,
> There was a little bargain made
>   About my own.
>
> "'Ten guineas did not quite suffice,
> And so I sold my body twice;
> Twice did not do—I sold it thrice.
>   Forgive my crimes!
> In short I have received its price
>   A dozen times!'"

CHAPTER X

SCIENCE, like politics, makes strange bedfellows. Alliances between the most eminent anatomists and surgeons on the one hand, and the most despicable of grave-robbers on the other, was made imperative, less than a century ago, by the apathy, the ignorance, and the indifference of the so-called statesmen of the United Kingdom.

By the term "respectable resurrectionists" is meant those men who, actuated solely by the desire to advance their knowledge of anatomy and surgery for the benefit of mankind, often risked their freedom and sometimes their lives for the general good. From the time of Hippocrates to the present day, the history of the medical profession has been made glorious by the self-sacrificing spirit of its members. Whoever heard of physicians and surgeons ignoring the call of duty, or by unholy alliance agreeing to strike for higher fees? Thanks be to Almighty God, that priests, prelates, and physicians are of a weld and weave different from those of the roughscuff which now rules a large part of the so-called "civilised" world!

The list of "respectable resurrectionists" might be made a long one; but here only a few names will be mentioned. Andreas Vesalius, whom Mr Henry Morley named the "Luther of Anatomy," in 1536, secured his first human skeleton by stealing the remains of a hanged and roasted thief, outside the walls of Louvain.[1]

John Hunter's successful quest of the body of the Irish giant, O'Brien or Byrne, is an example of the criminal but commendable act of an honoured member of the medical profession. Ottley,[2] in his *Life of John Hunter*, gives the following account of the manner in which the body of this giant (whose skeleton, eight feet four inches high, now adorns the Hunterian Museum in the Royal College of Surgeons in London)[3] was obtained :—

"Byrne, or O'Brien, the famous Irish giant, died in 1783. He had been in a declining state of health for some time previously, and Hunter, anxious to procure his skeleton, sent his man Howison to keep watch on his movements, that he be sure of securing his body at his death. Byrne learned this, and as he had a horror of being dissected, determined to take such precautions as should ensure his not falling into the hands of the doctors : he accordingly left strict orders that his body should be watched day and night, until a leaden coffin could be made, in which it was to be inclosed, and carried out to sea and sunk. Byrne died soon after, and, in compliance with his directions, the undertaker engaged some men to watch the body alternately. Howison soon learned this, found out the house where these men went to drink when off duty, and gave information to Hunter, who forthwith proceeded

---

[1] Morley, *Anatomy in Long Clothes*. This was contributed originally to *Fraser's Magazine*, November 1853. It was used in an abbreviated form by Morley in the second volume of *Clement Marot and Other Studies*, in 1871, under the title of *Andreas Vesalius*.

[2] Palmer, *The Works of John Hunter, F.R.S., with Notes. Edited by James F. Palmer*. In four volumes, London, Longmans, 1835. With a Life, by Drewry Ottley. (American edition, Philadelphia, 1839.)

[3] There is another Hunterian Museum, the one in Glasgow, founded by William Hunter, elder brother of John, which contains a mass of treasures.

PLATE XLII

JOHN HUNTER (1728-1793)
Engraved by J. Caldwall, after a Model done from the *Life* by Mr Tassie

thither with the view of bribing them to allow the body to be carried off. He had an interview with one of the party at the ale-house, and began by offering him fifty pounds if he would allow the body to be kidnapped ; the man agreed, provided his companions would consent, and went out to consult them. He returned shortly, saying that they must have a hundred pounds. Hunter consented to this, and thought the affair settled ; but the men finding him so eager, soon came back with an increased demand, which was also agreed to ; when further difficulties were found, and larger and larger demands made, until, it is said, they raised the price to five hundred pounds! The money was borrowed from Pidcock to pay them ; and in the dead of night the body was removed in a hackney coach, and after having been carried through several streets, was transferred to Hunter's own carriage, and conveyed immediately to Earl's Court. Fearing lest a discovery should take place, Hunter did not choose to risk the delay which the ordinary mode of preparing a skeleton would require ; accordingly, the body was cut to pieces, and the flesh separated by boiling ; hence has arisen the brown colour of the bones, which in all other respects form a magnificent skeleton."

This Irish giant should not be confounded with another huge Irishman, Mr Patrick Cotter O'Brien (1760-1806), for whose portrait we are indebted to John Kay,[1] the celebrated miniature painter and caricaturist of Edinburgh.

Kay's picture shows the giant in the act of being measured for a greatcoat by his tailor, Mr William Ranken. O'Brien, while exhibiting himself in Edinburgh, in February 1803, took a fancy for a greatcoat.

[1] Kay, *A Series of Original Portraits and Caricature Etchings*, Plate No. ccx., vol. ii., Edinburgh, 1877.

The order was forthwith given, says Kay, "*not* to Convener Ranken, as the print would infer, but to Deacon Jollie, a tailor in extensive business, and whose shop was at the head of the Old Assembly Close."

Patrick Cotter O'Brien was eight feet one inch in height, and weighed five hundredweight. An eye-witness thus describes his appearance :—" He was in fact a perfect *excrescence*. His hand was precisely like a shoulder of mutton. He had double knuckles— prodigious lumps at his hip-bones—and when he rose off the table, on which he always sat, his bones were distinctly heard as if crashing against one another. To support himself, he always placed the top of the door under his *oxter* (arm-pit)."

In the "lifting" of bodies, strategy and foresight were quite as necessary as brute force, and men of intelligence often succeeded where the resurrectionists failed, as in an instance related by Lonsdale[1] :—

" A country lad, whose enormously enlarged head had attracted the attention of many physicians, was buried in an exposed cemetery on the shores of the Firth of Forth, and for weeks thereafter his grave was guarded at night by trustworthy watchers. The agents of Monro, Barclay, and others tried to secure the subject, but all offers of money were refused."

After many weeks the contest between the "watchers" and the resurrectionists was abandoned by the latter ; " when one evening at dusk two well-dressed gentlemen, smoking their cigars, drove up in a dog-cart to the chief hostelry of the little burgh : they alighted, and requested that their horse might be taken care of for an hour. The 'whip-hand' gentleman told the ostler that he expected a livery servant to bring a parcel for him, which could be put in the box part of the conveyance,

---

[1] Lonsdale, *Life of Robert Knox*, London, 1870, p. 66.

to which the key was attached. In a short time a man in smart livery came to the stable-yard, deposited a bag under the seat of the dog-cart, pocketed the key, and walked off—'a canny silent man, or dull o' hearing.' Presently afterwards the two gentlemen returned to the inn, ordered out their 'trap,' and trotted off at a brisk pace. The sharp-eyed stable-boy could not help remarking that the 'liveryman' who brought the bag was deuced like the off-side gentleman, and fancied he saw a bit of the scarlet lining under the said gentleman's brown overcoat. 'Haud yer tongue, Sandie,' said the lad's superior; 'ye're aye seeing farlies.' Whilst the unknown gentlemen were trotting homewards at full speed, the watchers of the night, or rather the guardians of the hydrocephalic body, were approaching their post of duty. As usual on entering the cemetery, they looked at the grave to see that all was right; but to their astonishment found that it had been disturbed; nay, more, that the coffin was broken, and that the body was gone! What! abstracted in daylight—impossible, yet too true! The reader will have surmised that the 'dog-cart gentlemen' were the depredators, and most expert ones too; for they had done a piece of work that had baffled the ingenuity of the most experienced resurrectionists of Scotland. Availing themselves of the twilight just before the watchers appeared on the ground, they succeeded in disinterring the body and carrying it off in thirty minutes. Two such accomplished artists, in their own line, as Liston, the Edinburgh surgeon, and Crouch, the London resurrectionist, the world never saw before."

A terrible hue and cry was raised; the search extended to Edinburgh; detectives and all the agencies of the law were employed, but to no purpose. Years later, the skeleton of the hydrocephalic lad found its permanent home in the noblest anatomical collection in Britain—where it is No. 3489, and bears the name of its donor.

Robert Liston (1794-1847).

Liston was the pupil of Dr Barclay, the noted teacher of anatomy. After having taken the diplomas of the College of Surgeons both in London and Edinburgh, he began practice in Edinburgh, in 1818, and also lectured on anatomy and surgery. His surgical skill soon won for him a European reputation. He became Professor of Clinical Surgery in University College, London, in 1834. Liston was a brilliant and skilful operator. He introduced many new procedures : his flap-amputation, a shoe for club-foot, methods for reducing dislocations, and crushing or cutting for stone. He excised the upper jaw in 1836, described his method of laryngoscopy in 1837, wrote important and popular treatises on surgery, and, like the Bells, the Coopers, and other great surgeons of that period, continued his dissections all his life. He was an expert resurrectionist.

William Gibson, professor of surgery in the University of Pennsylvania, has given a pen portrait of Liston, as follows :—" Judge of my surprise, then, when I found a tall, robust, and elegantly-formed man approaching me, in whose handsome and regular features and penetrating eye, there was displayed a degree of intelligence, benevolence, modesty, and playfulness combined, I had seldom before met with ; which joined to a manner peculiarly winning, unassuming and courteous, served at once to assure me that all the idle and gossiping tales I had so readily listened to were mere creations of the fancy. It seemed to me

PLATE XLIV

ROBERT LISTON (1794-1847)

From a painting in the Royal College of Surgeons, Edinburgh

as if he could read my thoughts, and was pleasing himself with my agreeable disappointment." [1]

Liston possessed great strength. "His hand and arm, it was said, might have furnished models for a Hercules" (Bettany). Liston would amputate the thigh single-handed, compress the artery with the left hand, using no tourniquet, and do all the cutting and sawing with the right, aided only by an assistant to hold the leg and ligate the arteries. He was equally successful in operations requiring the most delicate manipulation. Liston's mind acted with lightning-like rapidity; he did not need time for reflection; he seemed to be prompted by a kind of intuition akin to genius, comprehending at a glance the requirements of any particular patient.

Liston's skill was shown often in a striking manner. In the summer of 1836, he was consulted by a poor girl who was suffering from a formidable tumour of the upper jaw. The mass protruded from the mouth, prevented swallowing except when the head was thrown back, and, indeed, threatened her life. She had been refused treatment by surgeons of several of the hospitals in London, but, hearing of the wonderful skill of Liston, she applied to him.

Liston at once determined to amputate the entire jaw, and this, says Clarke, [2] "he did in a manner and with a success that astonished everyone. He was lauded by the press, and his fame as an operator was of the highest. The result of this operation determined Liston to remain in London. He had seriously contemplated migrating to New York, and had consulted several persons on the matter." All of Liston's operations

---

[1] Gibson, *Rambles in Europe in* 1839, Philadelphia, 1841, p. 33.

[2] Clarke, *Autobiographical Recollections of the Medical Profession*, London, 1874, p. 391.

—except those done during the last year of his life—
were performed without anæsthetics.

Sir Charles Bell (1774-1842).

Sir Charles Bell, in his catalogue of anatomical and
pathological specimens contained in his museum, now
the property of the Royal College of Surgeons of Edinburgh, thus introduces his description of an osteomalacic
skeleton :—

"A skeleton of great value; in procuring this
skeleton I lost myself for two hours, and found myself
at two o'clock in the morning in the Court before
Pennycuick House."

This must have been in his Edinburgh days, for
Pennycuick House is not far from Edinburgh, and he
had plenty of time to get home before daylight;
the days when strength, youth, and activity, impelled
by scientific ardour, knew no law, no bounds, no
danger.

Granville Sharp Pattison (1791-1851).

About the year 1813, Mr Granville Sharp Pattison,
a clever anatomist and skilful surgeon, residing in
Glasgow, became the teacher of a band of students
who robbed many a churchyard in and near the western
metropolis. MacGregor states that their rooms were
in College Street, in the vicinity of the old University,
and there they conducted in secret the dissection of such
bodies as could be secured.

Pattison's students, says MacGregor,[1] "kept up a
system of espionage over the doctors in the city, learning
the details of any peculiar cases they might be attending;

[1] MacGregor, *The History of Burke and Hare*, Glasgow, 1884,
p. 35.

and in the event of death there was little scruple about raising a body from which they thought they were likely to gain information." Their plans were laid with great care, and for a time their efforts were successful; but gradually the suspicion grew on the citizens of Glasgow that the graves of their friends were being violated.

Matters of grave import were brought to a crisis in Glasgow when, in December 1813, resurrectionists, at work in Ramshorn yard, were detected by a policeman, who raised the alarm. The students escaped, but were seen to disappear in the vicinity of the College. On the following day, 14th December 1813, amid intense excitement, many persons visited the graves of their friends to see if all were well. It was found that the body of a woman—Mrs M'Alister by name—had been stolen. A mob formed and quickly rushed to the house of Dr James Jeffrey, Professor of Anatomy. His windows were broken and the police had to suppress the tumult.

Officers of the law, armed with the proper warrant, searched for the body of Mrs M'Alister. They visited the rooms of Dr Pattison, were shown over the apartments with apparent freedom, but they discovered nothing. "They had left the house when Mr Alexander" (a surgeon dentist who had attended the deceased to the day of her death) "thought they should have examined a tub, seemingly filled with water, which stood in the middle of the floor of one of the rooms." The tub was drained, and in it were found a jawbone with several teeth attached, some fingers, and other parts of a human body. The dentist identified the teeth as those which he had fitted into Mrs M'Alister's mouth. Dr Pattison and his companions were arrested, and were taken to jail amid the curses of a mob which would have murdered them but for the vigilance of the police. The flooring of Pattison's rooms was dug up, and beneath were found the remains of several bodies. Among them were portions of what was believed to be the corpse of Mrs M'Alister. The fragments were carefully sealed in glass receptacles for use against the accused at their trial.

On Monday, 6th June 1814, Granville Sharp Pattison, Andrew Russell, his lecturer on surgery, and several students, were arraigned in the High Court of Justiciary, at Edinburgh, charged with having violated the grave of the deceased lady. The prisoners were defended by eminent counsel—John Clerk and Henry Cockburn —who proved that the body, or parts of the body, produced in court, were not portions of the body of Mrs M'Alister. The result was an acquittal. So strong, however, was the public feeling, that Pattison had to emigrate to the United States (MacGregor).[1]

In our country Dr Pattison was welcomed, and here he attained an eminence in harmony with his abilities. For several years he was Professor of Anatomy in the Baltimore Medical College. Returning to Europe, he held the same Chair in London University. On again visiting the United States he taught his specialty in Jefferson Medical College, Philadelphia, until 1840, when he accepted the Professorship of Anatomy in the University of the City of New York, where he died, 12th November 1851.

Dr Pattison published a translation of J. N. Masse's *Anatomy of the Human Body*, and edited Cruveilhier's work on the same subject.

Dr Pattison wielded a facile pen. One of his

[1] MacGregor, *The History of Burke and Hare*, Glasgow, 1884, p. 37.

PLATE XLV

VALENTINE MOTT (1785-1865)

scholarly productions discusses the question : " Has the Parotid Gland ever been Extirpated ? "

The *raison d'être* of this booklet[1] was the denial, "by a gentleman holding an eminent situation in the University of Pennsylvania, that the parotid gland has ever been extirpated, and although the name of our Professor of Surgery, *who has removed it*, was not mentioned, he was evidently referred to, and that *in the most contemptuous language.*"

Students of the Jefferson Medical College, resenting the imputation that Dr George McClellan, their Professor of Surgery, was mistaken in his claim that he had removed the parotid gland, requested Dr Pattison to discuss the question.

The request was granted, and "on the evening of Tuesday the 22nd of January 1833," Dr Pattison delivered a lecture, with a demonstration of the parts concerned, which proved conclusively that McClellan and other surgeons had removed the entire parotid gland.

Valentine Mott (1785-1865).

The United States has had its full quota of "respectable resurrectionists," whose names will live in the annals of medical history. There was a time, however, when nothing of value was expected to come from this side of the Atlantic.

Our hopeless condition was mentioned in the *Edinburgh Review*, 1820, by that divine wit and essayist, Sydney Smith, whose pen was sharper than the point of a Damascus blade, in these words : " In

---

[1] Pattison, A lecture delivered in Jefferson Medical College, Philadelphia, 22nd of January 1833, on the question, *Has the Parotid Gland ever been Extirpated?* Philadelphia : published by the Students of Jefferson Medical College, and presented to the members of the profession with their respects, 1833. 8vo, pp. 16.

the four quarters of the globe, who reads an American book? or goes to an American play? or looks at an American picture or statue? What does the world yet owe to American physicians or surgeons?"

What a husky indictment! Yet, eleven years earlier a surgeon, by the name of Ephraim M'Dowell, living in the backwoods of Kentucky, had successfully removed an ovarian tumour—the first operation of its kind. And less than thirty years after Sydney Smith's screed, Americans had given to a waiting world its greatest blessing—Anæsthesia.

CHAPTER XI

By far the most interesting information concerning the "sack-'em-up men," and the way in which these burglars of the house of death carried on their work, is afforded by the *Diary of a Resurrectionist* (London, 1896), which was edited by James Blake Bailey, B.A., Librarian of the Royal College of Surgeons of England. The original document is absolutely authentic. It was presented to the College by the late Sir Thomas Longmore, who, in his early days, was dresser to Bransby Cooper, and assisted him in writing the *Life of Sir Astley Cooper* (London, 1843).

The diary was given to the late Sir Thomas Longmore by a former practitioner of the gentle art of body-snatching, who had retired from business. Unfortunately, Sir Thomas was unable to remember the name of the man from whom he received it. Feeling against the resurrection-men was so strong that, long after the year 1832 when anatomical study had been legalised, every effort was made to hide their identity. As late as 1843, Bransby Cooper, while he freely discussed other members of the resurrection-gang, carefully concealed the name of this man, who was described as N——. It is quite certain that the diarist was Joseph Naples, who was on board the *Excellent* in the action off Cape St Vincent. Bransby Cooper states that N——, having tired of the sea, "came to London, where he soon afterwards obtained the situation of a grave-digger to the Spa-fields burial-ground. Here he was entrapped into connection with the resurrectionists by a Scotsman of the name of White, who, although never personally engaged in the business of exhumation, made a considerable profit by disposing of the bodies raised by grave-diggers and other inferior functionaries attached to the various burial-places in London."

This human document is written on sixteen leaves, and covers the period between 28th November 1811 and 5th December 1812, and thus may be taken as a record of one year's operations by the gang to which its author belonged. There are no entries in May, June, and July. During these months there would be little demand for subjects, as the session of the anatomical schools ran from October to May.

The Diary records the activities of the chief gang of resurrectionists who were operating in and around London during the early part of the nineteenth century ; and nearly always they are spoken of by their Christian names, as, for example, Ben [Crouch], Bill [Hartnett], Jack [Hartnett], Tom [Light], and Holliss. Other members were Daniel and Butler.

Interesting biographical sketches of these men are given in Bransby Cooper's *Life of Sir Astley Cooper* (London, 1843).

The leader of the gang was Ben Crouch. " He was a tall, powerful, athletic man, marked with the small-pox, and was well known as a prize-fighter. He used to dress in very good clothes, and wore a profusion of large gold rings, and a heap of seals dangling from his fob." . . . " Crouch was always rude and offensive in his manners, exceedingly artful, very rarely drunk, but, when so, most abusive and domineering. In his prosperous days he was the councillor, director, comptroller, and treasurer of the whole party, and in dividing the spoils, took especial care to cheat every one. This was very easily effected, for usually he himself was the only one who had any clear-headedness by the time, when the general accounts were gone through. He continued actively engaged in the business till about 1817, when he gradually withdrew from it, and occupied himself principally in obtaining and disposing of teeth. He went abroad several times, and followed this occupation, both in the Peninsula and France."

The final days of the resurrectionists were unhappy ones. Crouch, who at one time was wealthy, died in poverty. Bill Hartnett contracted consumption and died in St Thomas's Hospital. During his illness he exhibited a singular horror of being dissected. His wish, that he be buried without any mutilation whatsoever, was respected. Holliss, having inveigled a man named Page into a snare, turned him into the custody of officers, and thus led to his execution, was shunned by every one of his acquaintance and died in a state of wretchedness and poverty. Jack Hartnett, nephew of Bill Hartnett, left an estate of £6000.

Butler's career was spectacular. Bransby Cooper describes him as "a short, stout, good-tempered man, with a laughing eye and Sancho Panza sort of expression." He had been a porter in the dissecting-room at St Thomas's, and afterwards followed his father's business of an articulator, and dealer in bones. After many adventures, he was convicted of connection with the robbery of the Edinburgh mail, and was sentenced to death. For some unknown reason his execution was postponed ; and Butler having expressed to the governor of the jail a desire to pass his time as an articulator,[1] was furnished the body of a horse. The bones of this animal were prepared in the usual way,

[1] This was the man who prepared the skeleton of the elephant which Sir Astley Cooper dissected.

and were placed in the hands of Butler who proceeded to articulate them so as to form the skeleton.

It chanced in this year that two Archdukes of Austria visited Edinburgh, where, during an inspection of the various public institutions, they observed Butler hard at work in his cell, articulating the bones of this horse. This circumstance made such an impression on their Imperial Highnesses as to cause them to ask for the pardon of the condemned man. After much difficulty, this was granted, on condition that he left the country never to return.

Naples, granting that he was " N—— " of Bransby Cooper's text, spent much of his time in jail, and on each occasion in consequence of information given by Crouch, or some of his party. Sir Astley Cooper, through his influence with the Secretary of State, enabled N—— to escape the severe penalties of the law. The place, date, and circumstances of his death are not known. He was "a civil and well-conducted man, slight in person, with a pleasing expression of countenance," says Bransby Cooper.

It is impossible to identify many of the burial-grounds from which bodies are said in the Diary to have been stolen. Many of these were private, and the name given in the Diary probably is that of the proprietor or the caretaker.

The Diary is composed of laconic entries, as, for example, the following :—

"Thursday, 28th (November, 1811). At night went out and got 3, Jack & me Hospital Crib,[1] Benjn, Danl & Bill to Harpers,[2] Jack and me 1 Big Gates,[3] sold 1 Taunton Do St Thomas's."

[1] Slang for a burial-ground.
[2] Harper is probably the name of the keeper of the burial-ground.
[3] This evidently is the name of the rendezvous of the resurrection-men. Bailey states that it cannot be located.

PLATE XLVI

THE DISSECTING ROOM (Rowlandson)

The figure standing up above the rest is William Hunter; his brother John is on his right hand, and Matthew Baillie is next to William Hunter on the left; Cruikshank is seated at the extreme left of the picture, and Hewson is working on the orbit of the subject on the middle table

(Courtesy of Messrs George Allen & Unwin, Ltd.)

The second notation concerns the activities of Friday, 29th November 1811 :—

"At night went out and got 3, Jack, Ben & me got 2, Bethnall Green, Bill & Danl 1 Bartholow. Crib opened[1] ; whole at Barthw."

Tuesday, 10th December 1811, is noticed as follows:—

"Intoxsicated all day ; at night went out & got 5 Bunhill Row. Jack all most buried."

A profitable expedition is recorded under date of Wednesday, 8th January 1812 :—

"At 2 A.M. got up, the Party went to Harps, got 4 adults and 1 small, took 4 to St Thomas'. Came home, went to Mr Wilson & Brookes, Danl. got paid £8, 8, 0, from Mr Wilson. I recd. £9, 9, 0 from Mr Brookes. Came over to the borough, sold small[2] for £1, 10, 0. Recd. £4, 4, 0 for adult. At home all night."

"Friday, Aug. 28, 1812. Separated to look out ; brought the F. from Bartholm. to St Thomas, having got settled took from Hollis £1, 0, 0, afterwards met at St Thos. & went to St Jns. Ben not with us work'd two holes one bad, drew the C.ns. (opened two graves ; one body too decomposed to bring away, so they drew the canine teeth and sold them) & took the above to St Thos."

The greatest value of this Diary lies in its frank recital of the names of individuals and institutions receiving stolen bodies. The list of the names of individuals is an imposing one : John Taunton, founder

[1] This means that a body, which had been subjected to a *post-mortem* examination, was removed from the burial-ground attached to St Bartholomew's Hospital.

[2] A "small" was a body under three feet long. These were sold at so much per inch ; they were classed as "large small," "small" and "fœtus."

of the City of London Truss Society, a demonstrator
of anatomy at Guy's Hospital under Cline ; J. C. Carpue,
the founder of the Dean Street Anatomical School ;
Dr Frampton, of the London Hospital ; James Wilson,
of the Great Windmill Street School ; Joshua Brookes,
founder of the Blenheim Street, or Great Marlborough
Street, Anatomical School ; Sir Charles Bell, of the
Great Windmill Street School ; Sir Astley Cooper ;
Edward Stanley, Surgeon to St Bartholomew's Hospital.

CHAPTER XII

THE bodies which were supplied to the anatomical schools came from different geographic locations; and not all of them were obtained by exhumation. Many were secured by bribery or by subterfuge before burial; others were stolen by breaking into houses in which the coffins awaited the funeral services; and doubtless some few were obtained by murder.

It would have been impossible for the resurrection-men to have obtained so large a number of bodies, except for their alliance with bribable custodians of the different cemeteries. Grave-diggers and custodians often gave information to the resurrectionists, and sometimes assisted in the stealing of bodies. The slightest vigilance on the part of the custodians would have made it impossible for the resurrection-men to have spent the time necessary for their labour without detection. The ranks of the ghouls were largely recruited from the custodians of cemeteries, men who had lost their positions.

Many devices were tried to keep bodies from falling into the hands of the anatomists. In a few instances the sea was chosen as the resting-place, but this last wish of the deceased was not always consummated. For example, O'Brien, the Irish giant, left strict orders that his body, enclosed within a leaden coffin, should be carried out to sea and sunk: the coffin was duly sunk with its cargo of stone, while John Hunter was hastening towards London with the body of the giant.

Spring-guns were set in many cemeteries. Such weapons, however, often were made harmless by the female confederates of the resurrectionists. If the men wished to rob a grave so guarded, late in the afternoon a spurious sorrowing mother, or a bereaved widow, would express her grief by cutting the connecting wires.

Attempts to protect newly-made graves by means of strong iron fixtures, known as mortsafes, were made long before the public was aroused by the crimes committed by Burke and Hare. Perhaps the best existing examples of mortsafes are the few now remaining in Greyfriars Churchyard, Edinburgh.[1]

Security from the resurrection-men also was sought by burial in iron coffins. The merits of these, and of other patent coffins, were set forth in newspaper advertisements. Bailey cites such an advertisement which appeared in *Wooler's British Gazette*, 13th October 1822, with a rough cut of the coffin and its iron clamps as an appropriate heading. This curious announcement says :—

"Many hundred dead bodies will be dragged from their wooden coffins this winter, for the anatomical lectures (which have just commenced), the articulators, and for those who deal in the dead, for the supply of the country practitioner and the Scotch schools. The question of the right to inter in iron is now decided." . . . "The violation of the sanctity of the grave is said to be needful, for the instruction of the medical pupil, but let each one about to inter a mother, husband, child, or friend, say shall I devote this object of my affection to such a

[1] Greyfriars Churchyard, Edinburgh, is an old burial-place where, in 1638, the "National Covenant" was signed. On a recent tour of inspection, accompanied by Mr D. M. Greig, Conservator of the Museum of the Royal College of Surgeons of Edinburgh, the author remarked that many graves were without protection. Mr Greig answered that, after the Anatomy Act had been passed (in 1832), most of these devices had been removed.

PLATE XLVII

MORTSAFE IN GREYFRIARS CHURCHYARD, EDINBURGH

purpose; if not, the only safe coffin is Bridgman's Patent wrought-iron one, charged the same price as a wooden one, and is a superior substitute for lead."

For brevity, clarity, and logic, this announcement of Mr Bridgman's wares should commend itself to the present purveyors of publicity.

Another maker of patent coffins, whose name is unknown, was mentioned by Southey in his ballad called "The Surgeon's Warning":—

> " If they carry me off in the patent coffin
>   Their labour will be in vain,
> Let the undertaker see it bought of the maker,
>   Who lives in St Martin's Lane."

There is good reason to believe that the undertaker often forgot to fasten the fixtures of the patent coffins. Lack of confidence in all coffins, whether patented or not, was shown by a man of Dundee who placed an infernal machine, provided with an ample supply of gunpowder, over the box which enclosed the remains of his child.[1]

Sometimes loose stones were placed on the walls of the cemetery, to prevent scaling of the walls. In such a case, the resurrection-men would enter by way of the custodian's house, if it had a window overlooking the burial-place. Bereaved relatives often placed such objects as flowers or shells on the newly-made grave, so that disturbance of the soil might be noticed. These objects were carefully studied by the resurrectionists, and were put back in their exact places after the grave had been robbed. In some cemeteries houses were built in which bodies were kept until putrefaction had set in, thus making them useless to the resurrection-men. Such a house is still standing at Crail (Bailey).

---

[1] Bailey, p. 79.

Increasing demand for anatomical material led to the increased cost of bodies. Early in the eighteenth century the average price for a body was one guinea, in Dublin ; in a few years ten times this amount was often secured for a subject. The resurrectionists bribed sextons, grave-diggers, and undertakers' assistants, and thus secured information concerning impending funerals, the location of graves, and their depth. Sometimes the resurrectionists acted as assistants to undertakers—

" By day it was his trade to go,
   Sending the black-coach to and fro ;
   And sometimes at the gate of woe,
      With emblems suitable,
   He stood with brother-mutes to show
      That life is mutable.
   But long before they passed the ferry,
   The dead, that he had helped to bury,
      He sack'd (he had a sack to carry the bodies off in) ;
   In fact, he let them have a very short fit of *coffin*." [1]

Medical students sometimes dug up bodies and conveyed them on foot to the dissecting-room. Their plan was to place a suit of old clothes on the dead man, who, supported by a student on each side, was made to stagger along like a drunken man.

Many " free fights " occurred between guardians of graves and the " sack-'em-up men " ; and some of these encounters resulted in loss of life. Cameron states that the marks of bullets are still visible on some of the tombstones in Kilgobbin Churchyard, near the Dublin Mountains.

Resurrection-men who were caught in the act of conveying bodies for dissection, were fortunate to escape with only a ducking or a severe beating. " On one

[1] Hood, T., *Poetical Works*, item " Jack Hall."

PLATE XLVIII

ANOTHER FORM OF MORTSAFE IN GREYFRIARS CHURCHYARD, EDINBURGH.

PLATE XLIX

UPRIGHT MORTSAFE IN GREYFRIARS CHURCHYARD, EDINBURGH

occasion so severe a castigation with a wire cat-o'-nine-tails was administered to a sack-'em-up man that he expired from the effects " (Cameron). Another member of the fraternity was kicked to death.

Peter Harkan, who was demonstrator of anatomy in Philip Crampton's anatomical school in Dublin, often headed parties of students in search of bodies. One night, whilst exploring in " Bully's Acre," a party of "watchers of the dead" attacked him and his companions. " Harkan got all his assistants over the cemetery wall, but whilst crossing over himself his legs were captured by the watchers. His pupils, seizing him by the opposite extremity of his body, partially pulled him from his captors, who succeeded in drawing him back ; these operations were repeated several times before Harkan's escape was effected. The see-saw movement to which he was subjected on the crest of the wall injured him so severely that it is believed he never quite recovered from its effects " (Cameron).

Amusing anecdotes are told of hired resurrectionists and their conspiracies with grave-diggers and night watchmen. A hospital demonstrator was taken by one of these professionals to interview a grave-digger as to the "working " of a body. The grave-digger represented himself as so indignant at being asked to betray his trust, that he drew a huge horse pistol and pointed it at the demonstrator, adding a volley of oaths. Escaping from the house at the peril of his life, so he thought, he encountered the waiting "resurrection-man." " Now you see, sir, what desperate ruffians I have to deal with ; you'll need to give me something handsome to buy that man over."

Such a thing as honour was unknown among the cacodemons who plundered graves, betrayed one another, and extorted money from the anatomists. The resourcefulness of these fishermen[1] was shown by Edinburgh members of the guild when a resurrected body was sold to Lizars ; was stolen from his dissecting-room ; and then was sold over again to Dr Knox—all of which was done within the short space of one hour, the villains netting £25 by their work.[2]

In rare instances the resurrectionist was afforded an opportunity to profit by the sudden death of a person who was walking the street. In such an event the professional body-snatcher would rush to the aid of the sufferer, and would shed tears over the body of his dead cousin. After the coroner's inquest, the body was given to the grave actor who carried it to one of the teachers of anatomy.

The schemes and stratagems employed to ensure a safe deliverance of bodies procured at a distance from the centres of teaching were truly ingenious. The supply was sent in trunks and hampers, either anonymously, addressed or without any address. Previous to the trunk being sent to the depot or freight house, an invoice or a letter of advice was sent by mail, stating that on a certain train, and on a certain day, a body, packed in a particular box or trunk with a certain address, or marked "perishable, glass, to be kept dry," will be forwarded accordingly. A person is in waiting at the office to claim such package, pay the charges, and it is safely delivered at the proper destination. An amusing anecdote is told of how packages sometimes got mixed in delivery. A porter one day brought a box to a certain lecture room, and as this box was very similar to those in which bodies

[1] Mr Jerry Cruncher, one of the characters raised by Dickens in *A Tale of Two Cities*, was a fisherman whose angling was done at night, with "a sack, a crowbar of convenient size, a rope and chain, and other fishing tackle of that nature."

[2] Lonsdale, *Life of Robert Knox*, London, 1870, p. 71.

generally came, and without any address or mark, it was understood by the porter and by those to whom it was delivered that it contained a body. Some little time after the porter was gone the box was opened, but to the utter astonishment of those present, instead of a dead body it contained a very fine ham, a large cheese, a basket of eggs, and a huge ball of yarn—a present no doubt, from a country cousin, and intended to have reached a different destination. A body in a box without address had come by the same conveyance, and had no doubt been changed by mistake, but what the feelings were of the party who received it can only be guessed.

Bodies, when sent from the rural districts to London, were packed in containers such as were used for transporting goods of local manufacture. Crates, ordinary packing-cases, or casks, were used in harmony with the local custom. Most shipments went without accident to their respective destinations. A notable exception, however, concerned the discovery that three casks of "Bitter Salts," placed on a Liverpool dock for shipment to Leith, on 9th October 1826, contained eleven human bodies. Four other casks, holding twenty-two bodies, were discovered in the cellar of a house in Hope Street. All were intended for use in Edinburgh.

Exhumation Methods of the Resurrectionists.

Methods whereby bodies were secured by the "sack-'em-up men" must have differed with varying conditions, such as depth of the grave, the kind of soil around it, the material of which the coffin was constructed, etc.

Although several writers have described what they believe to have been the methods of exhumation employed by the resurrection-men, it is by no means certain that their accounts exhaust the subject. In fact, it is quite probable that not a few of their secrets died with them.

The rapidity in their operations was well known, says Bransby Cooper, "but the means by which it was accomplished was one of the mysteries of their occupation. This was never fathomed by the public, and curiously enough, no accidental circumstance occurred to furnish the solution."

The doings of the resurrectionists have been described in the *Autobiography of Sir Robert Christison, Baronet*, with so much relish as to lead to the conclusion that the author must have taken part in the unhallowed sport. He says: "The time chosen in the dark winter nights was, for the town churchyards, from six to eight o'clock; at which latter hour the churchyard watch was set, and the city police also commenced their night rounds. A hole was dug down to the coffin only where the head lay—a canvas sheet being stretched around to receive the earth, and to prevent any of it spoiling the smooth uniformity of the grass. The digging was done with short, flat, dagger-shaped implements of wood, to avoid the clicking of iron striking stones. On reaching the coffin, two broad iron hooks under the lid, pulled forcibly up with a rope, broke off a sufficient portion of the lid to allow the body to be dragged out; and sacking was heaped over the whole to deaden the sound of cracking wood. The body was stripped of the grave-clothes, which were scrupulously buried again; it was secured in a sack; and the surface of the ground was carefully restored to its original condition—which was not difficult, as the sod over a fresh-filled grave must always present signs of recent disturbance. The whole process could be completed in an hour, even though the grave might be six feet deep, because the soil was loose, and the digging was done impetuously by frequent relays of active men. Transference over the churchyard wall was easy on a dark evening; and once in the street, the carrier of the sack drew no attention at so early an hour." In country churchyards the work was undertaken at a later hour when the neighbourhood was asleep.

CHAPTER XIII

THE universal interest which was aroused by the crimes of Burke and Hare found an outlet through various channels, of which one of the most expressive was the production of a mass of fugitive literature.

Newspapers, a century ago, were practically limited to towns and to the higher and middle ranks of life. The lower orders had to trust to loose sheets, and to the spoken word. Hence the fugitive literature. This comprises broadsides, chap-books, pamphlets, etc., many of which make up in virility what they lack in literary finish. They now are among the rare items which are seized eagerly by the medical historian; and few collectors are so fortunate as to possess two or three of these exemplars.

By sheer good luck, fortified by a cablegram, the author secured a volume made up of what the bookseller described as "A wonderful collection of items on the West Port Murders, Burke and Hare of Edinburgh, who systematically committed murders and sold the bodies for dissection; 10 items in 1 vol., 8vo."

The first item is entitled *West Port Murders* (Edinburgh, 1829, 8vo, 362 pages, with portraits and views). The author's name does not appear.

The first item, *West Port Murders*, is well written and evidently has been produced by a man who was resident in Edinburgh before, during, and for some time after Burke and Hare had carried on their

WEST PORT MURDERS;

OR AN

AUTHENTIC ACCOUNT OF THE ATROCIOUS MURDERS

COMMITTED BY

BURKE AND HIS ASSOCIATES;

CONTAINING

A FULL ACCOUNT OF ALL THE EXTRAORDINARY CIRCUMSTANCES
CONNECTED WITH THEM.

ALSO,

A REPORT OF THE TRIAL

OF

BURKE AND M'DOUGAL.

WITH

A DESCRIPTION OF THE EXECUTION OF BURKE,

HIS CONFESSIONS, AND MEMOIRS OF HIS ACCOMPLICES,

INCLUDING

THE PROCEEDINGS AGAINST HARE, &c.

ILLUSTRATED BY PORTRAITS AND VIEWS.

" O horror ! horror ! horror ! tongue nor heart
Cannot conceive nor name thee !"

Macbeth.

EDINBURGH:
PUBLISHED BY THOMAS IRELAND, JUNIOR,
57, SOUTH BRIDGE STREET.

1829.

TITLE-PAGE OF "WEST PORT MURDERS" (Edinburgh, 1829).

murderous work.   Here are the opening sentences of
this monograph :—

"We have heard a great deal of late concerning
'the march of intellect,' for which the present age
is supposed to be distinguished ; and the phrase has
been rung in our ears till it has nauseated us by its
repetition, and become almost a proverbial expression
of derision.   But we fear that, with all its pretended
illumination, the present age must be characterised by
some deeper and fouler blots than have attached to any
that preceded it ; and that if it has brighter spots, it
has also darker shades and more appalling obscurations.
It has, in fact, nooks and corners where everything
that is evil seems to be concentrated and condensed ;
dens and holes to which the Genius of Iniquity has
fled, and become envenomed with newer and more
malignant inspirations.   Thus the march of crime has
far outstripped 'the march of intellect,' and attained a
monstrous, a colossal development." . . .

"No one who reads the following report of the
regular system of murder, which seems to have been
organised in Edinburgh, can doubt that it is almost
wholly without example in any age or country."

The author of *West Port Murders* concludes his
brochure with these sensible words (pp. 361-362) :—
"It is admitted by all enlightened people, that subjects
must and will be procured, and that severe legislative
enactments only tend to increase the difficulty, and
enhance the price.   The recent proceedings present a
fearful illustration of this opinion ; but out of evil, if
properly considered, good may be extracted ; and these
transactions will, indeed, have failed in their effect,
should some plan not be devised which, while it saves
the feelings of relatives from outrage, may 'prevent a
recurrence of such frightful scenes."

AUTHENTIC
CONFESSIONS
OF
WILLIAM BURK,

Who was Executed at Edinburgh, on 28th January 1829, for Murder, emited before the Sheriff-Substitute of Edinburgh, the Rev. Mr Reid, Catholic Priest, and others, in the Jail, on 3d and 22d January.

EDINBURGH :

Printed and Sold by R. Menzies, Lawumarket.

1829.

Price Twopence.

TITLE-PAGE OF " AUTHENTIC CONFESSIONS OF WILLIAM BURK."
(Edinburgh, 1829.)

The *Authentic Confessions of William Burk* is classed as a chap-book. It consists of eight octavo pages, printed on thin and cheap paper. On page seven there is a crude woodcut portrait of "Daft Jamie." The paternity of this literary gem is disclosed by a note at the bottom of the last page, which says : "Extracted from the *Edinburgh Advertiser* of the 6th February 1829."

The next item is a broadside, measuring approximately 5 by 10 inches. It is entitled, *Elegiac Lines on the Tragical Murder of Poor Daft Jamie.* The verses are arranged in two columns. At the top of the sheet is the picture of a barrel, bearing these words : "Alas ! Poor Daft Jamie's Pickled."

It is with a sense of relief that we turn from the "Elegiac Lines" to a more substantial production. It bears this title : *Reflections suggested by the Murders, etc., being an Epistle to the Right Hon. Robert Peel, M.P., Secretary of State for the Home Department.* This is a well-printed pamphlet of fifty octavo pages, and was written "By a Medical Officer in the Royal Navy." It was published at Glasgow, by W. R. M'Phun, in the year 1829. This letter bears the date, "21st January 1829." On its title-page are the following lines :—

> "Oft it was wondered why, on Irish ground,
> No poisonous reptile ever could be found ;
> Revealed the secret stands !—of nature's work,
> She saved her venom to create a Burke !"—*Law.*

The anonymous "Medical Officer in the Royal Navy" addresses the Right Hon. Robert Peel in chaste and courteous language :—

"I presume not to approach you, Sir, in any other character than that of an humble individual, who deems the atrocities now undergoing inquiry a disgrace to his country, and the reproach of that legislature by which his country is governed ; while, at

ELEGIAC LINES

ON THE

𝔗ragical 𝔐urder

OF

POOR DAFT JAMIE.

ATTENDANCE give, whilst I relate
How poor Daft Jamie met his fate ;
'Twill make your hair stand on your head,
As I unfold the horrid deed :—

That hellish monster, William Burke,
Like Reynard sneaking on the lurk,
Coyduck'd his prey into his den,
And then the woeful work began :—

" Come, Jamie, drink a glass wi' me,
And I'll gang wi' ye in a wee,
To seek yer mither i' the town—
Come drink, man, drink, an' sit ye down."

" Nae, I'll no' drink wi' ye the nou,
For if I div 'twill mak' me fou ;"
" Tush, man, a wee will do ye guid,
'Twill cheer yer heart, an' warm yer bluid."

At last he took the fatal glass,
Not dreaming what would come to pass ;
When once he drank, he wanted more—
Till drunk he fell upon the floor.

" Now," said th' assassin, " now we may
Seize on him as our lawful prey."
" Wait, wait," said Hare, " ye stupid ass,
He's yet too strong—let's tak' a glass."

Like some unguarded gem he lies—
The vulture waits to seize its prize ;
Nor does he dream he's in its power,
Till it has seized him to devour.

The ruffian dogs,—the hellish pair,—
The villain Burke,—the meagre Hare,—
Impatient were the prize to win,
So to their smothering pranks begin :—

Burke cast himself on Jamie's face,
And clasp'd him in his foul embrace ;
But Jamie waking in surprise,
Writhed in an agony to rise.

At last, with nerves' unstrung before,
He threw the villain on the floor ;
And though alarm'd, and weaken'd too,
He would have soon o'ercome the foe :

But help was near—for it Burke cried,
And soon his friend was at his side ;
Hare tripp'd up Jamie's heels, and o'er
He fell, alas ! to rise no more !.

Now both these blood-hounds him engage,
As hungry tygers fill'd with rage,
Nor did they handle axe or knife,
To take away Daft Jamie's life.

No sooner done, than in a chest
They cramm'd this lately welcom'd guest,
And bore him into Surgeons' Square—
A subject fresh—a victim rare !

And soon he's on the table laid,
Expos'd to the dissecting blade ;
But where his members now may lay
Is not for me—or you—to say.

But this I'll say—some thoughts did rise :
It fill'd the Students with surprise,
That so short time should intervene
Since Jamie on the streets was seen:

But though his body is destroy'd,
His soul can never be decoy'd
From that celestial state of rest,
Where he, I trust, is with the bless'd.

Written by J. P.

N. B.—There will be published on Monday first, by the same Editor, a LACONIC NAR-
RATIVE of the LIFE and DEATH of POOR JAMIE ; to which will be added, a few Anecdotes relative to him, and his old friend BOBY AWL :—PRICE THRIP PENCE. The work
will be embellished with a striking Portrait of Jamie.

Published by WILLIE SMITH, No. 3, Bristo Port.
PRICE ONE PENNY.

" ELEGIAC LINES ON THE TRAGICAL MURDER OF POOR DAFT JAMIE."
(Edinburgh, n.d., but issued early in 1829.)

the same time, he thinks it foul scorn that his profession should ever have been necessitated to traffick in the bodies of murdered men.

"I make my present advance to you, Sir, because, as His Majesty's Principal Secretary of State for the Home Department, to you is confided the police of Great Britain; and on you the responsible duty devolves of providing preventatives against the commission of crime, not less than of enforcing punishment when crime has been perpetrated. The propriety, therefore, of making my appeal to you cannot, I imagine, be disputed, if your official situation alone be regarded. I conceive it admits of as little doubt on the part of any one who with me has delighted to mark your progress as a statesman, or, by the hearing of the ear, has become acquainted with your character as a philosopher and a philanthropist." . . .

In place of wasting time and words in denouncing the monster, Burk, or Burke, this unknown "Medical Officer in the Royal Navy" at once gets into the heart of the question, saying—

"I prefer sitting down to follow his deeds of darkness to their source, and studying to contrive how a repetition of such iniquities may be most effectually prevented.

"In pursuance of these two objects, it may not be amiss to state the following, which are facts not admitting of doubt, far less of denial. The criminal, Burke, has committed several murders. He entered upon the sanguinary office of an assassin because it promised to be at the outset, what he afterwards found it in reality was, a most lucrative one; for, for the bodies of *his* slain there was always a market at hand, and customers that asked no questions, in the dissecting-rooms of anatomists. The improvement of anatomical science, by dissection of the human corpse, is indirectly contrary to the law of this land; while the exhumation of cadavera for the use of medical students is in direct defiance of a legal statute, and not infrequently made a pretext for visiting upon those that resort to the practice, the penalty of other and graver offences. The robbery of churchyards, notwithstanding its illegality, is a distinct art followed as a trade by a separate body of men, and affording subsistence to a great number of people. To all the medical profession, anatomical knowledge is of great value—to surgeons, it is indispensably necessary. The knowledge of anatomy required by both physicians and surgeons may be best attained in the dissecting-room ; that which is essential to the surgeon can be obtained in no other way. Medical practitioners are liable to civil actions, if injurious effects result from their malpractice or neglect ; nor is a plea of unavoidable ignorance admitted in law, as either justifying or extenuating the errors of practice, or the evils of negligence, although, as has been already stated, legal impediments oppose the acquisition of that knowledge by which alone can ignorance be avoided, and the ills from it prevented.

"For the greater convenience of discussion, I shall reduce the facts now stated to a few propositions, each of which it is my design to consider in succession.

"I.—The present state of the laws affecting that part of medical education which depends on anatomy, makes it impossible to study that science efficiently, without incurring some degree of criminality.

"II.—It is impossible for a surgeon, or surgeon-apothecary, to practise his profession independent of an intimate acquaintance with the structure of the human frame, and at the same time consistently with the safety of the public, his own comfort, and the security of his property.

"III.—When the legislature requires one thing, and necessity demands another, not only *must* the enactment of the *former* be disregarded, but, in process of time, temptations will accumulate to supply the wants of the *latter* by unlawful as well as by illegal means.

"IV.—All laws, whether private or public, the tendency of which is to increase crime, by increasing the temptations thereunto, are unjust, cruel, iniquitous, and non-obligatory.

"V.—When an actual increase in the crimes of a country may be proved to be a consequence of any of its laws, the guilt incurred belongs as much to that law, or those laws, as to the perpetrators of all the crimes originating therefrom.

"VI.—The existing legal impediments to the study of

anatomy, by dissection of the human frame, are not only opposed to the necessities of the medical profession, but have been the remote causes of increased, and are so still, of increasing crime.

"VII.—The murders committed by Burke and his associates having had a legal origin, the law which divides the guilt with him ought to share his reproach."

This "Medical Officer in the Royal Navy" then proceeds, in a calm, logical, and convincing manner, to prove the correctness of his seven propositions.

He writes of the earnest medical student, who tries to obtain a sufficient knowledge of the human frame to justify him, at a later date, in operating on the living body, as acquiring his anatomical knowledge, "in the dissecting-room, where, seated among putrefying corpses, inhaling the stench of dead bodies, and exposed to the danger of losing health and life," he still carries on. And, further : "While he toils thus anxiously, and in the midst of disagreeables unparalleled in any other course of study ; while he perils his health by exposure to the pestilential atmosphere of a dead-house, and endangers his life by braving the accidents too common to anatomists,[1] and which the experience of ages affirms to have been too frequently fatal—he finds himself opposed to the legislature of that country which, on his mother's breast, he learned to love and venerate, because his own, and worthy of honour." He calls attention to the injustice of the law, and the persecution of members of the medical profession who had been found in possession of bodies which had been "resurrected" ;

---

[1] The medical student of to-day whose dissections are made often in a modern palace, and on bodies which are carefully injected and are in no way offensive, cannot imagine the conditions under which, only a century ago, practical anatomy was studied. Every winter session, not a few students died from human virus which entered the system through a minute wound.

he cites instances "of civil actions successfully instituted, for pecuniary damages, against surgeons and general practitioners, on account of some evil produced, or alleged to have been produced, through their insufficient acquaintance with anatomy." He details gross surgical blunders—all of which arose from ignorance of anatomy. He carries on with argument so clearly stated and convincing that no fair-minded man can oppose him. In his argument he calls up the light artillery, the massed troops, and then his heaviest guns, leaving the Law and Government as then constituted without a leg to stand on. His pamphlet is worthy of a Junius, albeit the language is milder. But the effort did no good. Possibly it may have happened that the Right Hon. Robert Peel, M.P., read the entire fifty pages; but this is doubtful, for at this time the Right Hon. Robert probably had his full share of troubles in the parliamentary debates over the Irish question and the Catholic Relief Bill.

Be that as it may, the fact remains that Government did nothing for the relief of the medical profession, or for the furtherance of anatomical study, until after crimes, like those committed in Edinburgh, had aroused the citizens of London. The London murderers, vile as they were, did a good turn in this respect, that they furnished the last straw which broke the indifference of Government, and paved the way for the passing of Mr Warburton's Bill.

The execution of Burke gave the phrenologists an opportunity to climb into the limelight. Prior to the public dissection by Professor Monro, Burke's body was examined privately by a number of gentlemen, amongst whom were Mr Liston, Mr George Combe and his philosophical opponent Sir William Hamilton, and Mr Joseph, the sculptor.

Combe, the apostle of phrenology, and Sir William Hamilton, the metaphysician, waged a terrible war of printed words over the conclusions to be drawn from the measurements of Burke's head. Much good paper was wasted in the numerous pamphlets on the subject.

Apparently nothing was settled by the wordy war; phrenologists remained phrenologists and the scoffers continued to scoff. The collection of resurrectionist literature which we have been describing contains a *Letter on the Prejudices of the Great in Science and Philosophy against Phrenology: addressed to the Editor of the "Edinburgh Weekly Journal,"* by George Combe, Edinburgh, 1829, 8vo, 27 pages.

This pamphlet was answered by Thomas Stone, Esq., President of the Royal Medical Society, in a paper which he read before the Society.[1] Here is the opening paragraph : " The circumstance of a regular course of lectures on Phrenology being yet publicly delivered in this city, and the acknowledgement that some individuals, not aware of the extent of the Phrenological delusion, yet hesitate to pronounce any opinion, either favourable or unfavourable to its pretensions, must alone plead my apology for directing the attention of a scientific institution to an hypothesis which has been decidedly rejected by the most enlightened men in Europe, and which, from its earliest existence, has appealed rather to the credulity of the vulgar, than to the judgment of men of science. Astrologers, Metoposcopists, Physiognomists, and Chiromancers, have in every age arrogated to themselves a peculiar and superior insight into human nature ; and, by pretending to predicate, by external signs, the faculties and dispositions which influence the destiny of mankind, they have not failed to impose repeatedly on

---

[1] Stone, *Observations on the Phrenological Development of Burke, Hare, and other Atrocious Murderers, etc.*, Edinburgh, 1829, 8vo, pp. 75.

A

ᴸᴬᶜᴼᴺᴵᶜ ᴺᴬᴿᴿᴬᵀᴵᵛᴱ

OF THE

LIFE & DEATH

OF

JAMES WILSON,

KNOWN BY THE NAME OF

DAFT JAMIE.

IN WHICH ARE INTERSPERSED,

SEVERAL ANECDOTES RELATIVE TO HIM AND HIS OLD
FRIEND BOBY AWL, AN IDIOT WHO STROLLED
ABOUT EDINBURGH FOR MANY YEARS.

———◆———

He's to be pitied, that's such a silly elf,
Who cannot speak nor wrestle for himself.
Jamie was such a simpleton,
He'd not fight with a boy;
Nor did he ever curse or swear,
At those who'd him annoy.

———◆———

PUBLISHED BY W. SMITH,
Bristo Port, Edina.

PRICE **THRIP** PENCE.

1829.

REPRINTED (1881) BY A. & G. BROWN.
15 Bristo Place and The Mound, Edinburgh.

the understanding of the ignorant, and by appealing to accidental contingencies, which for a moment seem to favour their empirical speculations, they have occasionally taken by surprise the judgment of better educated individuals, who, after receiving the grossest fictions, in the belief that they are the soundest facts, become prepared to listen with a kind of religious gravity to the most ludicrous and incongruous assertions."

Of course, Mr Combe had to furnish an *Answer* to Mr Stone's attack ; and Mr Stone, in turn, had to come back with *A Rejoinder*, while lesser luminaries invited themselves into the fray.   All of which happened in the Athens of the North, in the year 1829.

Of all the horrid deeds committed by Burke and Hare, not one "aroused in the community of Edinburgh greater sympathy with the victim or a more vehement desire for vengeance on the murderers than did the slaying of James Wilson.   The Scottish people have ever regarded with especial tenderness those unhappy beings, called by our custom 'innocents,' upon whom, though adult, an inscrutable Providence has seen fit to lay the blight of intellectual infancy ; and any offence done to such helpless folk was properly deemed a crime as heinous as one wrought against an actual child."[1]

James Wilson, better known by the name of "Daft Jamie," was born in Edinburgh, 27th November 1809. He was murdered by Burke and Hare in October 1828, and on the same day his body was turned over to Paterson, the doorkeeper of Dr Knox's establishment. When the report reached No. 10 Surgeons' Square that Jamie was amissing, his body was promptly dissected.   The fate of poor "Daft Jamie" was not clearly determined until Burke had made his confession.

[1] Roughead, *Burke and Hare*, " Notable British Trial Series," Edinburgh and London, 1921, p. 30.

PLATE L

PORTRAIT OF "DAFT JAMIE." (Edinburgh, 1829)

The fate of Jamie peculiarly affected the public mind, and caused much fugitive literature to be written. Ballads in the form of broadsheets were hawked upon the streets. One of these is shown on page 159. An account of "Daft Jamie's" life appeared early in the year 1829, entitled, *A Laconic Narrative of the Life and Death of James Wilson, known by the name of Daft Jamie*. It has thrice been reprinted in facsimile. The title-page, as shown on page 165, bears these lines :—

> " He's to be pitied, that's such a silly elf,
> Who cannot speak nor wrestle for himself.
> Jamie was such a simpleton,
>   He'd not fight with a boy ;
>   Nor did he ever curse or swear,
>   At those who'd him annoy."

Jamie was a quiet, harmless being, and gave no person the smallest offence whatever. He was by no means quarrelsome, and would refuse to defend himself no matter how ill-used he might be, or howsoever insignificant his tormentor. Small boys, aged five or six years, often would try to engage him in battle, but Jamie would always run away. Plate L. shows a portrait of "Daft Jamie," and bears an appropriate legend.

As concerns resurrectionist literature of a more elaborate and a more lasting type, it must suffice to mention Dr D. M. Moir, in his *Mansie Wauch, the Tailor of Dalkeith*, Alexander Leighton, in his *Court of Cacus*, Charles Dickens, in his *Tale of Two Cities*, and Robert Louis Stevenson, in his *Body-Snatcher*. Each of these literary luminaries has had his tilt at this hair-raising subject.

CHAPTER XIV

THE real or imagined activities of the "sack-'em-up men" have furnished the *motif* for a not inconsiderable amount of literature, which, with the exception of. humorous poems, has been produced by three classes of writers : (1) Those who have told the truth ; (2) those who have written fiction ; and (3) those who, apparently inspired with the sole desire to blast the reputation of a great anatomist, have scrambled a minimum of truth with a maximum of falsehood.

The third class was poor in number but rich in venom. Chief among these literary ruffians was John Wilson, better known as "Christopher North," a noted writer and Professor of *Moral* Philosophy, who, two months after Burke in his confession had exonerated Robert Knox of all blame, did all in his power to ruin the reputation of the unfortunate anatomist. Wilson's article appeared in *Blackwood's Magazine*, March 1829, in its "Noctes Ambrosianæ." In this ambrosial effort, its writer, not content with his attack on Knox, did not hesitate to apply his literary scalping knife and tomahawk to an unoffending anatomical class for showing loyalty and respect to their great teacher.[1]

Alexander Leighton's romance, *The Court of Cacus, or the Story of Burke and Hare*, shows its author's prejudices "on every page" (Lonsdale).

In Robert Louis Stevenson's story, *The Body-Snatcher*, he depicts under thin disguise Dr Knox

[1] Lonsdale, *Life of Robert Knox*, London, 1870, p. 81.

and some of the other figures in the Edinburgh tragedy. This additional shaft, however, could not sink into the soul of the great anatomist, or disturb the repose of the grave.

Writers of fiction have revelled in body-snatching. In his *Diary of a Late Physician*, Samuel Warren, who had studied medicine in Edinburgh for a brief period, has given us a chapter on "Grave Doings," which probably was founded on fact. In this case, however, the grave was robbed in order to obtain a pathological specimen—a diseased heart. Warren states that this was his first and last experience as a resurrectionist.

To his credit it must be said, that Warren's chapter on "Grave Doings" opens with a plea for the legalisation of dissection. He addresses the reader in these words—"You expect us to cure you of disease, and yet deny us the only means of learning *how*? You would have us bring you the ore of skill and experience, yet forbid us to break the soil, or sink a shaft! Is this fair, *fair* reader? Is this reasonable?"

Several writers have given a gruesome turn to their stories by making the body, when uncovered, turn out to be that of a relation or friend of some one of the party engaged in the exhumation, or of some one of the anatomical class. While such a *dénoûment* often has been a choice morsel for the fictionists, an identical situation has truly occurred.

Thus, the *Monthly Magazine* for April 1827 records the story of a sailor who aided a party of students in robbing a grave. When the subject had been brought to its new home, the sack was found to contain the remains of the sailor's sweetheart who had died a few days before his return from the sea.

Another instance of the same kind occurred in St Thomas's Hospital. The body of a child was brought to the medical school by Holliss, a well-known resurrectionist. The body was at once recognised by one of the students as that of his sister's child, and was immediately buried before any dissection had taken place.[1]

Dr Francis J. Shepherd, formerly Demonstrator of Anatomy, M'Gill University, Montreal, in a book printed for private circulation only,[2] relates the following:—"I remember on one occasion a student finding his uncle on the table. He was a Frenchman, and said to me, 'What for you got mine oncle here?' I said I did not know it was his uncle; had I known I should never have received him. I added if he paid the expenses of removal he could have him. He thought awhile and said, 'S'pose mine oncle come, s'pose he stay,' and he did stay and was properly dissected."

David Macbeth Moir (1798-1851), who at the age of eighteen years received his surgeon's diploma at the University of Edinburgh, and for the rest of his life practised his profession by day and wrote prose and poetry at night, has portrayed the resurrection-men in *The Life of Mansie Wauch, Tailor in Dalkeith: written by Himself.* This, the most valuable of Moir's numerous writings, was commenced in *Blackwood's Magazine* in 1824, and was there published serially for nearly three years. It appeared in book form in 1828, and was so popular that many editions (the latest in 1913) were published in Great Britain. The work was reprinted in America and in France.

This from *Mansie Wauch:*

"About this time there arose a great sough and surmise, that some loons were playing false with the kirkyard, howking up the bodies from their damp graves, and harling them away

---

[1] Bailey, *The Diary of a Resurrectionist*, London, 1896, p. 16.
[2] Shepherd, *Reminiscences of Student Days and Dissecting-Room*, Montreal, 1919, p. 25.

to the College. Words cannot describe the fear, and the dool, and the misery it caused. All flocked to the kirk-yett; and the friends of the newly buried stood by the mools, which were yet dark, and the brown newly cast divots, that had not yet taken root, looking, with mournful faces, to descry any tokens of sinking in.

"I'll never forget it. I was standing by when three young lads took shools, and, lifting up the truff, proceeded to houk down to the coffin, wherein they had laid the grey hairs of their mother. They looked wild and bewildered like, and the glance of their een was like that of folk out of a mad-house; and none dared in the world to have spoken to them. They did not even speak to one another; but wrought on with a great hurry, till the spades stuck on the coffin lid—which was broken. The dead-clothes were there huddled together in a nook, but the dead was gone. I took hold of Willie Walker's arm, and looked down. There was a cold sweat all over me;—losh me! but I was terribly frighted and eerie. Three more graves were opened, and all just alike; save and except that of a wee unchristened wean, which was off bodily, coffin and all."

Edward Bulwer Lytton, in *Lucretia, or the Children of Night* (London, 1846), portrays a resurrectionist along with worse criminals. At its first appearance, certain criticisms on *Lucretia* were made the vehicle for a savage attack on the author's general writings. Lord Lytton then wrote "A Word to the Public," a critical essay which is still appended to *Lucretia*.

In *A Tale of Two Cities* Charles Dickens (1812-1870) has given a good description of a resurrectionist in the person of Mr Jerry Cruncher.

"Father," said Young Jerry, as they walked along: taking care to keep at arm's length and to have the stool well between them: "what's a Resurrection-Man?"

Mr Cruncher came to a stop on the pavement before he answered, "How should I know?"

"I thought you knowed everything, father," said the artless boy.

"Hem! Well," returned Mr Cruncher, going on again, and lifting off his hat to give his spikes free play, "he is a tradesman."

"What's his goods, father?" asked the brisk young Jerry.

"His goods," said Mr Cruncher, after turning it over in his mind, "is a branch of Scientific goods."

"Persons' bodies, ain't it, father?" asked the lively boy.

"I believe it is something of that sort," observed Mr Cruncher.

"Oh, father, I should so like to be a Resurrection-Man when I'm quite growed up!"

Mrs Crowe, in *Light and Darkness*, and Miss Sergeant, in *Dr Endicott's Experiment*, have figured the resurrectionist in their novels.

Thomas Hood's Humorous Poem, "Mary's Ghost."

Body-snatching was not without its humorous features and its comic poems. Hood's poem, " Mary's Ghost, a Pathetic Ballad," was inspired by the story of Sir Charles Bell's haunted house.

For a number of years Sir Charles Bell lived in a large, old-fashioned house in Leicester Square, London, that formerly belonged to a gentleman named Onslow. Bell, who paid only a small rental for it, was boasting of his bargain to Garthshore, an eccentric old physician, when the latter said, in a peculiar, significant way, "Never mind, my friend, you'll pay dearly enough for it at last; you might as well have a wife and seven children, or a millstone about your neck; it's a divil of a house, an awful place, and you'll have a divil of a time in it I'm thinking." Bell thought little of these remarks at the time, but later had good cause to recall them, as Gibson [1] relates :—

" Months rolled away, however, and nothing occurred

---

[1] Gibson, *Rambles in Europe in* 1839, Philadelphia, 1841, p. 142.

PLATE LI

MESSRS CRUNCHER AND SON

to disturb his tranquillity. The lectures went merrily
on, and pupils were dropping in, and he was then a
bachelor, and had nothing to care for ; but, at last, his
servants began to leave, one by one, and, as fresh ones
were engaged, they, in turn, in a week or two, cleared
out ; his house-pupils, too, who at first preferred single
rooms, were not satisfied until they could be crowded
together into one or more beds, as far as possible
from the Anatomical Theatre. All this, however, was
mystery to Sir Charles, for as often as he asked what
was the matter, what had got into the heads of the
cooks, and chamber-maids, and waiters, and into the
minds of his pupils, he was only answered, 'Nothing,
sir, nothing in the world.' He got reconciled, at last,
to the thing, and thought no more of it, until one night,
after a hard day's work, being restless, excited, and not
very well, and tossing about, half asleep, half awake, as
he supposed, he felt his foot suddenly grasped by an
ice-cold hand—but for how long it was impossible to
say—such was the horror inspired even by the thought,
much less the reality of such an event. All he
remembered, afterwards, was pacing the floor industri-
ously, for some time, to shake off the effect of his *dream*,
for from such source, no doubt, had the impression he
experienced been derived. Upon talking with his pupils
next day on the subject, he heard, for the first time, the
cause of their clustering together in one chamber ; and
was distinctly told that everybody in London believed
Onslow House *haunted* by a beautiful young woman,
who died, whilst engaged to be married, and whose body
was dissected by different London surgeons. This
accounted for Garthshore's remarks, and, perhaps, for
the pathetic ballad soon after published, under the name
of 'Mary's Ghost.'"

In the following comic poem by Tom Hood the

closing stanzas explain the distribution of a lady's parts among the anatomical teachers of London.

MARY'S GHOST: A PATHETIC BALLAD.

'Twas in the middle of the night,
　To sleep young William tried,
When Mary's ghost came stealing in,
　And stood at his bedside.

O William, dear! O William, dear!
　My rest eternal ceases;
Alas! my everlasting peace
　Is broken into pieces.

I thought the last of all my cares
　Would end with my last minute;
But tho' I went to my long home,
　I didn't stay long in it.

The body-snatchers, they have come,
　And made a snatch at me;
It's very hard them kind of men
　Won't let a body be!

You thought that I was buried deep,
　Quite decent-like and chary,
But from her grave in Mary-bone
　They've come and boned your Mary.

The arm that used to take your arm
　Is took to Dr Vyse[1];
And both my legs are gone to walk
　The Hospital at Guy's.

I vow'd that you should have my hand,
　But fate gives us denial;
You'll find it there, at Dr Bell's,[2]
　In spirits and a phial.

[1] Dr Vyse cannot be traced.
[2] Sir Charles Bell, demonstrator of anatomy at the Middlesex Hospital.

As for my feet, the little feet
　　You used to call so pretty,
There's one, I know, in Bedford Row,[3]
　　The t'other's in the city.[4]

I can't tell where my head is gone,
　　But Doctor Carpue can[5];
As for my trunk, it's all pack'd up
　　To go by Pickford's van.

I wish you'd go to Mr P.[6]
　　And save me such a ride;
I don't half like the outside place,
　　They've took for my inside.

The cock it crows—I must be gone!
　　My William, we must part!
But I'll be yours in death, altho'
　　Sir Astley[7] has my heart.

Don't go to weep upon my grave,
　　And think that there I be;
They haven't left an atom there
　　Of my anatomie.

"The Surgeon's Warning."

To foil the resurrection-men strong iron guards or
mortsafes sometimes were placed over the grave. Iron
coffins also were used. The undertaker often arranged
that the coffin fastenings were an easy kind. The newspapers of the day advertised patent coffins. Southey in

---

[3] Abernethy lived for many years at 14 Bedford Row.

[4] The Aldersgate City School of Anatomy.

[5] Joseph Constantine Carpue, the head of a great private school of
anatomy.

[6] Mr Richard Partridge, demonstrator of anatomy at King's College
Hospital.

[7] Sir Astley Cooper.

(These footnotes are found in Sprigge's *Life of Thomas Wakley*, London,
1897, p. 27.)

his ballad, "The Surgeon's Warning," represents the fear of a dying surgeon buried in one of these, lest his apprentices should serve him after death as he had served others during his life.

All kinds of carcasses I have cut up,
   And the judgment now must be!
But, brothers, I took care of you,
   So pray take care of me!

I have made candles of infants' fat,
   The sextons have been my slaves,
I have bottled babes unborn, and dried
   Hearts and livers from rifled graves.

And my 'prentices will surely come,
   And carve me bone from bone,
And I, who have rifled the dead man's grave
   Shall never rest in my own.

Bury me in lead when I am dead,
   My brethren, I entreat,
And see the coffin weigh'd, I beg,
   Lest the plumber should be a cheat.

And let it be solder'd closely down,
   Strong as strong can be, I implore,
And put it in a patent coffin,
   That I may rise no more.

If they carry me off in the patent coffin,
   Their labour will be in vain;
Let the undertaker see it bought of the maker,
   Who lives in St Martin's Lane.

And bury me in my brother's church,
   For that will safer be,
And I implore, lock the church door,
   And pray take care of the key.

And all night long let three stout men
  The vestry watch within,
To each man give a gallon of beer
  And a keg of Holland's gin ;

Powder, and ball, and blunderbuss,
  To save me if he can,
And eke five guineas if he shoot
  A resurrection-man.

And let them watch me for three weeks,
  My wretched corpse to save,
For then I think that I may stink
  Enough to rest in my grave.

The surgeon laid him down in his bed,
  His eyes grew deadly dim,
Short came his breath, and the struggle of death
  Distorted every limb.

They put him in lead when he was dead,
  And shrouded up so neat,
And they the leaden coffin weigh,
  Lest the plumber should be a cheat.

They had it solder'd closely down,
  And examined it o'er and o'er,
And they put it in a patent coffin,
  That he might rise no more.

For to carry him off in a patent coffin
  Would, they thought, be but labour in vain,
So the undertaker saw it bought of the maker
  Who lives by St Martin's Lane.

In his brother's church they buried him,
  That safer he might be,
They lock'd the door, and would not trust
  The sexton with the key.

And three men in the vestry watch,
　To save him if they can,
And should he come there to shoot, they swear,
　A resurrection-man.

So all night long, by the vestry fire,
　They quaff'd their gin and ale,
And they did drink, as you may think,
　And told full many a tale.

They look'd askance with greedy glance,
　The guineas they shone bright,
For the sexton on the yellow gold
　Let fall his lantern light.

And he look'd sly, with his roguish eye,
　And gave a well-timed wink,
And they could not stand the sound in his hand
　For he made the guineas chink.

And conscience late, that had such weight,
　All in a moment fails,
For well they knew, that it was true :
　A dead man told no tales.

Then, though the key of the church door
　Was left with the parson, his brother,
It opened at the sexton's touch,—
　Because he had another.

They laid the pick-axe to the stones,
　And they moved them soon asunder,
They shovell'd away the hard-prest clay,
　And came to the coffin under.

PLATE LII

HENRY WARBURTON (1784?-1858)

Painted by Sir George Hayter and engraved by W. H. Mote

CHAPTER XV

FINALLY it became evident that the time had arrived for the legalisation of the study of anatomy. During the long struggle which preceded the passage of the Anatomy Act, the name of Mr Henry Warburton constantly appeared as the courageous and practical champion of the true interests of the medical profession in Parliament.

Mr Henry Warburton (1784?-1858), philosophical radical, was educated at Eton and at Trinity College, Cambridge. He was elected F.R.S. in 1809. He was one of the leading supporters of Brougham in founding London University, and was a member of its first council in 1827.

At the general election of 1826 Warburton was returned to Parliament in the radical interest for the borough of Bridport, in Dorset.

Mr Warburton's maiden effort on behalf of the medical profession occurred on 20th June 1827, when he presented to the House of Commons a petition of Members of the Royal College of Surgeons in London, asking that the Charter of the College be abrogated for numerous, good, and sufficient reasons.

The governing body of the College of Surgeons was an oligarchy composed of twenty-one councillors who were elected for life and were privileged to name their successors. This autocratic body failed to keep pace with the improved medical education of the time, much of which advancement was due entirely to the private schools of anatomy. The governing body of the College was part and parcel of a coterie, or ring, whose object was to maintain a monopoly of offices, emoluments, and honours, regardless of the best interests of the public or of the profession, and with an utter contempt for the ability and learning of the extra-mural teachers. Nepotism held sway everywhere in medical London.

Little of good, and much of evil, was the inevitable result of such a system. In the main it meant mismanagement in hospital administration; malpractice in medical and surgical treatment; and stagnation in medical education. It put a ban on independent research, discouraged individual effort, and frowned upon the labours, thoughts, and deeds of all men who were not nepotists. For many years—be it said with shame—this condition ruled medical London. When the revolt came, however, it was short and terrible. A spade was called by its real name, and not a few idols were ruined.

The imperious and unjust acts of the Royal College of Surgeons had long been the subject of criticism, but no concerted effort had been made to correct the abuses. When, however, in March 1824, the College passed a by-law which made it compulsory for medical students to attend the lectures of certain hospital officials; and when the College decreed: "that certificates of attendance at lectures on anatomy, physiology, the theory and practice of surgery, and of the performance of dissections be not received by the Court except from the appointed professors of anatomy and surgery in the University of Dublin, Edinburgh, Glasgow, or Aberdeen, or from persons teaching in a school acknowledged by the medical establishment of one of the recognised hospitals, or from persons being physicians or surgeons to any

of these hospitals" then it was that Thomas Wakley
trained his guns on the Court of Examiners of the
Royal College of Surgeons.

The real purpose of the by-law was to destroy the
private schools of anatomy and surgery, which were
conducted for the most part by the ablest teachers to
be found in London, and to aggrandise the hospital
surgeons.

Thomas Wakley was the knight errant who devoted
his life to the correction of abuses which existed in, and
outside of, the medical profession. His career was a
stormy one, and his opposition was most formidable.
His life reads like a romance. Neither the burning of
his house, the attempt which was made to murder him,
the starting of suits at law, the occurrence of personal
encounters, nor the attempts at social and professional
ostracism, could cause this Knight of the True Cross
to stop his fight for medical reform.

Six months prior to the enactment of the offensive
by-law, Thomas Wakley had founded *The Lancet*, a
medical journal which was destined to become the leader
of its class.[1] It was in the columns of *The Lancet* that
year after year attacks were made on abuses to which
the medical profession was subjected.

A fierce indictment of the College authorities, with
a summary of the more obvious grievances of its
members, appeared in *The Lancet*, 27th August 1825,
in the form of an "Open Letter addressed to the Court
of Examiners of the Royal College of Surgeons," over
the signature "Brutus." The "Brutus" in this case
was none other than James Wardrop (1782-1869), an

---

[1] The first number of *The Lancet* was issued on 5th October 1823,
which was a Sunday. It was "Printed and published by G. L. Hutchinson,
at *The Lancet* Office, 210 Strand, London." It is a significant fact that
the names of the printers and publishers of this "stormy petrel" were
omitted from the imprints after the second number.

able surgeon, best known now for his treatise on ophthalmic pathology, and his operation for aneurysm.[1]

In his letter "Brutus" charged that the corporation, since the year 1744, had received the sum of £80,000, and that during the same period they had put £16,000 into their own pockets! "They take our money, give us *ex post facto* laws, lock up our property, insult us with mock orations, live at our expense, and refuse to call us by our proper names!"

Other letters from "Brutus" followed the one mentioned above, and all showed an intimate knowledge of the constitutional history of the Royal College of Surgeons, and a thorough appreciation of the mal-administration of its affairs. The bitter epistles from "Brutus," and the thunderous editorials from Wakley, continued to appear in *The Lancet*, and finally caused that revolt of the members of the College which found expression in Mr Warburton's petition.

The House acceded to Mr Warburton's motion and the College was called upon to render an account of its stewardship from 1799 to 20th June 1827; and to furnish specific information concerning grants made for the purchase, building, and repairing of the College, and for the purchase of John Hunter's Museum. A temporary victory was thus gained by the members.

Public sentiment at last forced Parliament to action, and a parliamentary committee, with Mr Warburton as chairman, was appointed to inquire into the study of anatomy as practised in the United Kingdom and into the best method of obtaining bodies for dissection. Its sittings began on 28th April 1828, its first witness being Sir Astley Cooper. Among the other witnesses

[1] Wardrop was an Edinburgh graduate who came to London in his twenty-seventh year and attained eminence in surgery and also in ophthalmology.

PLATE LIII

THOMAS WAKLEY (1795-1862)

Reproduced from a bust, a replica of one executed by John Bell, in the Hall of *The Lancet* Office. (Courtesy of Messrs Longmans, Green and Co., 39 Paternoster Row, London. From Sprigge's *Life*, 1897)

were Brodie, Abernethy, Joshua Brookes, and Wakley. After various measures were introduced into Parliament from March 1829 to December 1831, it was not until August 1832 that Mr Warburton's famous Anatomy Bill finally passed safely through both Houses and became the Anatomy Act. The murder of the Italian boy, 5th November 1831, helped to hurry the slow progress of legislation.

The Act provided that the Secretary of State for the Home Department in Great Britain, and the Chief Secretary in Ireland, were empowered to "grant licences to practise anatomy to any Members of the Royal College of Physicians or Surgeons, or to any graduates or licentiates in medicine, or to any professor of anatomy, medicine, or surgery, or to any student attending any school of anatomy, the application for such licence being countersigned by two justices of the peace ; and persons so licensed may receive or possess for anatomical examination, or examine anatomically under such licence and with such permission as aforesaid, any dead body ; but no anatomical examination is to be conducted save at some place of which the Secretary of State has had a week's notice, and the Secretary of State may appoint inspectors for all such places, who are to make quarterly returns as to the dead bodies carried in for examination there."

By this Act "it is provided that the executor or other person having lawful possession of the body of a deceased person, and not being entrusted with it for interment only, may permit the body of such person to undergo anatomical examination, unless in his life-time the deceased shall have expressed, in such manner as in the Act specified, a wish to the contrary ; or unless the surviving husband, or wife, or known relation of the deceased shall object."

If a person had expressed a wish to be dissected, this was to be done unless a known relative raised an objection. A body could not be moved for dissection until forty-eight hours after death, nor until the expiration of twenty-four hours' notice to the inspector of anatomy ; and not then unless a proper death certificate had been signed by the medical attendant. Provision was made for the decent removal of all bodies, and for their burial in consecrated ground. No licensed person was liable to prosecution or punishment for having a body in his possession for anatomical purposes according to the provisions of the Act.

One of the most important parts of the Act was Section XVI., which did away with the dissection of the bodies of murderers. It orders, "that the sentence to be pronounced by the Court shall express that the body of such Prisoner shall be hung in Chains, or buried within the Precincts of the Prison, whichever of the two the Court shall order."

The old law requiring "that the Body of every Person convicted of Murder shall, after Execution, either be dissected or hung in Chains, as to the Court which tried the Offender shall deem meet," was abrogated. No longer were members of the medical profession forced into the disgustful and disgraceful alliance with the hangman.

The attitude of the public on important questions, its way of arriving at conclusions, and its mode of expressing its sentiments—whether of approval, or of hostility—are matters which are not always explicable by the rules of logic. A curious example of mob psychology is afforded by the popular prejudice, which existed a century ago, against the setting aside of the bodies of any particular class of citizens for anatomical study. The old law, which consigned the bodies of

PLATE LIV

JAMES WARDROP (1782-1869)
From vol. ii., *Pettigrew's Medical Portrait Gallery*, London, n.d.

legally-executed murderers to the limbo where the anatomists gleefully sharpened their knives, and joyously converted human flesh into mince-meat, excited the belief, in the minds of many persons, that there was something degrading in the very idea of anatomising a human body. The process carried with it this thought : that it was a punishment by mutilation, which should be inflicted only upon the bodies of the most degraded criminals. Illogical as was this view, it served for three centuries to retard the study of anatomy in Scotland and in England (Lonsdale).

It was not to be expected that the Anatomy Act should be a perfect document. It was a decided step in advance, and its excellence is attested by the few changes which have been made in it between the year 1832 and the present day. Its defects were those of omission ; and these did not escape the aquiline eye of Wakley, who voiced his objections in the columns of *The Lancet*. Wakley found fault with Warburton's Act because : (1) it left the parochial authorities free either to dispose of the bodies or to bury them as they pleased ; (2) it did not compel parochial, hospital, and asylum authorities to forward notice to the inspector of anatomy whenever a dead body should be in their possession ; and (3) it did not say that bodies should be distributed to all the schools in proportion to the number of students.

Mr Wakley made these criticisms because of his desire to secure fair and just treatment for all the schools. He wished to defeat the manœuvring of the large hospitals against the small ones and against the private schools. Looking ahead, he could see the large and rich hospitals obtaining bodies to the exclusion of rival institutions, where often better instruction was given at lower fees. The validity of Mr Wakley's criticisms was soon demonstrated by numerous facts, of which only two will be cited :—

I. " *The Conduct of the Treasurer of Guy's Hospital.*—Three years after the passage of the Anatomy Act, this gentleman offered that Guy's should receive all the sick paupers of the Southwark Union and all incurables, without the usual weekly subsidy from the guardians — provided that every body available should be sent to his school and to no other ! [1]

II. " *The Decline of Edinburgh as a Medical Centre.*— Edinburgh began to show a loss in numbers about 1835, and continued declining for many years thereafter. This situation was the result of several factors, as, for example : the improved character of the London and Dublin schools; the rise of provincial medical institutions; the extension of the curriculum and advance in fees; and the retention of senile professors in certain chairs in the University—yet, the chief cause was the lack of anatomical *matériel.*" [2]

The lack of bodies for dissection was felt most acutely in Edinburgh. "Warburton's Act," says Lonsdale, "did not work well in the North ; the Whigs and 'Little John' Russell were passive upon all matters but holding place ; and no impress could be made upon the town authorities." During the sessions of 1834-35-36, at public meetings of students, the policy of the parochial and other authorities was exposed, and the University monopoly was denounced. Indifference of those in power caused many students to enter schools in Glasgow and Dublin, where *matériel* was more abundant.

Administration of the Anatomy Act was followed by success. The serious defects, existing at the time of its birth and discussed by Mr Wakley, have long since been removed, some by time and some by law. No

[1] Sprigge, *Life and Times of Thomas Wakley*, London, 1897, p. 438.
[2] Lonsdale, *Life of Robert Knox*, London, 1870, p. 196.

provision was made in the Act for the punishment of grave-robbing : this was an offence at common law.

What Mr Henry Warburton accomplished for mankind, when, after years of struggle, his Bill for the legalisation of anatomical study was made law and became the Anatomy Act of 1832, never will be appreciated properly by the present generation. The Act which bears his name has done these things :—

It has legalised human dissection in Great Britain and Ireland ;

It has permitted cultured, brave, and honourable members of the medical profession to escape the slimy tentacles of the resurrectionists ;

It has provided the student of to-day with facilities for anatomical study, under such surroundings and with such abundance, as would have brought pæans from the lips of Andreas Vesalius, William Harvey, and John Hunter ;

It put an end to the vocation of the "sack-'em-up men " ; and,

To the public—the always indifferent and stuporous public—it has given original, brilliant, and life-saving surgical operations.

The long delay in the legalisation of anatomical study in Britain forms one of the most disgraceful chapters in the history of the Empire. Members of Parliament who, in 1832, converted Mr Warburton's Bill into the Anatomy Act, could take but little "flattering unction" to their souls. Nothing less than foul murder, oft repeated, could move those lawgivers from the point of stagnation to that of action. It would seem that the anatomical construction of the English politician of 1832 was quite the same as that of the American congressman of this year of grace, 1928, in one respect at least—in the elephantine thickness of his cuticular covering.

It is doubtful sportsmanship for me, whose Scottish ancestors came to the New World two and a half centuries ago, to throw any new units into the rockpile of English legislative indifference. Let the missiles be furnished by a true Englishman, Mr J. F. Clarke,[1] a Member of the Royal College of Surgeons, and for many years one of the writers on the editorial staff of *The Lancet*, in these words :—

"Here it may not be out of place just to say a few words respecting the position of the anatomical schools, teachers, and students, previous to the passing of the Anatomy Act. Nothing could have been more unsatisfactory and disgraceful to us as a civilised nation. The outrages against decency, the misdemeanours, which the law was compelled to wink at, continued long after the necessity for a change had been demonstrated."

Terms and Provisions of the Anatomy Act.

Bishop and Williams, the London Burkers, were executed 5th December 1831, only four days after the jury had found them guilty. Ten days later, while the danger attending the procurement of anatomical material was still fresh in the minds of the public, Mr Henry Warburton again introduced his Bill, slightly altered in details, into the House of Commons. On 29th January 1832 it went to a second reading. After it had passed through the usual stages in committee, Mr Warburton, on 11th April, asked that it be re-committed because deputations from the College of Surgeons in Dublin, and another medical body, desired its provisions to be extended to Ireland. The Bill passed the House of Commons on 11th May 1832, and shortly thereafter

---

[1] Clarke, *Autobiographical Recollections of the Medical Profession*, London, 1874, p. 103.

it received the approval of the Upper House. It received the Royal assent on 1st August 1832, and is technically known as 3 and 4 Geo. IV., c. 75, the short title being *An Act for regulating Schools of Anatomy.* The following are its terms and provisions :—

"Whereas a knowledge of the causes and nature of sundry diseases which affect the body, and the best methods of treating and curing such diseases, and of healing and repairing divers wounds and injuries to which the human frame is liable, cannot be acquired without the aid of anatomical examination: And whereas the legal supply of human bodies for such anatomical examination is insufficient fully to provide the means of such knowledge: And whereas in order further to supply human bodies for such purposes, divers great and grievous crimes have been committed, and lately murder, for the single object of selling for such purposes the bodies of the persons so murdered: And whereas, therefore, it is highly expedient to give protection, under certain regulations, to the study and practice of anatomy, and to prevent, as far as may be, such great and grievous crimes and murder as aforesaid: Be it therefore enacted by the King's most excellent Majesty, by and with the advice and consent of the lords spiritual and temporal and commons, in this present Parliament assembled, and by the authority of the same, that it shall be lawful for his Majesty's principal secretary of state for the time being for the home department in that part of the United Kingdom called Great Britain, and for the chief secretary for Ireland in that part of the United Kingdom called Ireland, immediately on the passing of this Act, or so soon thereafter as may be required, to grant a licence to practise anatomy to any fellow or member of any college of physicians or surgeons, or to any graduate or licentiate in medicine, or to any person lawfully qualified to practise medicine in any part of the United Kingdom, or to any professor or teacher of anatomy, medicine, or surgery, or to any student attending any school of anatomy, on application from such party for such purpose, countersigned by two of his Majesty's justices of the peace acting for the county, city, borough, or place wherein such party so applying is about to carry on the practice of anatomy.

"2. And be it enacted, that it shall be lawful for his Majesty's said principal secretary of state or chief secretary, as the case may be, immediately on the passing of this Act, or as soon thereafter as may be necessary, to appoint respectively not fewer than three persons to be inspectors of places where anatomy is carried on, and at any time after such first appointment to appoint, if they shall see fit, one or more other person or persons to be an inspector or inspectors as aforesaid ; and every such inspector shall continue in office for one year, or until he be removed by the said secretary of state or chief secretary, as the case may be, or until some other person shall be appointed in his place ; and as often as any inspector appointed as aforesaid shall die, or shall be removed from his said office, or shall refuse or become unable to act, it shall be lawful for the said secretary of state or chief secretary, as the case may be, to appoint another person to be inspector in his room.

" 3. And be it enacted, that it shall be lawful for the said secretary of state or chief secretary, as the case may be, to direct what district of town or country, or of both, and what places where anatomy is carried on, situate within such district, every such inspector shall be appointed to superintend, and in what manner every such inspector shall transact the duties of his office.

" 4. And be it enacted, that every inspector to be appointed by virtue of this Act shall make a quarterly return to the said secretary of state or chief secretary, as the case may be, of every deceased person's body that during the preceding quarter has been removed for anatomical examination to every separate place in his district where anatomy is carried on, distinguishing the sex, and as far as is known at the time, the name and age of each person whose body was so removed as aforesaid.

" 5. And be it enacted, that it shall be lawful for every such inspector to visit and inspect at any time any place within his district, notice of what place has been given, as is hereinafter directed, that it is intended there to practise anatomy.

" 6. And be it enacted, that it shall be lawful for his Majesty to grant to every such inspector such an annual salary not exceeding one hundred pounds for his trouble, and to allow such a sum of money for the expenses of his office as may appear reasonable, such salaries and allowances to be charged on the consolidated fund of the United Kingdom, and to be payable quarterly ; and that an annual return of all such salaries and allowances shall be made to Parliament.

" 7. And be it enacted, that it shall be lawful for any executor or other party having lawful possession of the body of any deceased person, and not being an undertaker or other party intrusted with the body for the purpose only of interment, to permit the body of such deceased person to undergo anatomical examination, unless, to the knowledge of such executor or other party, such person shall have expressed his desire, either in writing at any time during his life, or verbally in the presence of two or more witnesses during the illness whereof he dies, that his body after death might not undergo such examination, or unless the surviving husband or wife, or any known relation of the deceased person, shall require the body to be interred without such examination.

" 8. And be it enacted, that if any person, either in writing at any time during his life, or verbally in the presence of two or more witnesses during the illness whereof he died, shall direct that his body after death be examined anatomically or shall nominate any party by this Act authorised to examine bodies anatomically to make such examination, and if, before the burial of the body of such person, such direction or nomination shall be made known to the party having lawful possession of the dead body, then such last-mentioned party shall direct such examination to be made, and in case of any such nomination as aforesaid, shall request and permit any party so authorised and nominated as aforesaid to make such examination, unless the deceased person's surviving husband or wife, or nearest known relative, or any one or more of such person's nearest known relatives, being of kin in the same degree, shall require the body to be interred without such examination.

" 9. Provided always, and be it enacted, that in no case shall the body of any person be removed for anatomical examination from any place where such person may have died until after forty-eight hours from the time of such person's decease, nor until twenty-four hours' notice, to be reckoned from the time of such decease, to the inspector of the district, of the intended removal of the body, or if no such inspector have been appointed, to some physician, surgeon, or apothecary residing at or near the place of death, nor unless a certificate stating in what manner such person came by his death, shall previously to the removal of the body have been signed by the physician, surgeon, or apothecary who attended such person during the illness whereof he died, or if no such medical man attended such person during such illness, then by some physician, surgeon, or apothecary who shall be called in after the death of such person, to view his body, or who shall state the manner or cause of death according to the best of his knowledge and belief, but who shall not be concerned in examining the body after removal; and that in case of such removal such certificate shall be delivered, together with the body, to the party receiving the same for anatomical examination.

" 10. And be it enacted, that it shall be lawful for any member or fellow of any college of physicians or surgeons, or any graduate or licentiate in medicine, or any person lawfully qualified to practise medicine in any part of the United Kingdom, or any professor, teacher, or student of anatomy, medicine, or surgery, having a licence from his Majesty's principal secretary of state or chief secretary as aforesaid, to receive or possess for anatomical examination, or to examine anatomically, the body of any person deceased, if permitted or directed so to do by a party who had at the time of giving such permission or direction lawful possession of the body, and who had power, in pursuance of the provisions of this Act, to permit or cause the body to be so examined, and provided such certificates as aforesaid were delivered by such party together with the body.

" 11. And be it enacted, that every party so receiving a body for anatomical examination after removal shall demand and receive, together with the body, a certificate as aforesaid, and shall, within twenty-four hours next after such removal, transmit to the inspector of the district such certificate, and also a return stating at what day and hour and from whom the body was received, the date and place of death, the sex, and (as far as is known at the time) the Christian and surname, age and last place of abode of such person, or if no such inspector have been appointed, to some physician, surgeon, or apothecary residing at or near the place to which the body is removed, and shall enter or cause to be entered the aforesaid particulars relating thereto, and a copy of the certificate be received therewith, in a book to be kept by him for that purpose, and shall produce such book whenever required so to do by any inspector so appointed as aforesaid.

" 12. And be it enacted, that it shall not be lawful for any party to carry on or teach anatomy at any place, or at any place to receive or possess for anatomical examination, or examine anatomically, any deceased person's body after removal of the same, unless such party, or the owner or occupier of such place, or some party by this Act authorised to examine bodies anatomically, shall, at least one week before the first receipt or possession of a body for such purpose at such place, have given notice to the said secretary of state or chief secretary, as the case may be, of the place where it is intended to practise anatomy.

" 13. Provided always, and be it enacted, that every such body so removed as aforesaid for the purpose of examination shall, before such removal, be placed in a decent coffin or shell, and be removed therein ; and that the party removing the same, or causing the same to be removed as aforesaid, shall make provision that such body, after undergoing anatomical examination, be decently interred in consecrated ground, or in some public burial-ground in use for persons of that religious persuasion to which the person whose body was so removed belonged ; and that a certificate of the interment of such body shall be transmitted to the inspector of the district within six weeks after the day on which such body was received as aforesaid.

" 14. And be it enacted, that no member or fellow of any college of physicians or surgeons, nor any graduate or licentiate in medicine, nor any person lawfully qualified to practise medicine in any part of the United Kingdom, nor any professor, teacher, or student of anatomy, medicine, or surgery, having a licence from his Majesty's principal secretary of state or chief secretary as aforesaid, shall be liable to any prosecution, penalty, forfeiture, or punishment for receiving or having in his possession for anatomical examination, or for examining anatomically, any dead human body, according to the provisions of this Act.

" 15. And be it enacted, that nothing in this Act contained shall be construed to extend to or to prohibit any post-mortem examination of any human body required or directed to be made by any competent legal authority.

" 16. And whereas an Act was passed in the ninth year of the reign of his late Majesty, for consolidating and amending the statutes in England relative to offences against the person, by which latter Act it is enacted, that the body of every person convicted of murder shall, after execution, either be dissected or hung in chains, as to the court which tried the offence shall seem meet, and that the sentence to be pronounced by the court shall express that the body of the offender shall be dissected or hung in chains, whichever of the two the court shall order.   Be it enacted, that so much of the said last recited Act as authorises the court, if it shall see fit, to direct that the body of a person convicted of murder shall, after execution, be dissected, be and the same is hereby repealed; and that in every case of conviction of any prisoner for murder the court before which such prisoner shall have been tried direct such prisoner either to be hung in chains, or to be buried within the precincts of the prison in which such prisoner shall have been confined after conviction, as to such court shall seem meet ; and that the sentence to be pronounced by the court shall express that the body of such prisoner shall be hung in chains, or buried within the precincts of the prison, whichever of the two the court shall order.

" 17. And be it enacted, that if any action or suit be commenced or brought against any person for anything done in pursuance of this Act, the same shall be commenced within six calendar months next after the cause of action accrued ; and the defendant in every such action or suit may, at his election, plead the matter specially or the general issue Not Guilty, and give this Act and the special matter in evidence at any trial to be had thereupon.

" 18. And be it enacted, that any person offending against the provisions of this Act in England or Ireland shall be deemed and taken to be guilty of a misdemeanour, and being duly convicted thereof, shall be punished by imprisonment for a term not exceeding three months, or by a fine not exceeding fifty pounds, at the discretion of the court before which he shall be tried; and any person offending against the provisions of this Act in Scotland shall, upon being duly convicted of such offence, be punished by imprisonment for a term not exceeding three months, or by fine not exceeding fifty pounds, at the discretion of the court before which he shall be tried.

" 19. And in order to remove doubts as to the meaning of certain words in this Act, be it enacted, that the words " person and party " shall be respectively deemed to include any number of persons, or any society, whether by charter or otherwise; and that the meaning of the aforesaid words shall not be restricted, although the same may be subsequently referred to in the singular number and masculine gender only."

CHAPTER XVI

In a country as young as the United States, as Krumbhaar[1] remarks, "it is a comparatively easy matter to trace the growth of a science from its earliest beginning, and medicine is no exception to this rule."

We know that Thomas Wootton, the "Chirurgeon Gentleman" of Captain John Smith, accompanied the expedition that sailed from England on 19th December 1606, to found Jamestown; that Samuel Fuller, physician and divine, accompanied the Pilgrims on the *Mayflower* in 1620; that Sebastian Crol and Jan Huyck came with Peter Minuit, and other Dutchmen, in the migration of 1626; and that three Welsh physicians—Thomas Lloyd, Griffith Owen, and Thomas Wynne—arrived with William Penn in the *Welcome*, in 1682, to help to found Philadelphia and Penn's Sylvania. From the earliest times the need for dissection was recognised, and it found expression in occasional *post-mortem* examinations and in suggestions for the teaching of anatomy in brief courses.

The Earliest Recorded Autopsies in America.

John Eliot (1604-1690), usually styled Apostle to the Indians, as early as 1647, stated that the "young Students in Physick," of that day, were "forced to fall to practice before ever they saw an Anatomy made." Up to that time there had been "but one Anatomy in

[1] Krumbhaar, "The Early History of Anatomy in the United States," *Annals of Medical History*, September 1922.

PLATE LV

THOMAS CADWALADER (1708-1779)

From a Portrait in possession of the Pennsylvania Hospital. The Original, by Charles Wilson Peale in 1770, is owned by Mr John Cadwalader, of Philadelphia (Krumbhaar, *Annals of Medical History*, September 1922, p. 272)

PLATE LVI

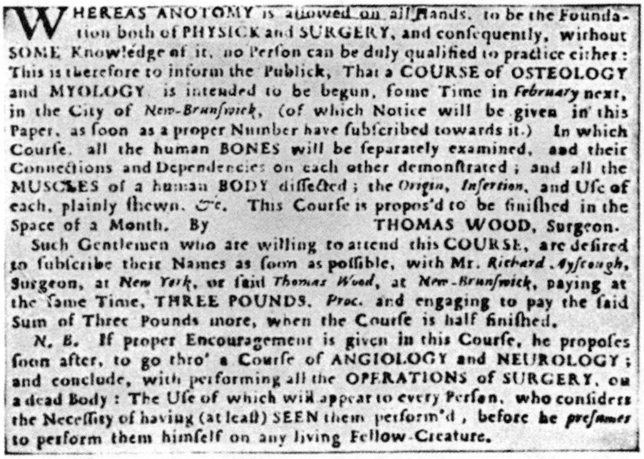

WHEREAS ANOTOMY is allowed on all Hands, to be the Foundation both of PHYSICK and SURGERY, and consequently, without SOME Knowledge of it, no Person can be duly qualified to practice either: This is therefore to inform the Publick, That a COURSE of OSTEOLOGY and MYOLOGY is intended to be begun, some Time in *February* next, in the City of *New-Brunswick*, (of which Notice will be given in this Paper, as soon as a proper Number have subscribed towards it.) In which Course, all the human BONES will be separately examined, and their Connections and Dependencies on each other demonstrated ; and all the MUSCLES of a human BODY dissected ; the *Origin*, *Insertion*, and Use of each, plainly shewn, &c. This Course is propos'd to be finished in the Space of a Month. By　　　　　　THOMAS WOOD, Surgeon.

Such Gentlemen who are willing to attend this COURSE, are desired to subscribe their Names as soon as possible, with Mr. *Richard Ayscough*, Surgeon, at *New York*, or said *Thomas Wood*, at *New-Brunswick*, paying at the same Time, THREE POUNDS. *Proc.* and engaging to pay the said Sum of Three Pounds more, when the Course is half finished.

N. B. If proper Encouragement is given in this Course, he proposes soon after, to go thro' a Course of ANGIOLOGY and NEUROLOGY ; and conclude, with performing all the OPERATIONS of SURGERY, on a dead Body : The Use of which will appear to every Person, who considers the Necessity of having (at least) SEEN them perform'd, before he *presumes* to perform them himself on any living Fellow-Creature.

Thomas Wood's Announcement in the *New York Weekly Postboy* of 17th January 1752, of the First Course of Anatomical Lectures given in British America (Krumbhaar, *Annals of Medical History*, September 1922, p. 286)

the Countrey, which Mr Giles Firman (Firmin) (now in England) did make and read upon very well."[1] This, says Hartwell,[2] was "the earliest utterance in America, in recognition of the importance of anatomical studies." In his letter, dated "Roxbury, 24 September, 1647," John Eliot informs the Rev. Thomas Shepard (Shepherd), of "Cambridge in New England," of his efforts to instruct the Red Men in Anatomy and Physick, saying : "Some of the wiser sort I have stirred up to get this skill; I have showed them the anatomy of man's body, and some generall principles of Physick." Hartwell, however, thinks that Eliot's instruction did not comprise dissections.

In the diary of Judge Samuel Sewall, of Boston, under date of 22nd September 1676, is an entry, stating : "Spent the day from 9 in the M. with Mr (Dr) Braken-bury, Mr Thomson, Butter, Hooper, Cragg, Pemberton, dissecting the middle-most of the Indians executed the day before."

Packard[3] has recorded six autopsies reported in New England between the years 1674 and 1678 ; and Hartwell found a manuscript order of the Council of Lord Baltimore, dated "St Marys, in Maryland, July 20 1670," directing two "Chyrurgeons" to view on Monday, 8th August 1670, the head of one Benjamin Price, supposed to have been killed by the Indians.

For a long period, Toner[4] and others erroneously believed that the first recorded autopsy in this country

[1] Eliot's Letter is in a book by Thomas Shepherd entitled, *The Cleare Sun-Shine of Gospel breaking upon the Indians of New England*. (Reprinted in the *Coll. of the Mass. Hist. Soc.*, 1834, 3rd ser., iv. 37.)

[2] Hartwell, "The Hindrances to Anatomical Study in the United States," *Annals of Anatomy and Surgery*, January-June 1881, vol. iii. p. 209.

[3] Packard, *The History of Medicine in the United States*, Philadelphia, 1901, p. 62.

[4] Toner, *Contributions to the Annals of Medical Progress and Medical Education in the United States*, Washington, 1874.

was that held in 1691, on the body of Governor Slaughter of New York, who had died so suddenly as to cause suspicions of poisoning. The examination was made by Dr Johannes Kerfbyle, a graduate of the University of Leyden, who was assisted by five physicians. These gentlemen received £8, 8s. for their services.

Early Lessons in Practical Anatomy.

The honour of initiating the teaching of practical anatomy in this country belongs to Dr Thomas Cadwalader (1708-1779), of Philadelphia, who began his course of dissections in 1750. To complete his medical education he had been sent to the University of Rheims and to London, where he studied under William Cheselden.

In the same year (1750) Dr John Bard and Dr Peter Middleton, in New York City, injected and dissected the body of Hermanus Carroll, an executed criminal, "for the instruction of the young men then engaged in the study of medicine."

The earliest printed announcement of lectures on anatomy in this country appeared in the *New York Weekly Postboy* of 17th January 1752, over the name of Thomas Wood, Surgeon, who announced that he would give "a Course of Osteology and Myology," in the following month, "in the City of New Brunswick." (Plate LVI.)

Wood's announcement of lectures antedated by two years the better known anatomical course which a Scotsman, William Hunter (1720[1]-1777), a student of Alexander Monro *primus*, and a relative of the famous brothers—John and William Hunter—gave at Newport,

[1] The date of Hunter's birth is given 1720 by Krumbhaar, and as 1729 by Packard.

R.I., on the "History of Anatomy and Comparative Anatomy in 1754, 1755, and 1756" (Norris).[1]

These and many other isolated and sporadic examples of medical teaching show that, in the Colonies, there was a slowly growing but sincere demand for instruction in the medical sciences—a demand which could be filled only by the founding of a medical college.

It must not be thought an extraordinary circumstance, that more than a century and a half should have elapsed between the first colonisation and the founding of our earliest medical school. The hardy pioneers of the New World were aware of the importance of general education ; and they were desirous of founding institutions of learning, but with them the welfare of the Church and their political economy were always first in mind. The peculiar circumstances surrounding their immigration to this country, the desperate situation in which, only too often, they found themselves after their arrival, and their dependence upon the physicians and surgeons whom they had brought from Europe, combined to make the early establishment of a medical school unnecessary, if not impossible, during the first century of American life.

In course of time, after other institutions had been established, many of the ablest young men, when desirous of studying medicine, crossed the Atlantic and received instruction in the famous schools of London, Edinburgh, Leyden, and Paris. At this period the duties of physicians and surgeons were most onerous owing to the scattered condition of the settlements. It was not an uncommon experience for a noted surgeon to travel one hundred or more miles, by horse or

[1] Norris, *The Early History of Medicine in Philadelphia*, Philadelphia, 1886, p. 211.

by stage, to perform an important operation; and as late as the middle of the eighteenth century an American patient crossed to London to have a lithotomy done by Cheselden.

Among the young Americans who crossed the Atlantic to complete their medical education were two— William Shippen, jun. (1736-1808) and John Morgan (1735-1789)—who were destined to become the founders of the first medical school in the United States. Both were natives of Philadelphia, and both while abroad attended the lectures and demonstrations of the most eminent physicians, surgeons, and anatomists of the Old World.

Dr Shippen returned from Europe in 1762, and in the autumn of the same year he began to teach anatomy to a private class of ten or twelve students. In 1765 Dr John Morgan, whom Norris[1] styles "the Founder of American Medicine," returned from Europe loaded with literary honours. In the same year he persuaded the trustees of the College of Philadelphia to inaugurate medical teaching. On 3rd May 1765 Dr Morgan was elected Professor of the Theory and Practice of Physic, a post which he retained until his decease. In September 1765 Dr William Shippen, jun., was elected Professor of Anatomy and Surgery. Such was the initiation of medical teaching in the United States; and such was the beginning of that pre-eminence in medical instruction which Philadelphia still retains.

Shippen's elucidation of anatomy was aided by the use of a series of beautiful charts and by a set of anatomical casts which Dr John Fothergill (1712-1780) of London, presented to the Pennsylvania Hospital in 1762.

[1] Norris, *The Early History of Medicine in Philadelphia*, Philadelphia, 1886, p. 46.

PLATE LVII

WILLIAM HUNTER (1720-1777) OF NEWPORT, R.I.
Painted by Cosmo Alexander, now owned by Mr A. F. Hunter of Newport
(*Annals of Medical History*, September 1922, p. 284)

PLATE LVIII

WILLIAM SHIPPEN, JUN. (1736-1808), THE FIRST PROFESSOR OF ANATOMY
IN BRITISH AMERICA

(Krumbhaar, *Annals of Medical History*, September 1922, p. 278)

PLATE LIX

PORTRAIT OF JOHN MORGAN (1735-1789), FOUNDER OF MEDICAL INSTRUCTION
IN BRITISH AMERICA

From the Original Painting by Angelica Kauffman, reproduced in Norris's *Early
History of Medicine in Philadelphia*, Philadelphia, 1886

PLATE LX

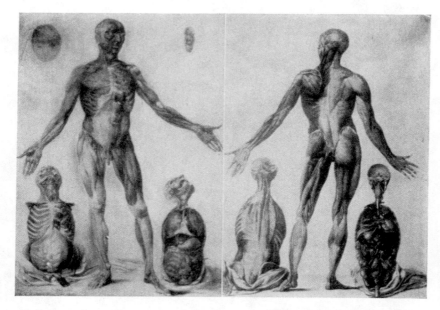

TWO OF THE FOTHERGILL CRAYONS, AT THE PENNSYLVANIA HOSPITAL,
WHICH WERE USED BY WILLIAM SHIPPEN, JUN., IN HIS LECTURES ON ANATOMY

These beautiful anatomical charts were made in 1755 by J. Van Riemsdyck, the artist employed by William Hunter to illustrate his work on the gravid uterus, from preparations made by Jenty, a well-known London dissector (Krumbhaar, *Annals of Medical History*, September 1922, p. 279)

Anatomy Riots in British America.

The opening of an anatomical theatre created great alarm among some of the citizens of Philadelphia, and on several occasions Dr Shippen's labours were interrupted by rioters. In one of these attacks the anatomist escaped "by passing out through an alley, while his carriage, which stood before the door with its blinds raised, and which was supposed to contain him, received, along with a shower of other missiles, a musket ball through the centre of it" (Norris). More than once Dr Shippen had to desert his home and conceal himself, in order to avoid bodily harm. Several times Dr Shippen addressed the populace through the public papers, assuring them that he had not disturbed private burial-grounds; and stating that the subjects anatomised by him were either persons who had committed suicide, or such as had been publicly executed—except, he naïvely adds, "now and then one from the Potter's Field." His tactful and honourable deportment led many of the respected citizens and the authorities to give him their support.

The Anatomy Riot in New York City.

The inauguration of anatomical instruction in Philadelphia, then the largest city in British America, was soon followed by the development of anatomical courses in New York City, which ranked second in point of population.[1] Our second medical school was founded in 1768, as the medical department of King's (now Columbia) College. The New York school, like that of Philadelphia, arose from private teaching. In 1763, one year after Dr Shippen had begun his course,

---

[1] The first U.S. Census, taken in 1790, showed a total population of nearly 4,000,000. Philadelphia had 45,250 ; New York, 33,131 ; Boston, 18,038 ; Charleston, 16,359 ; and Baltimore, 13,503 inhabitants.

an anatomical course was started in New York by Dr Samuel Clossy, a graduate of Trinity College, Dublin, who had accepted the Chair of Natural Philosophy in King's College. On 25th November 1763 he began to deliver lectures on anatomy to the collegians; and five years later he became Professor of Anatomy in the new school, holding the Chair until a short time prior to the Revolution. Dr Clossy spent his remaining years among his Tory friends, and, according to Cameron,[1] he died in London.

The popular prejudice against dissection often has found expression in acts of violence; and New York City, which has furnished several of the most serious and spectacular examples of mob rule to be found in American history, in April 1788 staged what has been given the dignified but illogical title of "The Doctors' Mob." A more appropriate appellation would be "The Doctors Mobbed," or "The Mobbed Doctors."

The outbreak occurred on Sunday, 13th April 1788, in and around the New York Hospital. "This," says Thacher,[2] "was in consequence of a suspicion that the physicians of the city had robbed the graveyards to procure subjects for dissection. The concourse assembled on this occasion was immense, and some of the mob having forced their way into the dissecting-room, several human bodies were found in various states of mutilation. Enraged at this discovery, they seized upon the fragments, as heads, legs and arms, and exposed them from the windows and doors to public view, with horrid imprecations. The rioters had now become so outrageous, that both the civil and military authorities were summoned to quell the tumult, and the medical

---

[1] Cameron, *History of the Royal College of Surgeons in Ireland*, Dublin, 1886, p. 36.

[2] Thacher, *American Medical Biography*, Boston, 1828, vol. i., p. 52.

students were confined in the common prison for security against the wild passions of the populace." The riot continued for two days. Baron Steuben and Secretary Jay endeavoured to reason with the rioters and to quiet them by speeches, but both were injured by flying missiles.

Thacher states that the disturbance was quelled without the loss of lives. A different version is given by Packard,[1] in these words: "Baron Steuben was knocked down. As he fell he cried to the mayor, James Duane, 'Fire, Duane, fire!' The militia fired a volley, which killed seven of the rioters and wounded seven or eight." James Hardie, in his description of the City of New York (1827), says: "Five persons were killed and seven or eight severely wounded."

In his valuable article on "The Hindrances to Anatomical Study in the United States," Hartwell[2] reprints newspaper accounts of this riot.

The anatomy riot in New York City had a stimulating effect on legislation, judging from "An Act to prevent the odious practice of digging up and removing, for the purpose of dissection, dead Bodies interred in cemeteries or burial places," which was passed 6th January 1789, and constitutes Chapter III. of the Laws of the 12th Session of New York.

Hartwell states that the first statutory provision regarding anatomy in America seems to be that of the Massachusetts Act of 1784, by the terms of which the bodies of persons killed in duels, and of those executed for killing another in a duel might be given up to the surgeons "to be dissected and anatomised." In 1831

---

[1] Packard, *History of Medicine in the United States*, Philadelphia, 1901, p. 364.

[2] Hartwell, *Annals of Anatomy and Surgery*, Brooklyn, N.Y., 1881, p. 220.

Massachusetts anticipated all her sister States, and England as well, in legalising the "study of Anatomy in certain cases."

The Baltimore "Burking" Case.

An incident which appears to be unique in the annals of American medicine was the celebrated "Baltimore Burking Case." For the following account the author is indebted to Dr Arthur M. Shipley, of Baltimore, who has searched the files of the *Sun*, a leading daily paper of that city.

THE STORY OF EMILY BROWN.

Caleb Brown of Easton, Talbot County, Maryland, was the proprietor of the "Old Brick Hotel." These were the times when the innkeeper was in his glory. He had three children—- Arthur, Emily, and Elizabeth. Caleb Brown lived for his children and his one idea and purpose was to accumulate enough to keep them happy and comfortable. In this, however, he was not successful and on his death his children had to seek their own means of livelihood.

Elizabeth married a young man of Easton, whose name was William Austin, but Emily remained single. The trio (Elizabeth, her husband William Austin, and Emily) lived the quiet life of a country town. Arthur, true to the promise of his boyhood, won a more and more prominent place in the estimation of the public, and at last people began to predict great things for the editor and proprietor of the *Journal*, for such position he had attained. In 1850 we find the sisters opening a dressmaking and millinery establishment, and this they kept up together for sixteen years, when Arthur sold out the *Journal* and bought a mill property near Richmond, Virginia. Arthur was single, so Emily went to Richmond to keep house for him, as it was a day when few people of any account boarded. For eleven years brother and sister lived together, caring for each other and each taking a share of work and responsibility; he at the mill and she around the house. No doubt these were the happiest years of her life.

In 1877 Arthur died. Her knowledge of property and of legal forms was very meagre, so that out of what she had worked to establish she could recover nothing, and finally she drifted away from Richmond and was forgotten by all who knew her there.

Merchants doing business on Baltimore Street, Baltimore, Md., began to notice, in 1879, a woman of about fifty years of age who solicited alms of the charitable. To those who would listen, she told a pitiful story. She had seen better days, and bitterly did she rail against those whom she claimed had defrauded her by keeping from her her brother's property. There was even a suggestion of fallen respectability about the woman that touched many hearts and she often received liberal charity, but after a while it was noticed that her speech was maudlin and her eyes bleared. These evident marks of indulgence in liquor got to be more and more frequent, till pity gave place to disgust and the coins that were dropped into her outstretched hand were few. If anyone had followed that wretched creature some night, he would have found her going to a miserable den in a place known as " Pig Alley." There a negress lived, whose name was Mary Bluxom. She had been a slave once and was the mother of eighteen children, of whom the eldest was a repulsive brute called Ross, her son by a former marriage. In this abode of squalor Emily Brown made her home. Two dollars and a half a week she had agreed to pay Mary Bluxom, but even that meagre sum was more than she could compass. Gradually she gave less and less, till finally she was in debt and living on the unwilling charity of the least respectable of negroes. Probably no sadder story could be written than this, but the last act of the tragedy added a peculiar horror to what has already been narrated.

Living with the Bluxom woman was a half-paralysed negro named Perry, who was employed about the Maryland University, and into his depraved mind came the idea of not only getting rid of the useless old white woman, but of making something out of the transaction as well. At least, that was the story told by Ross, who in an evil moment killed old Emily in order to sell her body for the dissecting-room. Ross claimed his tempter was Perry, whose promise of fifteen dollars was the inducement to commit the crime. Doctors, upon examination of the subject brought to them, discovered what they thought to be indisputable signs of violence, and immediately reported the case to the *Sun*. A thorough search was instituted by them and it was finally found out that old Emily Brown, who had been living in " Pig Alley," had disappeared from her accustomed haunts, and little Sarah Bluxom was taken to identify the body. This she did fully, her recognition of the clothing worn by Emily and especially of a curious red flannel patch on her dress being unhesitating. The child also told how " Uncle Perry," who had received the subject, was an inmate of the same house, and that Emily had given him his coffee on the morning before. This information led to Perry's arrest, who at first refused to talk, but later gave in and implicated Ross as the man who had done the deed. In a few hours Ross and his companion, Hawkins, were found. There was not sufficient condemnatory proof against Hawkins, however. Ross's confession followed. It was full and complete and given without inducements or threats. Ross, whose full name was John Thomas Ross, was condemned, sentenced, and executed, on 9th September 1887, but the trial of Perry did not result in his conviction and he was finally liberated.

This crime, usually alluded to as the great " Burking Case," stands almost, if not quite, alone in the criminal annals of America.

The "Resurrection" of Mr John Scott Harrison.

One of the most widely heralded and distressing examples of grave-robbery, occurring in the United States, was perpetrated in the year 1878. Mr John Scott Harrison, who had been an honoured member of the United States Senate and was the son of the ninth President of the United States, died 26th May 1878. He was buried three days later in a cemetery at North Bend, Ohio. A few days later his son, Benjamin Harrison, who was elected President of the United States in 1888, went to Cincinnati, Ohio, and searched the Ohio Medical College for the remains of a friend. Much to his astonishment he found in that institution the body of his father. It is not advisable at this time to disclose all of the details of this affair. However, in justice it must be said that the officials of the Ohio Medical College were not responsible for this act. The true story will not be published in our day.

INDEX